Anne-Marie Sutton

Gilded Death

A Newport Mystery

Written by

Anne-Marie Sutton

authorHOUSE®

AuthorHouse™
1663 Liberty Drive, Suite 200
Bloomington, IN 47403
www.authorhouse.com
Phone: 1-800-839-8640

First published by AuthorHouse   8/19/2008

ISBN: 978-1-4389-0626-3 (sc)

Library of Congress Control Number: 2008907481

Printed in the United States of America
Bloomington, Indiana

This book is printed on acid-free paper.

For my wonderful husband Dexter

Author's Notes

When I wrote my first Newport mystery, *Murder Stalks A Mansion*, I had no idea how it would be received by readers. I knew and loved Newport, Rhode Island, but I didn't know how much interest there would be in a mystery set in the city. I have been delighted with the response to the book by both the area's residents and visitors to the city and pleased with the many requests from readers to continue writing about mystery in Newport.

Gilded Death marks the second in the series, and I am now writing a third Newport mystery novel, *Keep My Secret*, also featuring the team of amateur sleuth Caroline Kent and Newport Police Detective Hank Nightingale.

In *Gilded Death*, as in the first story, many of the Newport places mentioned do exist. But the two houses, Kenwood Court and Mon Plaisir, are my own creations. The Kents and the Revels, as well as all the other characters, are fictitious. But they exist in Newport in my imagination and I hope that you, the reader, will welcome them into yours.

Prologue

Hugh Dockings was dead. That this was true, no person in the elegant crowded ballroom who had heard the last gasp of life expel from his shaking body could doubt. A few of the guests had been close enough to see his startled face, that first stunned expression which was rapidly overtaken by the recognition that something was terribly wrong. Then the look of final panic when Dockings's whole being realized the useless fight he was making to forestall the inevitable.

What were his last thoughts? Surely his entire concentration was on survival, not the flashing of the fifty-five years of his life before him, nor the fear for what hellish place would be his in after-death.

He must have heard the music stop. The interruption was triggered not by Hugh Dockings's falling, for that was out of the sight of the string quartet, but by the sound of the woman screaming. The music's amiable melody was sharp in its stop, right in the middle of a Mozart trill.

High above the startled guests, smoky rays from the June sun continued down through the room's towering Gothic windows of ancient stained glass which traced its lineage back to the thirteenth century in France. The huge ballroom was one of Newport, Rhode Island's finest architectural wonders. It was a refined setting with walls of French silk damask set in panels outlined in carved oak and ceilings dotted with brilliant chandeliers in the curling style of the French Renaissance.

At the sound of the scream, waiters held their heavy silver trays laden with champagne glasses and wine goblets suspended in mid-air. Waitresses at the overflowing buffet table stared in astonishment. Conversations, some even clever from the effect of the expensive stimulants, ceased. The perfect atmosphere, designed only to celebrate the next day's wedding ceremony, had been shattered like the crystal goblet which had dropped from Hugh Dockings's hand.

Only one strident, shouting voice was heard over the paralyzed quiet.

"Hugh, Hugh, what's wrong with you? Hugh! Get up. Can't anybody help him? Hugh! Get up." The piercing sound made by the tall, black-haired woman's words was unpleasant to hear.

Claude Revel, the gathering's host, stepped into the scene. He was barely medium in height, with the outline of a paunch beginning around his waist. Despite his approaching sixtieth birthday, there were no discernable traces of greying among the shiny black hair which trimmed his round balding head.

"Imogen, be quiet," he said to his sister in his deep, rich voice. "You're not helping." He grasped her long arm with a firm hold and looked around the hushed gathering for his wife.

Standing close by, Pamela Revel had been watching the frightened face of her sister-in-law Imogen as her fiancé Hugh Dockings fell stricken in front of her. There would be no wedding tomorrow. Inside her chest Pamela felt a sense of pleasure involuntarily well up, and she set her jaw. It wouldn't do to let her delicate face, artfully made up to cloak the effects of time on her fading beauty, give away her feelings.

Imogen's tall, agitated figure began to pull away from her brother to reach for the unmoving form of Hugh Dockings on the floor. Claude found his wife's eyes, and they met, unspeaking but saying what needed to be said. Pamela moved quickly past her bewildered guests and clutched firmly onto Imogen Revel. "Come away, Imogen," Pamela said without feeling. "You shouldn't stay here."

"Hugh." The woman gave out a moan. "What's wrong with him? Why won't he move?" Her large black eyes were opened wide, and she pulled wildly on a clump of her hair.

"He's dead," Pamela said. "Surely you can see that." She tried once again to move her sister-in-law away from the man lying on the floor.

Imogen would not budge. Her solid weight and broad shoulders made her an uneven match for the effort of the short, slim frame of her sister-in-law. Pamela sighed. She nodded to Claude, and he dropped to his knees over the prostrate body of Hugh Dockings. Wincing as her husband's knee dipped into a puddle of red wine from the dead man's fallen glass, Pamela suppressed an admonition for Claude to avoid the stain. Instead, a quick, involuntary action made her dig her long pink finger nails into Imogen's arm.

Imogen flinched, but refused to make a sound. Determinedly, her big eyes wet with tears, she stared as her brother ceremoniously put his own face close to the purple, distorted one on the floor. Imogen watched as Claude felt under the fleshy jaw line for the pulse and listened to the still chest for sounds of breathing. No physicians at the gathering had rushed to this duty and so it fell to Claude Revel, a fourth generation merchant banker, to pronounce the words in a way which made them final at last.

"Hugh Dockings is dead."

Pamela was easily able to take her hands away as the virginal, middle-aged woman, whom Hugh Dockings had promised to marry on the following day, dropped gracelessly in a crumpled faint by his side. There was no question in Pamela's mind. The deep red stain seeping into the yellow silk of Imogen's new dress would never come out.

1

Caroline Kent had been standing less than two feet from Hugh Dockings when he fell to the floor. She was doing her social duty, listening as old Dorsey Revel, the youngest brother of Claude's late father, was repeating for the third, or possibly it was the fourth time, "We all miss Reed. That we do. Claude was saying it again only last week. 'If only Reed Kent were still alive, Uncle Dorsey. He would have handled this business with the Swiss discreetly.' My nephew Claude did not want to get directly involved, Caroline, I can tell you. But that fellow Jenkins made such a botch of the negotiations." He paused to take a drink of his wine, and his black eyes twinkled at her from over his glass.

Dorsey Revel had been retired from Syndicat Revel, the Revel family's bank, for over ten years, but he liked to keep up with the gossip. He was old enough to be her grandfather, and Caroline couldn't check the feeling that she must be courteous to him. Dorsey enjoyed feminine company. His wife Helen had died over twenty years ago. The couple had had no children.

"I don't mind admitting it, Caroline, that I thought Reed awfully young when he was first given all that responsibility at the bank. But my brother Henri had known your father-in-law, and didn't we all know the story of Frederick Kent's losing all that money in that old oil deal in the Far East? That was the beginning of the end, wasn't it?"

"No, Caroline, Henley Jenkins is not the man your late husband was," Dorsey said, shaking his head. "But, of course, I needn't tell you that about Reed. Such a brilliant career he was building. And to have it all end in a car crash."

Caroline willed her ears to stop listening. She shifted her eyes over Dorsey's head to where his niece Imogen was standing talking to her niece, Claudine. All the male Revels were short. This masculine family gene of strong proportions was not in the females of the line, everyone of whom towered over their male relations. It was their particular dark coloring which every Revel shared. The members of the family gathered in the ballroom at Mon Plaisir this afternoon to celebrate the betrothal of Imogen Revel to Hugh Dockings were all easily identified by their heavy black Gallic eyes and thick black hair.

As her fiancé joined her and Claudine, Caroline saw the look of excitement come over Imogen's plain face. The middle-aged Imogen Revel had never seemed interested in the opposite sex, and the news of this engagement to her colleague at the Connecticut boarding school where they both taught had caught Newport society by surprise. They were to be married on the following day in a private family ceremony.

"Louise was such a saint through everything, Caroline," Dorsey was saying. "I haven't seen much of your mother-in-law this afternoon." His eyes grazed around the room, and he turned back disappointedly to Caroline when he did not find the object of his search. "Such a lovely woman. And always so loyal to Frederick. Even though he practically left her penniless when he died. And Reed was still in law school."

"Caroline, are you listening, my dear?"

"That was a difficult time," Caroline said mechanically. She saw Hugh reach for the wine glass in Imogen's hand. From his flushed appearance he must already have had a great deal to drink.

Hugh Dockings was looking straight at Caroline now, and she stared back into his astonished eyes. The liquid was in his throat, and he was teetering past Imogen toward her. Drops of perspiration collected around his temples and unkept, abundant eyebrows.

"And when Reed had to put Kenwood up for rent," Dorsey continued, "Louise must have been mortified. Of course I know that the Newport property was really all that was left in the estate, and Louise badly needed the income."

"Those Texans!" Dorsey declared with exaggerated angst in his voice. He couldn't see the man behind him whose bloodshot, watering eyes beseeched Caroline.

Hugh touched for his tongue, and Caroline would remember for a long time the picture of the thick square fingertips and the ugly red gash of an unhealed scrape across the middle knuckle.

"You wouldn't have believed them. Of course they wanted to meet everybody in Newport."

Hugh's knees were buckling.

"Waiters with white gloves at dinner. Pamela refused to go back to Kenwood as long as they were living there, and I can tell you that Claude --"

Imogen screamed as the man beside her dropped to the floor. The music stopped. Dorsey allowed an irritated look to cross his face.

"He's dead," Caroline said silently to herself. She had been hearing of her husband being spoken of as dead, and now this man lay dead before her. Imogen was screaming and calling for Hugh to get up. Caroline stood and watched as Claude and his wife reached her and tried to restrain her.

"Hugh Dockings is dead," Claude Revel said.

"Dead?" Dorsey Revel repeated in an annoyed tone.

"Oh, dear," he clucked as his niece collapsed beside the lifeless form of her fiancé. "Imogen has always been so ungraceful, even as a child." Pamela bent down to save Imogen's small gold purse from sliding into a pool of wine on the floor.

Caroline didn't answer the old man. She was staring at the pieces of the broken wine glass, which had scattered on the polished wood

3

floor amid the smeared globules of red wine. Claude was also looking down at the wet, broken glass.

"Clean this up," Claude commanded to a waiter who was standing nearby. The waiter's dazed eyes were fixated on the dead man on the floor.

"No," Caroline heard herself saying. "No one should touch that or step near the body." She saw that Claude frowned as she spoke. "The police will want to see Hugh as he fell and examine that glass."

"I'm sorry this has happened," Claude said to the nearest onlookers. His tone was apologetic. "Pamela is seeing to my sister. Please, I hope you will all have something to restore you." He clapped his hands for the drinks' service to begin. "We will get a doctor for poor Hugh."

"We must call the police," Caroline whispered to Claude. The buzz of sound began to rise in the room as the guests reached for their glasses.

Claude smiled reassuringly around the room, but his lowered voice hissed angrily to Caroline. "What are you talking about, Caroline? I'm going to find Martin Stanton. He'll call for an ambulance."

"It's too late for Dr. Stanton. I'm sorry, Claude, but the death is suspicious. The police need to be called." She looked around the room and added, "I don't think the police will want anyone to leave before they can be questioned."

"About what?" Claude asked.

"Something was in the burgundy," Caroline answered. "Hugh knew it as soon as he drank it. I saw him."

"Do you think he was poisoned, Caroline?" Dorsey asked eagerly. Claude gave his uncle a look of warning, but the old man made no attempt to conceal his delight that the possibility existed.

"Uncle Dorsey," Claude said, "Hugh's had some sort of seizure. A stroke, perhaps. Or his heart. You can help by finding Martin Stanton. Perhaps he stepped out onto the terrace. Go look for him, will you, please? I can't imagine why all this commotion hasn't brought him over here."

"All right, Claude, I'll go. But I think you'd better listen to Caroline. We need the police. The man's dead." He paused and then added with a mischievous grin, "In suspicious circumstances."

"I'm sorry, Claude," Caroline repeated as Dorsey left them. "You didn't see him. I saw his face when he swallowed the wine. He tasted something wrong."

"Hugh had been drinking heavily all afternoon, Caroline. You didn't know him. He was a middle-aged man, at least twenty pounds overweight, who drank to excess and smoked. Let's not jump to other conclusions, shall we? I'm sure the good doctor will agree."

"I don't think the broken glass and wine ought to be cleaned up just yet. It might provide a clue to what made him die."

"All right," Claude said impatiently. His short, compact body was twitching with anxiety. "I think I had better go on and try to get an ambulance. I don't know when Dorsey will find Martin. We must get Hugh moved to a more suitable place."

"If you call 911, they will send the Emergency Medical Service. I don't think we should move Hugh until they get here."

"Fine, Caroline. Would you stay here with the body, if it doesn't upset you? I see Uncle Dorsey has stopped to fill Aunt Grace in on all the details. I'd better take care of things myself."

Before Caroline could form a reply, Claude Revel walked away.

She looked down at the face of the man on the floor. The fluid which had dribbled from his mouth was drying to a grey scum around his chin. Hugh Dockings was beginning to look forgotten. Imogen had been helped from the scene, and the guests were talking now. Few of the people in the ballroom had known Dockings personally. Most of the guests were family and friends of the Revels who, like herself, had met Hugh Dockings for the first time this afternoon. Caroline looked about the room. Were her suspicions about the wine in the glass correct? Was there someone at the party who wanted to deny Imogen her chance at happiness by doing away with her fiancé?

It was a beautiful afternoon in Newport, one of the last days of spring before the summer season began. Who would spoil it all with murder?

2

Claude Revel tapped lightly on the study door and, without waiting for an answer, opened it. His first view of the two women inside gave him some reassurance that things might be going better than he had dared hope. He walked quickly inside the dimly lit room and re-closed the heavy oak door. Shadows spread across the figure reclining on the brown leather sofa. Claude squinted to see in what condition he would find his sister Imogen.

"How is she?" He directed his question to his wife Pamela, an authority he trusted much more than Imogen.

"We're managing," Pamela said, a cautious tone in her voice. Her sister-in-law instantly picked up on the error and became agitated, waving her long arms about her as she tried to raise herself up on the sofa's soft leather surface.

"Be careful, Imogen," Pamela said, "You should remain lying down. You've had a shock."

Claude went to his sister's side and tried to settle her back against the large needlepoint pillow, a medieval scene of white unicorns floating against a background of red roses.

"Imogen, you must be brave."

"Hugh, oh, Hugh." Loud sobbing began, and Claude turned helplessly to Pamela as Imogen continued to cry the dead man's name.

"What is happening out there?" Pamela asked with some anxiety. "Are the guests leaving?"

"No," her husband said. "But I'm afraid that the police have been called."

"The police!" Imogen cried.

"It's usual," Claude began in what he believed to be a natural and comforting voice. "We have had an unexpected death. Martin Stanton assured me that the police will come as a formality. Nothing more."

"I must speak to whomever's in charge," Imogen said sobbing.

"Yes, yes, my dear," Claude said. "In due time. I'm sure the police will want to talk to you, also. I know you were standing by his side when it happened. Such a consolation I would say, wouldn't you, Imogen? To be with him at the end."

Pamela frowned and gave her husband a clear signal that he should stop speaking such nonsense.

"But I must speak to the police," Imogen said in a voice now becoming determined. "It's vital."

"Why?" Pamela asked.

"Because," Imogen said firmly.

"But why?" her sister-in-law pressed. "What do you have to tell them that is so important?"

"Everything," Imogen said. "Don't you see? It was my wine glass that Hugh drank from."

"What! Your glass? Are you sure?"

"Oh, yes."

"But how?"

"It was mine. I had taken the glass from the waiter's tray. It was the last glass of red wine on the tray, and Hugh asked him to bring some more. I said, 'Here, Hugh, take mine. I'll wait for another one'." At this point, Imogen lowered her voice to whisper a confidence. "Hugh liked to drink red wine, you know, sometimes too much for his own good. But I wasn't going to interfere with that once we were married. Oh, no," she continued, her voice resuming its normal timber, "I had no intention of being that kind of wife."

"He took your glass?" Claude prodded her back to the important topic. He had no interest in his sister's advice for a happy marriage.

"Hugh insisted that I keep mine, and he would wait. But that waiter didn't return, and Hugh -- well, I could see he wanted the drink. So I gave him mine," she sobbed.

"But you didn't drink from it?" Pamela's small hazel eyes had narrowed into tight slits.

"No. I wanted Hugh to have it. I was saving it for him."

"And you held it in your hand? You didn't put it down?"

"It's so difficult now to remember," Imogen said.

Pamela's mouth twitched with irritation.

"Think, Imogen, the glass." Imogen closed her eyes.

"There were so many people there. We were still talking to Claudine. We were all between two of the French windows. There is one of the tall plant stands there, the one with the palm --"

"Yes, yes, we all know where the damned plant is," Claude interrupted.

"Well," Imogen said, her voice sounding aggrieved, "I'm trying to remember exactly. The police will want exact information on this... I remember now." Claude stared at his sister, his heart pounding in his chest. "I was afraid someone would jar my hand while I was holding the glass. It was full, and I didn't want any wine to spill on my dress." Here, she looked at the folds of her yellow silk skirt. The wine stain, blossomed to a large jagged roundness, was drying to an ugly, uneven purple color. "Now, of course, it seems so unimportant." She whimpered.

"I sat the glass on the stand, on the ledge around the pot. It must have been there for a few minutes. Then, when Hugh remarked that the waiter had not come back, I convinced him that he should take my drink after all."

"What does it mean?" Claude asked. He turned to his wife for an answer.

"It means what your sister has already cleverly concluded, Claude. Imogen, and not Hugh Dockings, was intended to drink from that glass."

"But, that's ridiculous," Claude sputtered. "There was nothing wrong with our wine. Hugh had some sort of attack. Heart or... or a seizure. A stroke. Imogen, you know how he drank. You just said it yourself." His sister covered her eyes with her hands. "Oh, this is nonsense."

"No, Claude," Imogen insisted. "It's true. There was something wrong with that wine. I know it now. We must get it analyzed." Here her attempt to get up from the sofa was successful, and she stood looking down at her brother. "You didn't see Hugh's face as soon as he drank that wine. When it went down his throat, he knew right away there was something in the glass besides the burgundy. That's what killed him. We must tell the police."

"Let's not jump to conclusions," Claude said. He turned to his wife, who seemed riveted by Imogen's narrative, for support.

"Oh, my God," Imogen gasped. "He died in my place. Oh, my precious Hugh." She lifted her eyes upward, although Claude thought it a slim possibility that Hugh's new residence lay in that direction.

"Imogen," Pamela said. "You're beginning to sound like an utter fool."

"My life's in danger, Pamela, and you call me a fool. I could be dead on the floor out there. How would you feel then?" Imogen stopped and stared, her eyes blazing. "You both would be glad, wouldn't you? Hugh and I were definitely a nuisance to you and Claude, weren't we, Pamela?"

"Don't be ridiculous," Claude said. "We're your family."

"Yes, my family," Imogen said bitterly. "I'm not so sure you aren't the ones who put the poison in my glass."

"How could we have done that?" Claude asked helplessly.

"That's what the police will have to find out," his sister said.

"You've had a shock, Imogen. You must rest. Claude will talk to the police."

"Yes, Imogen. You must take some time to understand all that's happened. You must recover yourself. I'll get Aunt Grace to sit with you."

Imogen sat back down on the sofa. There was a look of sadness now about her eyes and mouth. She looked weak and vulnerable.

"Go out there, Claude," he heard his wife say. "Make sure you handle the police very carefully."

"Of course," he said.

"I would like Aunt Grace to come," Imogen said.

There was a firm knock at the door, and Claudine Revel came into the room.

"Father, the police are here," she said. Her intelligent black eyes came to rest on the stiff figure of her aunt, who was holding a monogrammed handkerchief to her eyes.

His daughter's entrance into the room brought Claude a feeling of relief. He adored his only child and often acted as her shield when others might be tempted to suggest that she was less than perfect.

"I'll come," Claude answered quickly. "Come with me, Claudine."

"I should see the police," Imogen said. "Have Claudine show whoever is in charge to me in here."

"They seem very busy in the ballroom, Aunt Imogen," Claudine answered. "The paramedics are here, also."

"Claude, you know I must see them immediately."

"Come along with me, Claudine," he said. "I'll need you to help me." He saw his daughter smile down at her aunt. Why must she do that, he thought as he drew Claudine out into the hallway.

"She's being disgusting," Claudine said.

"Claudine," her father said gently.

"I suppose we'll all be treated to her histrionics over this."

"Hugh is dead. You have to expect her to be distressed by what has happened."

"She didn't love him. She couldn't love anything."

Claude paused in the hallway and took his daughter's hand.

"Please, darling," he said, looking up at her. Her youthful face was handsome, not beautiful. "Will you please try to be kind to her? She's in shock, I think. Don't be harsh on her. You said you were going to be pleasant to her today. The house is full of guests. And the police will be watching everything we say and do. Do you understand?"

"Even though she hasn't been kind to me in the past?"

"For my sake?" She nodded. He knew she wouldn't let him down. "Good," he said with a smile. "I know you won't disappoint me."

"Of course, Father, I will do what you want. I've got to be in London for the bank by the end of the week, and I don't want anything to interfere with that."

"Of course not," he said, hiding his surprise that she expected that anything would *interfere with that*.

3

In the nineteen months since her husband Reed's death, Caroline Kent had frequently let her mind imagine the accident scene which she had never seen in real life. It was television, she supposed. The dramatic car crashes which were depicted nightly with their wailing sirens, the screech of the tires as the emergency response teams reached the scene, the lights, the blue-black streets. She saw Reed over and over, his car crumpled, the door impossible to open. People were bustling about, calling for action. If it hadn't happened that way to Reed, she remembered it that way.

The night Reed died she had been waiting for him to return from a short business trip to Albany where he had gone to appear before the banking commission on Syndicat Revel's behalf. There had been some discussion of whether he would spend the night if the proceedings went late. They had not, and Caroline knew Reed's telephone message, which had come while she was in rehearsal, by heart.

"Darling, good news. I'll be home at nine at the latest. If you're not too tired from the theater, we'll go to Mario's. I know you thought --" and here he laughed indulgently "-- that I wouldn't finish until late, but I'm done and coming home to see you."

Coming home to see you. She still heard the words in her head. And then he had ended with *I love you*.

She had saved the message on her cell phone for months, repeatedly listening to it and pressing the *SAVE* function. Later she had read that it was not an uncommon act. She was one of many who had lost a loved one and clung to the bits and pieces, scraps of a life, abruptly left behind.

The emergency workers bending over Hugh Dockings brought everything back to her. She was standing in the grand ballroom of the Revels' house, watching Hugh, thinking of Reed. And then the police had come, and that brought back the sounds of sirens and braking cars to her ears. Her head was pounding, and she wanted air.

"Caroline." She heard the soft voice at the same time she felt the gentle touch on her arm.

"Louise," she said with undisguised relief. "Do you think we can go outside for some air?"

"Of course, my dear."

Her mother-in-law led her toward the French windows.

"Here I am leaning on you again, Louise," she said quietly.

"We lean on each other, Caroline. I think you know that."

The two women reached the doorway and stepped out onto the terrace. There were a few others there, smoking. Life goes on, Caroline thought in her head, and she wanted so much to cry. But that was impossible to do in front of Louise.

"Is this better?" Louise asked.

"Yes," her daughter-in-law said. "I'll be fine now. I was standing near him when he died." Hugh she meant; Reed she thought of.

"It was a shock, dear. Hardly the thing we expected to happen on this fine afternoon."

Louise's clear blue eyes looked grave. She was diminutive in stature, with a cap of curly grey hair. Her friendship with the Revels had extended over many years, both in New York City and in Newport. That Reed had ended up in the family's merchant bank was, as Dorsey had recalled earlier, an explicit favor done by Henri Revel to his old friend's son. Not, of course, that Reed couldn't have done well on his own, but that was not the way things were done in these old families, and Reed had himself been a traditionalist in that regard. He had liked being part of the Revel banking history that went back four generations. After all, his father had seen to it that the Kents no longer had a family enterprise to maintain them. Reed was an attorney, not a banker, so he had not interfered with the Revel family's established line of succession. All in all, he had fitted in very nicely. It was to have been a good career.

"The police seem to be here in large number," Louise observed as a uniformed officer came to the door and surveyed the guests on the terrace. "Why do you suppose that is? Is there something wrong? I heard people saying that Hugh must have had a heart attack."

"I don't think it was his heart, Louise. It happened as soon as he drank some red wine. He tried to spit it out and then he began to choke."

"Something was wrong with the wine?"

"It's likely something was put in the wine," Caroline said in a low voice.

"You mean that... that Hugh Dockings..." Louise Kent's voice had dropped to a bare whisper. "Are you saying that Hugh Dockings was deliberately killed?"

"I'm afraid that possibility has to be considered."

"But, who would be that cruel to Imogen?" Louise asked.

"Imogen? Why do you think this was directed against Imogen?"

"I can't imagine anyone wanting to kill Hugh, Caroline. From all accounts I have had of him from Grace March, he is a most ordinary man."

"Why would anyone want to hurt Imogen?"

"I've no business conjecturing on who might want the death of either of them. I can only hope that it's all a mistake, and that Hugh did die of some natural cause. After all, it would mean that someone here is a murderer."

15

Caroline looked up at the facade of the house. The yellow limestone looked peaceful in the late afternoon sun. Mon Plaisir was a reproduction of a French chateau, designed to give pleasure to its wealthy owners. That was all any of the Newport mansions had been built for. Amusements and pleasure.

"It's unreal," Caroline agreed. "There has to be some perfectly reasonable explanation for the death of Hugh Dockings."

"It was cyanide poisoning. You don't see many cases of that, but this one is textbook."

Daniel Peters, the medical examiner, was describing his preliminary conclusions to Lt. Hank Nightingale and Sgt. Ben Davies of the Newport Police Department. The three men were seated in the morning room at Mon Plaisir where Claude Revel had shown them after Hank requested a room to use for interviews. From his chipper demeanor, which bordered on euphoria, Lt. Nightingale thought Dan Peters might have been describing a rare species of orchid he had just discovered growing wild in his back yard.

"Cyanide," Ben repeated with a look of amazement. "What do you know about that." He whistled.

"The effect of it combined with alcohol is particularly swift," Peters continued, "and I was given to understand that the deceased had ingested a large amount of red wine today. If he had eaten little or no food, that would make the absorption of the poison more rapid."

"Make a note of that, Ben," Hank said to his subordinate.

"The autopsy will tell us for sure," Peters said.

"And you think the cyanide was in the wine, Dr. Peters?" Ben asked.

"Most probably. That would explain the immediate reaction after swallowing by the deceased due to the intense burning sensation as the poison went down his throat. Prussic acid is my guess. It's liquid and could have been easily concealed in a small vessel until it was needed."

"In someone's pocket," Hank said. "Handy."

"Prussic acid," Daniel Peters repeated, still cheery. "Right out of a mystery story. No, sir, you don't see this everyday."

"I'm glad we could provide you with something out of the ordinary, Dan," Nightingale said.

"Is that the stuff that smells like bitter almonds?" Ben asked.

"You're thinking of potassium cyanide, Ben," the medical examiner said. "That's a solid. White granules. It's what's used in photography. That's how people usually get their hands on it. This, I think we'll find, was hydrocyanic acid. We'll know more after we get him on the table."

"That's got to be done right away," Hank said. "I've got two hundred assorted guests and hired help out there. The chief isn't going to like it if we keep several members of one of the city's rich and not-so-famous, but important nonetheless, families under the police microscope any longer than is necessary."

"I understand, Hank," Peters said. He rose from the chair and, still smiling, left the room.

"What did you learn from the daughter, Ben?" Hank asked after the medical examiner had closed the door. "Before she went to get her father."

"This is a party to celebrate her aunt's wedding tomorrow. Funny, isn't it? The wedding's tomorrow, the party's today." Ben shook his head. He was an affable policeman, his thin red hair greying and his freckled face beginning to show his age. He had been working with Hank for the last seven years, and his value to his superior often lay in his ability to see right to the center of things.

"What have you got on the deceased?"

"Hugh Dockings. Age, fifty-five. He was to marry the aunt tomorrow, as we said." Here Ben consulted his notebook and read off the name. "Imogen Revel. She's the sister of this Claude Revel who owns the house."

"Does she live here?"

"Nobody actually lives here. All year round that is. Ms. Revel, Claudine, made it clear that the family lives in New York City. She expressed to me that she hoped this event would not interfere with their returning there."

"Oh?" Hank raised his eyebrows.

"Rather officious young female, if you ask me, Lieutenant. Although it is true that she works down in Manhattan at the family bank. Family has its own bank, you see." Ben shook his head as if this were something to be ridiculed. Ben had the heart of a true populist.

"And the deceased? Where did he live?"

Ben consulted his notebook again and read from his notes. "Hugh Dockings. Retired last week, at the end of the term, from The Camden School." He looked up. "I was given to understand it's one of those fancy boarding schools in Connecticut."

"I've heard of its reputation," Hank said, and Ben resumed reading.

"Both he and Ms. Imogen Revel were teachers there, and both lived in a small town called Waterville. That's where the school is. This Dockings was retiring, and they were to be married tomorrow, Sunday."

"And was Ms. Revel retiring as well?"

"That I did not ask. They were leaving on Monday to fly to Greece for a sailing trip which was to be their honeymoon."

With that, Ben snapped the book closed.

"All right," Hank said. "We'll have Claude Revel back. He said that his sister wants very much to talk to us, but I want to get more background before I see her."

"Right. I'll have Officer Pearson find him."

Ben went to the door and conferred with the uniformed officer standing outside it. Hank took the opportunity to get up and stretch his long legs. He hated to admit it, but he was excited at the prospect of another murder investigation. Homicide, if indeed it was the case here, was a challenge he relished.

His thoughts were interrupted by the appearance of Claude Revel in the doorway of the morning room.

"Come in, Mr. Revel," Hank said. "Sit down." He gestured toward the chintz upholstered chair which he had recently vacated. Claude hesitated slightly, then took the seat. The peach color which predominated in the decorating scheme looked sallow without the backlighting of the morning sun, and the owner of Mon Plaisir looked grey in the room's shadows. Ben ceremoniously took out his notebook and poised his pen to write. As Claude watched the sergeant's motion as he annotated the top of the page, Hank closed the door to the room with a loud thud. Claude jerked his head toward the door.

Hank walked back to the center of the room and was pleased to realize that Claude Revel's eyes were following him.

4

As he watched Hank Nightingale walk back into the center of the morning room Claude Revel felt he was beginning to get his bearings at last. Nightingale's slamming the door to give the effect of being in control was, to Claude's mind, an absurd gesture. Perhaps, he thought recklessly, this won't be so bad after all. Claude crossed his legs and leaned back in the chair. He was used to keeping an unreadable face in negotiations. This experience couldn't be dissimilar.

"Your officers have been very polite to my guests, Lt. Nightingale, and I want to thank you for that." He allowed himself to study the policeman as he spoke. Nightingale was tall. Young, he thought. Less than forty. Nightingale's hair was black, thick and curly, and his eyes were a deep shade of blue. The detective had a handsome face, and Claude judged that Nightingale knew that.

"It's part of our training, Mr. Revel. The department serves the community. We try to do a good job of that."

"Yes," Claude said, "I can see that, Lieutenant." He didn't care for the conversational ball hit back to his court. "What will happen once your officers finish taking everyone's names and addresses?" The scene in the ballroom was beginning to resemble security check-in at the airport. The two hundred guests had been organized by the officers into orderly groups to process each individual's information.

The Revels' elegantly attired guests looked totally out of place in the new official setting.

"My people are making a list of everyone who is here. They'll screen for the ones they think we should interview further. The staff, also. I understand you employed caterers for this party."

"Oh, yes. We don't keep that much staff here. It's not like the old days in Newport when these kinds of parties and dinners were put on every night in the summer. There are several reliable firms that provide the food and the wait staff."

"But not the drink?" Nightingale's question was sharp, and Claude answered quickly.

"No, no, not the drink."

"And where did that come from?"

"Mostly from our own cellars. I like to lay down my own wines."

"And that's what you served? Wine only?"

"Predominately. The waiters carried champagne, white and red wine, and sparkling water on the trays. They were instructed to bring anything from the bar stock a guest might want. Hard liquor, or other soft drinks, if that was their preference."

"I'm told Mr. Dockings had been drinking red wine."

"That was his usual drink," Claude said.

"The medical examiner is far from satisfied with the look of the deceased."

"I think it was a heart attack myself."

"Had Mr. Dockings eaten anything at the party? Would you happen to know?"

"I doubt very much whether he had. My sister's fiancé was not a man of proper living habits. That's why I don't think you should rule out some sort of attack or a stroke. He was addicted to red wine. *Cheap* red wine. You don't know how it galled me to see him swill back my vintage French wines." The lieutenant's eyebrows rose at this comment, and Claude stopped speaking at once. What was he doing, running on like this? He stiffened his shoulders and closed his lips.

"We'll do an autopsy," the detective said.

"Yes, I expected that. Will there be anything else, Lieutenant?" Claude asked.

"Yes," Nightingale said. "Tell me why this party was held today and not tomorrow. That's when I understand the actual wedding ceremony was to occur."

"That," Claude said evenly, "was my sister Imogen's decision."

"Why was that, do you think?"

"My sister is not a young woman. I believe she felt that a private ceremony, just for the family -- we do have a large family, as I expect you'll learn -- was appropriate. In fact, she was insistent that there be no gifts from our guests today. Only their presence to wish her, and Hugh of course, well for their future."

"I see," Nightingale said. "How old is your sister, Mr. Revel?"

"How old?"

"Do you mind answering it?"

"No, I suppose the police can obtain any information they like. She is fifty-seven."

"Thank you."

"We were going to have the wedding in the chapel. That reminds me. I'd better have someone change the flowers there. They are festive, and some of the family will no doubt want to pray for Hugh's poor soul."

"You have a chapel in the house?" the sergeant asked.

"Yes. Our family is French and Roman Catholic. The house was built in the French chateau style, and it is quite usual to find a chapel in such houses in France."

"Are any of Mr. Dockings's relatives here today?" Nightingale asked. Claude shook his head. "Do you know if he had any close relatives?"

"I have no idea. He never spoke of anyone. Certainly he didn't ask us to invite them."

"How long had Ms. Revel and Mr. Dockings known each other?"

"For many years. They taught together at The Camden School in Waterville, Connecticut."

"What subject does your sister teach?"

"She has been a physical education instructor. She also coached several of the girls' sports teams. Of course, she has resigned to be married." Claude shook his head. He was beginning to understand that Imogen was not going to be married tomorrow, and that she -- and he -- would have to have some new plan for her life.

"And Mr. Dockings?"

"What about Mr. Dockings?"

"What did he teach?"

"Hugh? Some kind of science teacher. But, the only thing I ever remember his talking about was coaching the sailing team at the school. That's why they were coming to Newport."

"I'm afraid you've lost me, Mr. Revel."

"Imogen and Hugh planned to live in Newport all year round, for the sailing. I said before that Dockings was addicted to red wine, and I should have said sailing also. Red wine and sailing were his two passions."

"I wouldn't have thought they would mix," Davies commented.

"I've done plenty of sailing myself," the lieutenant said, "and they don't mix."

"Oh, Hugh could hold his alcohol. I'm not sure I've ever seen him drunk, although I suspect what he was like most of the time was because of the influence of the drink. One never knows. He had done quite a bit of sailing, though. I thought he knew his stuff there. Back and forth to Bermuda or the Caribbean at the drop of a hat. At least once across the Atlantic, that I know about."

"You said before," Nightingale began, "that your sister and her fiancé had known each other for many years. Had they always planned to marry when Mr. Dockings retired?"

"Oh, no. Imogen never said a word that suggested she might be thinking of marriage until last Christmas."

"And what happened at Christmas?"

"My sister invited Hugh to spend the holidays with us. She told me then that they had an *understanding*."

"Did you come here for the holidays?"

"We are usually at our house in New York City. We never spend Christmas in Newport."

"Where is your sister's home, Mr. Revel?"

"She rented a small house in Waterville for the school year. During holidays she lived with my family. She liked coming to Newport with us in the summer."

"And you indicated that she and Mr. Dockings were coming to live here all year round." The lieutenant looked about the room as if to indicate that *here* meant Mon Plaisir.

"In the main house?" Claude shook his head.

"Not here," Nightingale said. "Then, may I ask where, Mr. Revel?"

"Their home was to be at Des Arbres." Claude stood up and went to one of the tall windows and motioned for the detective to follow. "Can you see that square stone building across the lawn?"

The landscaping at Mon Plaisir was of a formal design, with the shrubbery and flowers placed in ornamental arrangements of various shapes and sizes. In the last reaches of the sweeping lawn stood a compact structure surrounded by billowing shade trees. It was two stories high and graced with three closely-placed arches across its front. The sergeant followed them to the window, and the two policemen looked in the direction of Claude's pointing finger.

"Days Arbra?" Davies repeated quizzically.

"It means *the trees* in French," Nightingale explained to Ben. "What is it?" he asked, turning to Claude.

"The English would call it a folly. My grandfather always insisted we use the French word for it, the *pavilion*. It's a garden house. Three rooms originally on the main level, and two more on top. I had it modernized for Imogen so she and Hugh could live there. Installed a kitchen on the ground floor and a bathroom upstairs."

"And your sister and her husband were to live there all year round?"

"For the present, that was their plan. Hugh was delighted to have his own place in Newport."

"You say it was *his*?"

"No. It belongs only to Imogen. I gave it to her as an engagement present. I had the papers drawn up to separate that end of the grounds from the main part. She owns the pavilion and the small plot of land on that corner."

"That was very generous of you, Mr. Revel."

"Very daring, you ought to say. Mon Plaisir has always passed intact to the surviving eldest son of the eldest son in the Revel family. By the terms of my great-grandfather's original will, he wanted no female members of the family to hold property. Also, no women were ever left money in their own right. We're French, you see, and my ancestor believed in tradition. It's been the same at Syndicat Revel. Only the male members of the family were to have held positions."

"Yet your daughter Claudine has a job there, I understand."

"She does," Claude said proudly, "and I was responsible for breaking that tradition as well."

"You could do that?"

"I am chairman of the bank. Claudine is my only child and my heir."

"But you said something about a will?"

"Oh, that," Claude said. "My lawyers were able to manage around the will as far as Des Arbres goes. And, for the bank itself, we have always followed family custom. My father did, as my grandfather, who was the original Claude Revel's son Henri, certainly did."

"Syndicat Revel has remained in your family for a long time."

"Our family has been blessed." Claude stopped, aware of the policemen's exchanging glances. "Until this business today. My sister Imogen is devastated. I can't but believe this was her last chance at happiness."

"You're equating marriage with happiness?"

"I may have a high position in the financial world, Lt. Nightingale, but I can assure you that it is my wife and daughter who are at the center of my life." He paused. "For the Revels, family is everything."

"I can appreciate that sentiment," Nightingale said.

"The Revels have sustained each other for almost a hundred and thirty years. That's when my great-grandfather came from Paris, married my great-grandmother Violet Bishop, started Syndicat Revel, and founded our family line in the United States."

"That's quite a history."

"Yes, Lieutenant. I never forget it."

5

"The important thing is that we all have alibis."

"What is yours, Dorsey?" Louise Kent asked.

"Why Caroline, of course." Dorsey smiled. "We will alibi each other, won't we, Caroline?"

The ballroom had begun to empty of guests, and it had been an easy task for Dorsey Revel to spot Caroline and her mother-in-law as they came in from the terrace.

"Yes, Dorsey. I don't see how you could have poisoned the wine."

"And I shall alibi you, Caroline. I can't wait to talk to the police lieutenant. Claude said he is digging into everything." Dorsey clapped his hands with relish.

"Lieutenant?" Caroline asked, her face alert. She saw Louise watching her. "What is his name? What did he look like?"

"Oh, I didn't see him. I don't know his name," Dorsey answered, ignoring Caroline's sudden frown. He turned toward her mother-in-law. "I'm sure I can be of immense help in this inquiry."

"I'd have thought you would want the police to respect your family's privacy."

"For what earthly purpose, Louise?" Dorsey asked with a laugh. "My life is dull these days, and I applaud Hugh Dockings's bringing some excitement into it."

"By dying?" Louise asked.

"Listen," Dorsey said, drawing his animated face close to Louise's head. He motioned for Caroline to bend down. "I've got something I'll tell you first. I know who the murderer is."

"What?" Caroline asked.

"Yes," Dorsey whispered. "I can point her out to you. She's in this very room. Right now."

Caroline looked around. She saw several familiar faces, and she trembled.

"Dorsey," Louise said and drew back from him. "I don't think this is the time nor the place for your games. I know you too well, and I know how you like to manipulate people for your own amusement. If you have real information, you should share it with the police. Otherwise, I think you should be quiet."

"Oh, I definitely intend to tell the police when I see them." He was undeterred by Louise's tongue lashing. "She's right over there."

Dorsey gestured toward the group of people standing about ten feet further along the wall. There were about seven or eight of them, both men and women, and it took Caroline several seconds to recognize their mutual identity as the staff members of The Camden School. At their center was the school's headmaster, Nicholas Pratt, to whom she had been introduced earlier that afternoon.

"The school?" Caroline asked. "You think it's someone from the school?" Besides Pratt there were two other men, and now she counted five women.

"That one," Dorsey said. "The one in the flower print dress. The mousey one."

"What's her name?" Caroline realized she was one of the women who had been smoking on the terrace earlier. She had a tired face and limp brown hair.

"Ah," Dorsey said, glowing with appreciation that Caroline was now cooperating, "I specifically asked the handsome Mr. Pratt to introduce me to her. You see, the interesting thing," and here Dorsey lowered his voice, "is that until my niece Imogen made her dramatic announcement of her engagement last December, that woman considered herself Hugh Dockings's girlfriend."

"Her name is Marilyn Hansen," Dorsey continued. "She's another teacher, and she has been keeping company with the late Mr. Dockings for the last ten or so years. It was she, and not our Imogen, whom everyone at the school thought would hook Hugh if anyone would. There was some feeling that Hugh was the perennial bachelor, and that was why Marilyn was content to be his companion and not his wife. Imogen's snaring him was certainly a shock to her, and according to Nick Pratt, Marilyn has made no secret of her anger over the turn of events. Made quite a scene when Imogen and Hugh told everyone they were engaged."

"And that's what you're basing your charge on?" Louise asked. "You don't kill a man because he leaves you."

"My dear Louise, you have led a sheltered life. Haven't you ever heard of Frankie and Johnny?" Here he winked at Caroline.

"Nick was telling me that this Hansen woman took up sailing even though it made her violently seasick. Nothing prevented her seasickness. She tried ginger tea, those wristbands, even --"

"Dorsey, please," Louise broke in. "You have nothing to base this on. You're just spreading gossip."

"Believe me, Louise, Nick has his suspicions, also. Don't you understand. Imogen stole Hugh from her. Revenge. It's one of the oldest motives for murder. And there's something else." He paused, hoping for some suspense to develop. "Do you know what Marilyn Hansen teaches?"

"What?" Caroline asked.

"Biology," Dorsey said with unconcealed satisfaction.

"I'm not sure I understand --"

"The poison, Caroline. She had access to the science laboratory. She could easily obtain chemicals which were poisonous to lace the fatal drink."

"Dorsey," Caroline said suddenly. "How well did you know Hugh Dockings?"

"Oh, I've been in his company a few times. Imogen has been bringing him home on week-ends to make plans for Des Arbres."

"Why do you think he was marrying Imogen?"

"Oh, for the money, of course. I don't think he loved her, if that's what you mean. Imogen's not a very lovable person. Hugh was retiring, and he didn't want to worry about his old age. That Marilyn Hansen doesn't have money. You can see that by her clothes."

"I see," Caroline said.

"Imogen was buying him a sailboat. Did you know that?" Caroline shook her head. "Hugh had always used the boats which the school owned. Once he retired, he wouldn't be able to sail any of those, now would he? He'd want his own sailboat. Last month he and Imogen went up to the Portsmouth yards to look at boats. They were going to get one when they came back from sailing in Greece on their honeymoon. Nick told me that the boat Hugh wanted was going to cost a quarter of a million dollars. It was to be Imogen's wedding present to Hugh."

"A very generous gift," Louise said.

"Mark my words," Dorsey said. "It was the Revels' money which attracted Hugh to Imogen. And Marilyn Hansen couldn't compete with that. I'm surprised, now that I think of it, that she didn't kill Imogen instead of Hugh. But of course Marilyn was the woman scorned, and I suppose she had to take it out on old Hugh." He glanced toward the spot on the floor where Hugh had died. "Poor Dockings. I suppose the fellow thought he had it made, marrying into the Revel family. It does get to people, you know, when they learn we have our own bank." He winked again at Caroline. "It does sound so impressive."

When Hank Nightingale and Ben Davies knocked at the study door, they were greeted by a tall, elderly woman wearing an ankle-length grey silk dress and supporting her weight with a dark wooden cane.

"You've come to interview Imogen," she said as she stood aside so that they could enter the room. "Claude said you would be coming. I'm Grace March, Imogen's aunt." Her voice was firm. "Imogen, the police are here."

Hank saw the tall figure on the sofa rise and come to greet them. Walking with a dignified step despite the incongruous purple stain on her wrinkled dress, Imogen Revel inclined her head slightly in greeting.

"Thank you, Aunt Grace," Imogen said. "It was kind of you to sit with me."

"Don't worry, my girl," Grace March said as she patted Imogen's hand briskly. "Time heals all wounds."

Imogen looked at her aunt, but failed to respond to her statement of the old adage. Undeterred, the aunt smiled on her niece and, leaning on the cane, walked with a steady step out of the room.

Hank was watching Imogen Revel. He noted her height, taller than her brother, and her coloring which did resemble his. Her thick black hair, stiffly styled in a conventional arrangement for the occasion, had become disheveled. Imogen offered him her hand, and as he shook it, he felt its strength. Her hands were large, yet surprisingly nimble.

"I appreciate your seeing us now, Ms. Revel. I know this must be a difficult time for you."

"I must help you," Imogen said. "Please sit down." She indicated for Hank to take the chair opposite the sofa where she resumed her seat. "And I would ask you one thing before we begin." Hank, in the act of sitting, paused. "Please call me *Miss* Revel."

"Of course," he said.

"You may think me old-fashioned, but I'm used to it. My students call me Miss, and I much prefer it to the newer title of Miz. So harsh, so awkward, I've always thought."

"No problem," Hank said as he settled himself. "Now, I'd like to begin by first getting your impressions of the time when Mr. Dockings suffered his attack."

"I'm sorry, Lt. Nightingale, but this was no ordinary attack caused by a medical problem. Hugh was murdered."

"And tell me exactly why you have come to that conclusion?"

"It's simple. The wine was drugged with something. Hugh knew it as soon as he tasted it. It spilled all over my skirt. I suppose you will want my dress to test the stain."

"Thank you, yes. We'll collect it before we leave today."

"Hugh did take such a big drink out of the glass. It was his habit, you know. He enjoyed his wine so."

"I have heard that," Hank said.

"Yes, well, I suppose Claude has been talking about it. But there's nothing wrong with drinking red wine. All the studies say it keeps you healthy."

"Yes." Hank was letting her talk.

"As soon as he swallowed it, he started gagging and shaking. It couldn't be anything but poisoning. I'm sure your police doctor will confirm it. And he died so quickly." She allowed a sob to escape from her throat. "I'm sorry. Everyone says I must be brave, and I'm trying to be."

"You're doing fine," Hank said. "Tell me. Do you know if your fiancé had eaten food during the party?"

"No, I don't believe he did," she said slowly. "Is it important?"

"I'm curious. The *post mortem* will tell us."

"Yes, that will have to happen, will it not?"

"Tell me about Hugh Dockings, Miss Revel. I need to learn something about him."

"You won't find he had any enemies if that's what you want to know."

"We must look for a reason for this tragedy, Miss Revel."

"I know the reason, Lieutenant. I can tell you right now."

"What is the reason?"

"The poison was meant for me."

"I don't understand. Mr. Dockings drank his wine --"

"No, don't you see? Mr. Dockings drank *my* wine."

"Your wine?"

"It was my glass. I had taken it first. I only gave it to Hugh when the waiter didn't come back with another one for him."

Hank listened as Imogen told her story. Ben wrote the details in his notebook.

"You're absolutely sure of everything you've said?" Hank asked when Imogen had finished. Her face was flushed with excitement.

"Oh, yes."

"The glass was untouched by you, not drunk that is, and for a time, several minutes perhaps, it sat on the plant stand. Is that correct?" She nodded. "Mr. Dockings did not touch the glass during that time?" Imogen looked at Hank open-mouthed.

"Miss Revel? Did Mr. Dockings go near the glass?"

"Why, no, I don't think he did." She paused and wrinkled her eyebrows. "No, I'm sure he didn't."

"Who else was standing near you during this time?"

"Well, that is hard to say. The ballroom was very crowded, and naturally many people wanted to speak to us during the afternoon." She looked away as if she were trying to envision the scene. "I had been talking to my niece Claudine when Hugh joined me. That was about the time the waiter came by. I took the last glass of red wine, as I said, and Claudine took champagne. She talked to Hugh... let me see, and I said for him to take my glass, and Claudine said he should because the waiter would bring me another. She knew I wouldn't mind waiting. I'm not much of a drinker, you see."

"But you drank red wine as a rule?"

"Lately I had. Hugh enjoyed it so, and I used to like to take a glass with him. It was something we could share."

"I see. Now who else do you remember seeing at that time?"

"Caroline Kent was standing in front of us. She was talking to Uncle Dorsey. She was facing us, while Uncle Dorsey had his back to us."

Hank looked across at Ben. "Make a note of Caroline Kent, Sgt. Davies." he said evenly. "I will see her next."

"What do you think, Lieutenant?" Imogen asked. "Doesn't it seem that the glass *was* intended for me?"

"Possibly," he answered slowly. He was making a great effort now to concentrate on the woman in front of him. Caroline here. He tried to push her face from his mind.

"What do you mean?" Imogen leaned forward. "Lieutenant?"

"Well, Miss Revel," Hank answered, refocusing on his interview. "It's also possible that the poison wasn't meant for you. If you said you were saving the glass for Mr. Dockings, and you put it down in the middle of a crowded room, perhaps whoever put the poison in the wine heard you say that you weren't going to drink it."

"I didn't think of that," she said in a hushed voice. "Oh, I'm so confused. Why would anyone want to kill either of us? We're two ordinary people, neither of us would hurt a fly."

And now she began to cry in earnest.

"Perhaps I had better get your aunt back, Miss Revel, to take care of you."

"Oh, leave me alone," Imogen moaned. "No one cares about me; no one ever has. Only Hugh, and now someone's killed him."

6

After his meeting with Imogen Revel was concluded, Hank made his way slowly back to the morning room. He suddenly felt very tired. The eagerness to get started with the investigation was fading as he contemplated this unexpected turn of events. Caroline, here at a probable murder scene. Was that to be their hallmark? Always meeting over dead bodies? He felt sick to his stomach.

He entered the dark morning room, not bothering to turn on a light, choosing instead to stand in the comfort of the dark shell. How long had it been since they had seen one another? But it was no use pretending he couldn't pinpoint the exact time and place. Valentine's Day. February 14. Their favorite table in The White Horse Tavern. The look of fear in her eyes as he tried in vain to convince her to accept that he loved her.

"That's not what I want now, Hank." She hadn't hesitated, her response had been quick. She had meant every word.

And then he had exploded. The couple at the neighboring table had stared at them, and the waiter had come rushing over. As Hank tried to dismiss the waiter, Caroline had taken the opportunity to get up from her chair.

"No," he had said in a loud voice. Once more the waiter turned back. And Hank had felt himself losing total control. Caroline was gone, and he was left sitting there, the lobster pie untouched at their two elegantly set places. The wine, lit by candlelight, glowing. He threw his napkin on top of his plate and summoned the now cowering waiter to bring the check. He wouldn't go after her.

Afterwards he wondered how she had gotten back to Kenwood. There were taxis, of course, and she could have telephoned her mother-in-law. In his immediate anger, he really hadn't cared. By the time he had gone out to the parking lot there was no trace of her, and he had driven to the bar of the Casino where he'd had far too much to drink and nothing more to eat.

That was February. March, April, May, June. He counted the months on his right hand. There had been no communication between the two during those four months.

Well, now there would be. A murder had seen to that.

"Lieutenant," he heard Ben announce, "Mrs. Kent is here."

Hank reached for the light switch and steadied his face before turning to meet the woman entering the room.

"Please come in, Caroline," Hank said. He saw the familiar bright green eyes. Her pale brown hair was arranged naturally, cut almost to her shoulders. She smiled tentatively at him, and he couldn't resist looking at her left hand. She was wearing the plain gold wedding band which had so come to symbolize his frustrations. He breathed deeply and tried to convince himself that he would take refuge in his duty to question her. He couldn't let his personal feelings interfere.

"Sit down," he said calmly.

She took a chair, and he sat behind the desk. Her silence was unsettling. Ben sat at the back of the room where Hank could see he was losing his battle with looking as if this was an ordinary interview.

"Well," Hank began. "I understand that you were at the scene of this death. I'm sorry."

"Yes," she answered, relaxing a bit in the chair. "It's all right. I —"

"Damn it, Caroline," he said, his voice rising. "How did you manage to get yourself mixed up in another murder?"

"It is murder," she said. "I thought so."

"The medical examiner hasn't given his opinion yet," broke in Ben.

"Oh, shut up, Ben," Hank said.

"Hank," Caroline said. "I'm sure that Ben only meant—"

"How did you get home that night?"

"What?"

"You heard me. When you ran out of The White Horse Tavern, how did you get home? Didn't you think I would worry about you?"

Get drunk over you, he wanted to say.

"You didn't call the next day to find out, and I didn't run out. I left when you were being unreasonable."

"Do you want me to leave?" Ben's voice came from the fringes of the room. As he was ignored, he remained seated.

"I was telling you how much I loved you, on Valentine's Day no less. And you made me feel like an ass."

"Oh, no, I didn't mean that at all. You know that," she said.

"You said you weren't ready to be loved. How could you tell me that?"

"Hank, could we not talk about this now?" Caroline's eyes were unhappy.

"When then? I'm not going to let you out of this discussion. We should have had it months ago."

"I know"" she admitted. "I didn't like leaving things like that."

There was a long silence. Hank didn't trust himself to say that he thought it was easier for her to run. Figuratively, if not in actual fact.

"O.K.," Hank said at last. "We agree on that."

Ben cleared his throat.

"Why don't you give me the details, Mrs. Kent? Where exactly were you standing when Mr. Dockings died?"

Caroline swallowed and began with details of the party and her conversation with Dorsey Revel. Hank focused back on her eyes and listened to everything she remembered about Hugh and the way he had gaped at her, and when he finally collapsed on the floor while Imogen was screaming. "There was something in the wine. I think he was poisoned, Hank," she concluded. He felt unusually pleased that she had said his name.

"That does tie in with the preliminary examination by the medical examiner, and we are proceeding along that line at the present," he said.

Caroline absorbed this information solemnly, and Hank prodded her memory as to the first time she had seen the glass of red wine.

"I think when Hugh took it from Imogen."

He continued with his questions. *Did you see the waiter come with the tray, who first took the glass, did Imogen drink from the glass, did she put it down. Did anyone come near it? Did Caroline remember seeing the potted palm?*

At every query she shook her head. She had been listening to Dorsey Revel gossip about his family, the bank, the upcoming wedding, the deeding over of Des Arbres to Imogen. The first she remembered seeing the glass was when Hugh's hand took it from Imogen's hand.

"You didn't notice which waiter brought the glass?"

"The waiter." She stopped as if she had remembered something, and Hank felt his heartbeat quicken. But then she shook her head again, and said, "Honestly, no. I can't."

"Who was standing near Dockings and Miss Revel? Can you remember that?"

"We were of course, Dorsey and I. Imogen had been talking to Claudine Revel, and her mother Pamela had paused to say something to her, I think. But, that was earlier, before Hugh joined them. I think George March came by. He's Imogen's cousin. His mother is Grace March. She's the sister of Dorsey and Imogen's late father."

"What about Imogen Revel? What can you tell me about her?"

"Imogen?"

"There is some question whether the wine was meant for Miss Revel or Mr. Dockings."

"Imogen is one Revel I don't know especially well. She's usually away at the school. We knew her brother Claude better because..." She hesitated but soon continued. "...Reed worked for him."

"Would you say Miss Revel is the type of person to have enemies?" he asked quickly before the mention of her husband's name could invade his mind.

Caroline shook her head. "Enemies? When I've been in her company at family and business gatherings, she's usually been very retiring. Forgive me for saying it, but I don't think she has had much of a life."

"What about Mr. Dockings? Would you think him the type to have enemies?"

"Hugh? It's strange that you should ask that."

"Is it?"

"I suppose you will hear about this soon enough, so I may as well tell you. There is some talk out in the ballroom. It's probably only gossip, but --"

"You'd better give it to me, Caroline. You know everything in a murder investigation needs to come out."

"A short time ago, Dorsey told me --"

"Excuse me, but who is Dorsey again?"

"Dorsey Revel. He's Imogen and Claude's uncle. He's the one I was talking to when Hugh died."

"Of course. Go on."

"He believes that one of the teachers at The Camden School might have a motive for the murder. Apparently Nick Pratt, who is the headmaster of the school, was talking to Dorsey this afternoon. Before Imogen was to marry Hugh, he had a long relationship with another teacher at the school."

"Was this teacher here at the party this afternoon?" Caroline nodded her head. "I see. Do you know her name by any chance?"

"Marilyn Hansen. Dorsey pointed her out to me before I came in here to see you."

"Did you see her near Mr. Dockings when he died?"

Caroline gave the question some thought before shaking her head. "I'm not sure," she said. "I may have, but I can't be sure. Perhaps out of the periphery of my eye... no, I can't say for certain."

"I will speak to Mr. Dorsey Revel and to Mr. Pratt. Ben, make a note of that, and Ms. Hansen's name, also."

Hank mused on this new information. It fit with the possibility that either Imogen or Hugh was the victim. A jilted woman might take her revenge on either.

"You've been very helpful, Caroline." He didn't know what else to say. Certainly the topic he had introduced earlier was off limits now.

"Thank you," she said as she stood. He rose in preparation of showing her to the door.

His hand was on the door's knob when he felt it turning from the other side. He let go, and the door flew open. Sgt. Keisha McAndrews was standing on the other side. She was a young black officer who'd been assigned to the detective squad last year. The look on her face gave away that she had important news.

"Sergeant?" Hank asked expectantly.

"Lieutenant, it's one of the waiters."

"What about him?"

"We can't find him."

"Who is he?"

"That's just it. Nobody knows. Jackson and I were interviewing the catering staff. The manager was on the premises because this is such an important job. He had the complete list of everyone, waiters, waitresses, the barmen, kitchen help. Everybody. We matched up everyone and took their statement. But then one of the waiters said there was another waiter who was serving drinks with him. But everyone was accounted for. The manager said there was no one else, but then one of the fellows who was manning the bar remembered this other one, too."

"But you don't know who he is?"

"No, sorry. But there definitely is someone who is unaccounted for. What do you want us to do?"

"Get a complete description. Talk to everyone on the catering staff."

He turned to Caroline. "You remembered a waiter, didn't you?" he asked. "What did you remember about a waiter? I noticed something when you were giving your statement."

"It was after Hugh died," Caroline said. She seemed to be remembering now. "Claude wanted to clean up the glass fragments and the wine spill, and I had argued with him, told him not to do it. One of the waiters was there. Claude told him to clean up the mess, but the waiter was looking down at Hugh's body. He was absolutely riveted to the spot and staring at him."

"Describe this man." Hank motioned for Ben to get her words down on paper.

"He was older. Most of the wait staff were young. But he was older. In his late forties, I would say. Maybe fifty. He was slight in build, thin, with greying blonde hair. Light eyes."

"That fits with the waiter we can't find," Keisha said.

"He was very sad-looking. As I said, bewildered. I thought he was shocked by the death."

"I want to get the police sketch artist to work up a picture with you," Hank said. "I'll call you tomorrow to set up a time."

She nodded.

He was thinking of enemies again, and which of his two victims had made an enemy of a slight, greying man with a sad face. "Sgt. McAndrews."

"Yes, sir."

"Go back to the caterers' people and see if anybody can put a name to this mysterious waiter. He had to be called something, and maybe somebody knows what it is."

"Yes, sir," McAndrews repeated.

"I also want you to find the waiter who delivered that last glass of wine to Imogen Revel. The one who was coming back with another glass for Hugh Dockings, but never did." He turned back to Caroline.

"I'll be in touch with you tomorrow. Will you be at home?"

"I have an inn to run, Hank. You know I'm always there." If she meant this comment to mean something more, he chose to ignore it.

"Are any of the Revels' guests staying with you?"

"No," she answered. "No one."

"All right." He hesitated, wondering if he could find another reason to come in person to Kenwood. Instead he said, "I'll call you tomorrow." He thought he had made progress with her, and he congratulated himself that he had the good sense not to screw that up.

7

Caroline was by training and education an actress. Her degree from Yale Drama School had once been a source of pride to her. But since Reed's death she had scarcely given her former life in the theater a thought. That was in New York. She hadn't been in the city for almost a year since she had made the decision to move to the Kents' house in Newport. As Dorsey had so well reminded her, Kenwood was all that was left in the Kent family's holdings, and the mortgage on it was still to be paid thanks to her late father-in-law's injudicious investments. Louise had opted for selling up. The older woman had wanted to make a clean break with the past.

Caroline, however, had looked at Newport as a new place to begin, and also a place connected to Reed. The idea of turning the house into an inn catering to visitors to Newport had come to her quite suddenly one night as she lay awake in her apartment, the familiar pictures of car accidents whirling in her head. Remembering the green lawns and ocean breezes she connected with Kenwood, she had made her decision, and nothing would change her mind.

Getting the inn up and running was hard work. She rose most mornings at six, working seven days a week. But she had thrown herself into her new life, embracing the work as if scrubbing and cleaning would some day erase the memories, which deep down she wanted to keep.

And then Hank had come into her life. One of her first guests, a wealthy businessman from Boston had been staying at the Inn at Kenwood Court, as she had dubbed her new venture. His violent death led to the murder investigation which Lt. Hank Nightingale of the Newport Police Department headed. He was so different from Reed. Hank was tall, dark, muscular, outspoken, ego-driven. All the opposites of her gentle first husband.

They had solved the murder of Maurice Hargreave together, and that camaraderie had blossomed into something more. They had begun to meet for quiet dinners, walks on the beach. She had pretended not to acknowledge where such romantic encounters generally led. Lonely and often stressed by the unexpected problems she encountered in her new hotel business, she had let Hank provide a sanctuary. But, in her need to make some fledgling effort to move beyond her grief, she had let him fall in love with her. And she hadn't wanted that.

When they had parted on the previous Valentine's Day, she had, in fact, been relieved. Hank was a complication, and she had been striving to simplify her life. Work, and more work. She was determined to stay focused on what she believed was best for her. Seeing Hank on the previous day had been easy for her, but not she saw, for Hank. Now they would be spending time together to discuss the case, and she felt sorry for him. She had realized yesterday how much he still cared for her. Her dramatic training still remained with her. She knew what his character, so familiar to her, was thinking.

Hank Nightingale's office was a drab cubicle on the second floor of the Newport Police Station with a window view of the parking lot. When he had arrived at his desk at 8:30 the next morning, Ben was already in the squad room which surrounded Hank's own space.

"Sorry to make you come in on a Sunday, Ben, but we've got to do the interviews today of the out-of-town guests at the Revels' party so we can let them go home."

"Oh, I understand. Jean's going to take the kids to her parents for dinner today. I can miss that. They've already faxed today's menu from the deli. If you're going to be in for lunch, may I suggest the special. It's called Thanksgiving dinner. White meat turkey, stuffing, cranberry sauce on a hard roll. Jackson's got the sign-up sheet. He'll pick them up at noon for us."

"Thanksgiving in June?"

"Have you ever eaten stuffing on a sandwich, Lieutenant?"

"No."

"It's my idea of heaven... in June."

"I thought Jean had you on a diet."

"That's at home."

"I'm sorry but I don't think you and I will be in for lunch. We've got to be out on the interviews. I've divided up the list. I want you to take some, and also Sgt. McAndrews."

"I can always stop by the deli on my way. Sure I can't pick up one for you? You could save it for your supper."

Hank grimaced. He lived alone and wasn't fond of cooking, but he could find better things for his Sunday dinner than a sandwich which was several hours old.

"Any word from the artist?" Hank asked. "I left a message on her answering machine last night." Ben shook his head. "I hope she's not away for the week-end."

"Are you going to see Mrs. Kent today?" Ben asked cautiously.

"Right now I don't think that's a priority for today. My first call is at the hotel where Nicholas Pratt is staying. And you don't have to walk on tip toes, Sergeant. Caroline Kent is a witness in this case." He stared at Ben. "I can separate things."

"I'm sure you can, Lieutenant."

"Good. We agree. Now today I want to understand our little love triangle, the one that includes Marilyn Hansen, Imogen Revel, and the murder victim." As much as he was impatient to meet Caroline again, his interest in the case was again first in his thoughts.

"How does the waiter tie in to that?"

"He doesn't." The missing waiter still didn't have a name. None of the caterer's staff knew it. The police had also failed to come up with any waiter who admitted to delivering the last, fatal glass of wine to Imogen Revel. The absent waiter had to be regarded as suspect number one at present. "But while we're waiting to locate him, we can't forget about our other suspects."

"Who are?"

"The Hansen woman, for now." Hank paused as Ben eyed him skeptically. "I know, it isn't much so far. I suppose anyone who came near Hugh Dockings while that glass was on the plant stand. Caroline Kent did say that Claude Revel's daughter Claudine was talking to her aunt and Dockings during the key time period. She had opportunity."

"What would be her motive?"

"Who knows? I'm just listing names at this point. You talked to her. Do you think she's a possible killer?"

"She struck me as pretty cool. Some of those financial people on Wall Street have ice water in their veins." Ben read popular fiction.

"Claude Revel and his wife and daughter will remain in Newport with Imogen for the time being. No doubt there will be some kind of funeral or memorial service for Dockings. Perhaps they are planning to have it in that chapel they conveniently have in their house. Handy for weddings, and funerals."

"Sounds morbid to me," Ben said.

"I'll call Claude Revel this morning to get the lay of the land. Meantime, find McAndrews and see what you two can do with these."

Hank reached into his pocket and pulled out the list he had made earlier that morning. He was saving the headmaster of The Camden School and Marilyn Hansen for himself, but he had given the rest of the faculty who had been invited to the party to Ben and Keisha McAndrews, along with several other names whose statements indicated they might be worth pursuing, including Imogen's cousin George March. Caroline had mentioned seeing March near Imogen shortly before Dockings took his fatal drink. March worked at Syndicat Revel. Was there some tie-in to the family bank? Hank couldn't see how that connected back to the two school teachers, Imogen and Hugh.

"Who's on your list, Lieutenant?" Ben asked as he studied his sheet.

"Just Pratt and Hansen so far. There's one name I haven't assigned yet. The gossip, Dorsey Revel. How do you feel about tackling him? I'd like to talk to him, but I have a feeling it will be a long interview."

"Why don't we save him for later? He had his back to the victim so he can't tell us anything we need to know immediately."

"Yeah, but sometimes these old chatterboxes let something out that is useful."

"Then he'll keep, Lieutenant."

Claude Revel walked slowly across the ample back lawn of his family's estate. In the quiet still of the morning's mist, he could almost believe that yesterday's tragedy hadn't happened.

He was in no hurry to reach his destination. His sister Imogen had insisted on spending the night alone in Des Arbres, and he was remembering now how relieved he had been while he watched her solitary figure cross this same space last evening on the way to her new home. She was a trial to him. And now? What lay in store for them now that Dockings was dead?

Mon Plaisir had been built in Newport by his great-grandfather, the first Claude Revel, in 1890. It was the year his youngest son Dorsey, named after his American grandfather Dorsey Bishop, was born. The nineteenth century Claude Revel had been an enthusiastic convert to Newport. He built Mon Plaisir during the decade when the two grandsons of Cornelius Vanderbilt would take their family's money made in railroad monopolies, and build their competing monuments to luxury, The Breakers and Marble House.

For his family's home, the first Revel had opted for a more refined look, which he had copied from the plan of a sixteenth century French country house. Mon Plaisir was built entirely to Claude's specifications. The house was everything Claude's expatriate imagination believed a French baron's country home should be, including the chapel. For in addition to reclaiming his French cultural birthright, Claude had, once in America, embraced the lost Catholic faith of his childhood.

Des Arbres had been added to the estate in 1923 by Claude's eventual heir, his second son Henri. His eldest son Dorsey had died of pneumonia during his sophomore year at Harvard. Henri had given the structure as a gift to his father whose hearing had seriously deteriorated with age. As a result of his inability to pick up conversation around him, the elder man had become reclusive and irritable. The idea behind *le pavilion* was to isolate him there with his papers and books. In his later life he was compiling a history of the Emperor Louis Napoleon. The book lay unfinished at his death in 1926, and in 2005 Claude Revel had for the first time removed the yellowed manuscript from the building and re-shelved it in the vast library shelves of the main house.

Imogen was waiting for Claude as he approached the door of Des Arbres. She was standing in the arched doorway, dressed in a severe black dress he had never seen before, the picture of a prim, old-fashioned school teacher. There was a wary look on her face. Did she think he was coming to reclaim his gift of the property? At all costs, he was determined not to argue with her. He smiled affectionately and kissed her on the cheek, an action which required him to stand up on his toes. He felt her body stiff and unbending, and as he came back down on his heels, he also took her right hand in his.

"Imogen, how are you?" He wanted to add *dear* to the question, but his voice wouldn't say the word.

His sister answered with a deep sigh and led him into the pavilion's small foyer. In front of them the stairway led to the second floor.

Imogen had furnished the small house by taking pieces from the storage rooms of Mon Plaisir. The decoration was a mix of Louis XV and Empire Style. The predominate color was the royal blue of the later period, mixed with the golden yellow of the earlier. Even to Claude's untrained eye, the scheme was inharmonious.

She led him into the living room, and they sat side by side on the high-backed mahogany and velvet sofa.

"Would you like to come up to the house for lunch, Imogen? Most of the family will be there. Uncle Dorsey, and Aunt Grace, the Marches, Hannah and Violet --"

"Are you having a party?" Imogen's voice was harsh and angry.

"No, no. Everyone wants to see you. We're all worried about you."

"Oh?" She sounded doubting.

"You know we are."

"I want to talk about the arrangements."

"What *arrangements*, Imogen?" He was thinking of the property arrangements.

"Hugh's funeral, of course."

"The funeral?"

"Don't be purposefully obtuse, Claude. We must plan the service. I've been thinking all morning of what I want."

His first instinct to disagree with her was quelled. "What would you like?" he asked.

"We'll have it in the chapel."

"But Hugh wasn't Roman Catholic."

"We were to be married in the chapel."

"Imogen, you know that Father Halloran was willing to marry you in the chapel because you yourself are a Catholic. Hugh is not, however, and we cannot have Father Halloran perform a funeral service for a non-Catholic. What religion was Hugh, anyway?"

"He did not attend church."

"There, you see. He would not want a Catholic ceremony, even if we could have one."

49

"I want a Catholic ceremony."

"Imogen," he began, his pulse beating more rapidly, "I don't think that's possible. Father Halloran --"

"We don't have to have Father Halloran."

"Oh, do we go to rent-a-clergy?" His pique spilled out, and he stopped talking so that he could regain his composure. "I mean that I wouldn't know where to begin. You're asking me to find a Protestant minister to come to our chapel? I don't think that's going to be possible. Perhaps if we call the funeral home who will be handling the arrangements, they can suggest something." She was frowning. "I was planning to call the Lunsford establishment later this afternoon," he lied.

Suddenly Imogen began to cry, and Claude awkwardly reached for her hand again.

"Oh, Claude, I'm sorry, but this has all been so much for me to cope with. Today... today, we... Hugh and I --" she sobbed, and he squeezed her hand. "Today was going to be my wedding day."

"I know, I know. The shock is wearing off. You must expect this. Yesterday I thought you were so brave. Today, you must grieve." He was proud of his phrasing, and he wondered what else he could offer to comfort her. "Have a good cry," he concluded.

"The police still have Hugh, don't they?" He nodded. "When can I have him back?"

Claude felt a pain in his stomach. The idea of that body returning after the ambulance had so neatly carried it away was grotesque.

"I don't know," he answered. "The authorities will tell us when they are ready. I'm sure there is nothing we can do to hurry the process."

"I want him back. I want to put him in the chapel where we all can see him."

"An open coffin?" Now he made no attempt to conceal the horror he felt at the prospect of seeing that distorted purple face again.

"I must see him."

"Imogen, think of what you are saying. Don't subject yourself to seeing him again. Please remember him as he was. Believe me, it's better not to have this memory as you go forward."

"Forward? What have I to go forward to?" She was weeping in a steady flow of feral mewling sounds. "You don't understand," she cried out. "You have your wife, Claude. You've never known what it is to lose the only person you've ever loved."

"I know," he said, "but you must think of your future. Perhaps you might want to return to Camden. I'm sure they would want you back."

"Why can't we have the funeral in the chapel?"

He sighed. "First let's find out when --" he paused before continuing "-- Hugh will be... ready. Perhaps Father Halloran can suggest a way to proceed."

"I'm sure he can," his sister said. She had stopped crying now. "I'm sure he'll come." Her voice sounded childishly happy.

"I wouldn't be too optimistic, Imogen. These Catholic priests have to follow a lot of rules, you know. They aren't free to act on their own."

"Then you must make him, Claude," Imogen said assuredly. "You can do that."

"Yes," he answered. Why did the women in his life constantly expect him to jump through the hoops they set up for him? If it wasn't Pamela, it was his sister expecting him to carry out all kinds of orders. Even at the bank, he was beginning to see the same trait coming out in Claudine. She had begun to put demands on him, always with the expectation that he wouldn't fail to execute her commands.

Claude sighed and, not for the first time, wished he had been able to have a son who could be his ally against the three determined females in his life.

8

Sundays were always a busy day at the Inn at Kenwood Court. Week-end guests were leaving, and their rooms had to be made up for the next arrivals. Guests who came for a stay of a week or more generally arrived on Saturday morning, and Sundays were for long, leisurely breakfasts in the dining room before setting out on the day's activities. It was always noon before Caroline felt she had had even a minute to herself.

Now at twenty minutes past twelve Caroline entered the kitchen with the last of the Sunday breakfast dishes from the dining room and began stacking them in one of the dishwashers. Karen Moore, the college student who generally worked on week-ends, was busy at the sink with the pots and pans. In addition to her mother-in-law, the indoor staff consisted of three part-time maids and the cook Mattie Logan, who lived in and had been with the Kent family for over forty years. Mattie had been against the plan to open up Kenwood to paying guests. She had been appalled that Louise would have to take on tasks Mattie felt did not befit the former mistress of the house. A great deal of the stress Caroline often felt was the tension in the kitchen when Mattie was present.

"Where is Mattie?" she asked Karen.

"She took Mrs. Kent some lunch. She's out in the garden. Mattie was fussing because your mother-in-law was going to do some work out there. Honestly, you have to feel sorry for her, Caroline. That woman terrorizes her."

"When it comes to my mother-in-law, Mattie thinks she knows best, Karen."

"I wouldn't take it. Mrs. Kent should speak up."

Before Caroline could reply, the telephone began to ring, and she picked up the kitchen extension.

"The Inn at Kenwood Court. How may I help you?"

The deep voice of Imogen Revel answered her. "Is this Caroline?"

"Yes, it is, Imogen. How are you?"

"Oh, you recognize my voice."

"Yes," Caroline said into the receiver.

"I was wondering, Caroline, if I could ask you a favor."

"Of course."

"Could you come to see me today?"

"Today?" Caroline was thinking of beds to be changed and rooms to be aired. "What time today?"

"Oh, whatever is convenient. I know you have the inn, and you must be busy with all you do."

"I, uh... let me see." Caroline was to meet later with the police artist, a fact she didn't want to share with Imogen. "I have an appointment later this afternoon. Would this evening be too late?"

"Why don't you come around seven? I can have something sent down from the main house for us to eat. Come to Des Arbres. That is where I'm living now."

"Seven? That will work, I think. All right. I'll see you then."

As she put down the telephone, Caroline was puzzled. Why did Imogen Revel want to see her of all people? They were barely acquaintances, and certainly not friends. Imogen had mentioned a favor. What could Caroline possibly do for her?

"Neither of them were very popular teachers. Personally I was happy at the prospect of replacing them both for the fall." The self-assured face of Nicholas Pratt smiled easily at Hank. They were sitting in the Camden headmaster's suite in the Marriott in downtown Newport. Pratt was well-dressed, wearing slim, grey silk slacks, and a white cotton T-shirt which Hank was sure hadn't come in cellophane packaging. Hank wondered how much a headmaster was paid. "I'll be that honest with you, Lieutenant. I don't see the point of beating around the bush in a murder investigation. You're sure it's murder, aren't you?"

"The autopsy is being done today, but we're looking at a suspicious death. I have to get as much information as I can before the guests leave town, Mr. Pratt."

"Call me Nick," Pratt said expansively. He allowed his eyes to drift over to the portable bar that was set up on one of the tables. A used glass with what Hank thought were the dregs of a Bloody Mary sat on the table. "Oh, damn it," Nick said suddenly. "I hope this won't make Imogen change her mind about resigning."

"Now that she's not marrying Hugh, she may decide to return next semester. I've already hired her replacement." His eyes radiated sensuality. "Lovely young woman from St. Andrew's in New Hampshire. Her girls' field hockey team have been champions for three years running. I was damned lucky to get her. Parents love a championship girls' field hockey team. One of the best recruiting tools we have in our business."

"And you definitely don't want Miss Revel back?"

"Frankly, no. I've been headmaster at The Camden School for six years now, and I've spent the entire time refining the staff. Not all that easy to do in education, you know. Tough to get rid of people. They all want to sue."

"Tell me what specifically were the problems with Miss Revel."

"No humanity. Parents like a bit of humanity. Encouraging the kids, building up their confidence. That's what the playing fields are supposed to do, Lieutenant."

"Miss Revel was hard on the students?"

"Oh, yes. Game days and field days were a nightmare. I used to beg her not to bark at the students in front of their parents."

"But she ignored you?"

"Yes. She thought she was right."

"Did the parents complain to you about her treatment of their children?"

"Oh, yes. I tried to get Imogen to see their point of view. But, as I said, she is one determined woman. Everything black and white."

"I don't suppose you could tell me of any incident in particular which might have made a parent hold a grudge against her, can you?"

"Enough to kill her?" The headmaster was intelligent, Hank thought. He picked that one up right away. "You think she might have been the target of the poisoning?"

"It's possible."

The headmaster appeared to be thinking hard. Finally he shook his head. "I don't know. There were quite a few students she harassed. But, I can't see one of the parents killing her because of it. More likely one of the students. Girls at that age can be vicious. Some of the situations I've had to deal with would shock even you, Lt. Nightingale."

"Let's turn to Hugh Dockings then. What can you tell me about him?"

Pratt leaned back against the sofa and clasped his hands across his trim abdomen. His tan arms were muscular.

"Dockings," he said slowly. "He taught chemistry."

"Was he a good teacher?" Hank prodded.

"He knew his subject. His students did all right in standardized testing. It was, I suppose, that hollowness of his manner. You do know he was quite a drinker?"

"Yes, that's been mentioned. Tell me, Nick. How did that affect his ability to teach?"

"I don't think it did. I think he was the same person underneath no matter what. He wasn't one of these people who get mean when they drink, if that's what you're thinking."

"But you don't see his making enemies among his students or their parents?"

"Not really. No."

"I understand Dockings also had coaching duties."

"Oh, yes. Sailing team. That was the one place where he allowed himself to show a little fire about life. He loved to sail. He often took one of the school's boats out on week-ends. He was allowed to, of course. He and Imogen were going to buy a boat, you know, and keep it here in Newport after they were married. Quite a nice one, I understand."

"Yes."

"Too bad about that. Hugh did seem excited about the boat. Sailing. That was what he loved."

"Not Miss Revel?"

"Love Imogen? A matter of convenience, I thought."

"The money was the reason for the marriage?"

"The Revels' money?" Hank nodded. "What else? Imogen seemed eager to spend it on Hugh."

"What about Marilyn Hansen?"

"You've heard about that. Well, she was the odd woman out. Hugh didn't need her any more. Not once Imogen came along with the offer of a boat and a residence in Newport."

"Do you think Marilyn Hansen was angry enough to take her revenge on Hugh Dockings?"

"Dockings or Imogen? You said before that it was possible Imogen was the victim."

"And you think Hansen was capable of killing either of them?"

"Marilyn was very angry. Everybody on the staff heard her in the faculty room the day after the Christmas break ended. When Imogen came back with the announcement that she and Hugh were engaged, Marilyn swore at them like a damned sailor."

"At whom was she most angry?"

"Hmmn," Pratt said, making a clicking noise with his tongue. "I would have to say Imogen. Women never blame the man, you know, Lieutenant. She called her a bitch. A rich bitch. Marilyn also indicated her strong belief that Imogen was still a virgin. She was quite cruel. Apparently Marilyn and Hugh had no qualms about sharing a bed, and she swore that Imogen was not only a rich bitch, but a frigid one as well."

"I see," Hank said. "So you think she would take out her anger on Miss Revel?"

"That would be my opinion. Yes."

"And Ms. Hansen teaches biology, I understand."

"That's right, and I see what you're thinking. She would definitely know something about poisons."

Yes, Hank said to himself, that is exactly what I am thinking.

9

The computer image of the missing waiter which Caroline had helped the police artist create was waiting on Hank Nightingale's desk when he returned to the station after his two interviews. His session with Marilyn Hansen had been far from productive, and he was in a miserable mood. What had initially seemed promising to him, armed with Nick Pratt's information, had not proved so in reality. Marilyn Hansen's stony responses to his questioning had been vexing.

"Of course I was upset when Imogen stole Hugh away from me. Who wouldn't be?" she had told him in an acid tone.

"Why did you come to the Revels' party?" he had asked.

"I was invited," she said obstinately.

"But, surely if you were distressed that Mr. Dockings was marrying Miss Revel instead of you --"

"Only because of the money," she interjected.

"But was, nevertheless, marrying her. Why did you come? Please answer the question, Ms. Hansen."

Her reply came in a cold voice. "I wouldn't let the two of them see that I cared. I wanted them both to think I didn't give a shit." Her use of the four-letter word caught Hank by surprise, and she smiled as she read the reaction on his face.

"There was no other reason?"

"Such as?" She lit a cigarette.

"You didn't think of getting revenge?"

"You think I poisoned Hugh?" She laughed bitterly. "Not on your life. Don't you see, Lieutenant? That marriage was my revenge. Hugh would have to live the rest of his life with Imogen Revel."

Standing in the doorway of his office, Hank realized that if Marilyn Hansen had brought the dose of prussic acid that killed Hugh Dockings, it would be hell to prove unless he could find a witness who saw Hansen tamper with the wine glass.

"Damn, damn, damn," he said out loud.

The picture on his desk finally attracted his full attention. He picked it up and studied the face. *Sad eyes*, Caroline had said, and he agreed. He returned to the doorway and looked around.

"Is Mrs. Kent still here?" he asked one of the uniformed officers. "She was working with Pam Dotson."

"Sgt. Davies took her down to the break room for some coffee."

Picture in hand, Hank headed for the station canteen. He found Caroline and Ben sitting at one of the tables, drinking coffee and chatting amiably. He slid into the seat next to Ben.

"Thank you for this," he said, holding up the waiter's face.

"Does it help?" she asked.

"Oh, definitely. Do you remembering seeing this man at any other time during the party? Did he serve you a drink by any chance?"

"I can't be sure. I'm sorry to sound like a snob, Hank, but one usually doesn't notice the face of the servers at a party."

"And you can't remember seeing him serving anyone else?"

"Such as Imogen?" She looked straight into his eyes.

"I don't mind telling you that it would help. But don't say anything you don't know for sure."

"Coffee, Lieutenant?" Ben asked.

"Thanks." Hank nodded and Ben went over to the machine.

"I don't think I saw Imogen take the glass from the waiter's tray."

"Do you remember her putting it down on the plant stand?" She shook her head. "All right. We'll leave it at that. But you *are* sure you saw this man standing by Dockings right after he fell to the floor."

"At some point he was there. I can't say it was as Hugh fell."

"Let it go for now. Something may return to your mind later." She smiled and sipped her coffee as Ben returned. Hank took the cup and passed him the picture.

"You may as well get this duplicated and in the pipeline, Sergeant. I'll need a copy to show Imogen Revel."

"Right. I'll see you upstairs when you're through. I'm putting my notes from today into the computer now."

As Ben left them, Caroline finished her coffee and leaned forward in her chair. "I may as well be going."

"Can you wait a few minutes?" Hank asked. "I'm interested in learning more about the Revel family."

"Have you talked to Claude's uncle, Dorsey, yet?"

"No, I haven't."

"He's the one who can tell you everything you want to know."

"I'd like your impressions. I will be talking to Dorsey Revel, also."

"I'm not sure how much I know."

"You were very helpful during the last case we worked on. I couldn't have made an arrest without your help."

She smiled as if recalling a pleasant memory and he pressed her. "Start with Claudine Revel. You said she was in the neighborhood of the murder scene."

"I don't think she was there when Hugh died. I think she had drifted off. I'm sure she was only talking to Imogen to be polite."

"They're not close? Claude Revel indicated that the Revels are a close family."

"In a way. It's family tradition that holds them all together."

"How would you describe the relationship between Claudine Revel and her aunt?"

"According to Dorsey, Imogen has been upset that her brother brought Claudine into the family bank, Syndicat Revel."

"That was Revel family tradition broken."

"Claude had talked about it for a long time. You've got to have women in management these days."

"There were no women in the upper echelons of Syndicat Revel?"

"A few, but no one on track to be chairman one day. That position has always gone to a male Revel."

"There are other male Revel family members employed in the bank. George March for one."

"That's right, but it's the old story of the eldest son of the eldest son inheriting. Claude is the eldest son, and he has a daughter."

"I see. But his sister was against his plan?"

"Imogen's old-fashioned, I suppose."

"Yes, she said just that. Claudine is young for such a responsibility."

"Twenty-nine, maybe thirty. She's extremely intelligent and well-educated. Harvard M.B.A."

"Boyfriends?"

"Claudine? I don't know. Why does that matter?"

"I don't know. Just asking, trying to figure her out."

"Frustrated woman turns on her aunt who has gotten a man? I think you have to do better than that for a motive."

"I know, I will," he said, chastised.

"I think Imogen will come around eventually about Claudine and the chairmanship. Imogen is very proud of being a Revel. Ultimately, I think she'll be pleased with the idea."

"You're giving her a lot of credit."

"Reed always said she could have gone into the family business. He thought she was sharp."

"That was very generous of him," Hank said.

"Thank you," was all she said before he saw a faraway look come into her eyes. He wouldn't be much of a detective if he couldn't figure out what -- and who -- she was thinking about.

After Caroline said good-by, Hank returned to his office. The energy with which he had started his Sunday was waning. He looked out the window. The parked vehicles below made for a dismal view, but high above them the sky was blue and bright. A light breeze ruffled the leaves of the trees. The leaves had yet to reach their full, mature size, and Hank could see spaces of light and sky through the broad thick branches. Little more than a mile away was the harbor. He thought of boats and sailing the glistening waters under the Newport Bridge. For several years now Hank had been part of a regular racing group, week-end sailors with a competitive spirit whose friendship he valued. Lately his work schedule seemed always to interfere with the race schedule, and he found himself less and less free on week-ends. Hank knew the racing was on for today, and he looked at his watch. It was 5:30. The race was probably finishing about now. *Fancy Boy*, the boat he raced, would be heading back to port to its snug berth at Bowen's Wharf where its crew would relax at dockside over drinks and relive the day's maneuvers.

Hank backed away from the window and pushed the thought from his mind. His work day was far from over. He picked up a copy of the face of the missing waiter.

"Who are you?" he asked out loud. "Where can I start to find you?" One sad-faced man, with no name. He supposed he could circulate the picture around the bars and restaurants in the hope that the man was a real waiter by trade. There could have been some mistake made by the caterers in leaving his name off the hiring sheet. Somehow, Hank thought not. His gut told him there was no error in the caterer's record. "I think you're important in this business, Pete." He looked like a Pete, or a Tom, or a Bob. An inconspicuous man. "Where are you now, Pete?" he asked the picture.

The picture didn't answer, but the telephone rang. Hank picked up the receiver.

"Nightingale."

"Lieutenant, this is Nick Pratt. I'm glad I caught you in. I've remembered something when I was out by the harbor, taking a walk past all the sailboats."

"What did you remember?"

"It all happened before I came to Camden. When I came onboard the school was finally getting over the scandal. All I was told by the trustees was to murmur my regrets if any prospective parents brought it up and say that it was a horrible accident. Accidents do happen, even in expensive boarding schools."

"What was this accident?"

"Camden's team was in Block Island to race in a big interscholastic race off the Island. The water is rough out there on the ocean."

"I know the waters."

"The team was training, doing a practice race against one of the other schools. It was near the end of the race. Camden's boat didn't have the lead, but they were fighting for it."

"Was Hugh Dockings the sailing coach at this time?"

"Oh, yes. Hugh was in the boat coaching the crew. They had to come about to make a turn. Do you know anything about sailing, Lieutenant?"

"Quite a bit."

"Then you know that when the boom comes flying around, everyone has to be alert. In a racing situation, with the crew moving in all directions, it's pretty hectic in the cockpit."

"There was an accident, I gather. Tell me what happened."

"One of the students was hit in the head by the boom and went overboard."

"My God," Hank said. He himself had been in some near misses onboard, with a few grazings by the heavy boom of the mainsail's brace on his own head more than once. But a hit so hard as to knock a man overboard had never been in his experience.

"How did they rescue him?"

"That's just it. They didn't try to right away. One of the crew wanted to throw him the line, but Hugh didn't let them adjust their course. There is some dispute over whether he actually said to go on with the race. It was just a practice, for Chrisakes." Nick's voice surprised Hank with its sound of pain. "The students were screaming to stop and finally they turned the boat around again, but by this time Dennis had disappeared under the water."

"Dennis?"

"The boy's name was Dennis Montgomery. He was sixteen. The body was never recovered."

"Horrible," Hank murmured.

"You wanted to know if either Imogen or Hugh had enemies. It came to me when I was looking at those sailboats today. Dennis's parents sued the school and collected for the accidental death. The board of trustees didn't put up much of a fight over the case. The bad publicity was worse to them than the settlement. They wanted it over with as quickly as possible."

"I see what you mean about enemies. The parents."

"Dennis's father Donald Montgomery blamed Hugh completely for the accident. The students gave statements. It seemed clear that at first Hugh did not react to the boy's going into the water as he should have."

"Dennis may not have been able to be saved. If he had been knocked unconscious, he might not have been able to grab the rescue buoy when it was thrown to him."

"Well, we'll never know."

"The parents wanted Hugh to be charged with manslaughter. They found out he drank, and they tried to bring into the case that he was drunk during the practice. I'm not really sure of the details. It was all before my time, as I said."

"But Mr. Dockings wasn't charged?"

"I don't think so."

"Well, I can get the records. Did you ever meet Donald Montgomery, Nick?"

"Me? No. There would have been no reason, Lieutenant."

"I see. Well, I appreciate the telephone call. Thanks for the information. I may be in touch."

As Hank slowly put down the receiver he looked down at the sad eyes of the waiter he had taken to calling Pete. Was it possible that melancholy look was caused by unrelenting grief, the deep sorrow that comes from the loss of a child?

10

Kenwood was situated on a majestic property overlooking the Atlantic Ocean. Many of the old Gilded Age houses, including the Vanderbilts' The Breakers, fronted the sea. All had the Newport Cliff Walk, the three mile stretch of public pathways and steps, erected along the high rocky sea wall of the ocean, between their property and the water's edge.

Caroline often used walking on the Cliff Walk for her daily exercise, and as she put aside her work later that same Sunday evening, she considered using the Cliff Walk to walk to Des Arbres to visit Imogen. While the Revels' estate Mon Plaisir was not located directly on the ocean, it was only a few minutes' walk inland. She looked at her watch. It was after 6:30. Best drive the short distance. It would probably be dark by the time she concluded her call on Imogen, and the unlighted Cliff Walk was not supposed to be used after dusk for safety reasons. The pathways were in a rough, natural state, and footing was treacherous in spots. There were only a few places where fencing to protect the pedestrian from the cliffs had been erected.

Imogen greeted Caroline at the door of the pavilion. She was dressed in black, and her face looked grey and tired. She led Caroline into the living room where a tray of drinks was waiting for them.

"What would you like, Caroline?" Imogen asked. "I've opened a bottle of red wine."

"That's fine for me. Thank you." Imogen carefully poured out the dark red liquid into crystal wine glasses. Instantly Caroline was reminded of Hugh Dockings's death. Once again she saw the image of the goblet dropping from his hand and crashing to the floor.

"I hope you like this particular wine, Caroline," Imogen said. Her attention was on the glasses, and she did not see Caroline shudder recalling those fingers with their red, scraped knuckles as they reached in agony for his throat. "It's Hugh's favorite." She handed Caroline a glass. "That is to say, it was."

Caroline looked at the bottle. It was a California merlot with which she was unfamiliar.

"To Hugh," Imogen said. She held up her glass to touch Caroline's. "I hope you don't find it morbid to drink to him." Caroline shook her head. Both women sipped their wine. "Do you like it, Caroline? All Claude keeps in his cellar are his precious French wines. He's such a wine snob. I had some of this merlot ordered for Hugh before he... died. It was to be a surprise." She began to whimper and Caroline touched her hand. "Thank you. I know you understand how I feel."

"I think I do," Caroline answered.

"We're planning the memorial service for Friday. I want you and Louise to come."

"Of course."

"You must tell me everything you did to cope with Reed's death. You can help me, Caroline, as no one else can."

Now it was Caroline's turn to feel tears. She had been thinking on the drive from Kenwood of how well she had been managing lately and how successful the inn was becoming. Now, suddenly, all her underpinnings felt weak. Caroline swallowed hard to regain her composure.

"You still miss Reed terribly, don't you?" Imogen asked.

"I do," Caroline admitted, "but it has been almost two years now, and I'm learning that life does go on."

"Oh, my life won't go on," Imogen cried in a loud voice which surprised Caroline in its intensity. "I've nothing left to live for."

"You mustn't give in to those feelings. I know you want to think that way." Caroline was remembering how much she despaired in the first few days after Reed died. The memory of the funeral flashed in her mind. She saw Louise's pale, drained face as she stood beside Caroline in the church. The smell of the flowers, the music's sounds, the hushed voices of the people who took Caroline's hand afterwards and said useless words of comfort. It was if the scene was only on the other side of the door she had passed through to enter Des Arbres.

"The beginning is very hard," Caroline said. "People try to comfort you, and it means so little."

"That's exactly how I feel now. I can't bear to be with any of my family up at the main house. They are smothering me."

"Your family means to be kind. Don't shut them out completely. They are feeling pain, too."

"No, they're not," Imogen said with bitterness. "Some of them are truly happy."

"No," Caroline said emphatically. "You mustn't think that."

"But I must." Imogen's voice was strong now. "One of them tried to kill me."

"When?" Caroline asked. She was confused.

"Yesterday. That glass of wine was meant for me. Lt. Nightingale was here earlier and tried to tell me that the poison was meant for Hugh, but he's wrong. He's got it all wrong."

"Did he show you the picture of a waiter?" Caroline asked. "Did you recognize him as the one who brought the wine to you?"

"Oh, he might be. I wasn't paying attention. It looked something like him, I think."

"The police think he could be the murderer."

"Why would a man I don't know try to kill me?"

"Is it someone Hugh might have known?"

"Oh, that detective had a theory about that, too. He said he might be the father of one of the Camden students."

"One of the students?"

"Yes. A boy who died in an accident while he was on the sailing team for the school. Apparently the police believe that this waiter might be his father."

"I don't understand."

"Hugh was the sailing coach. Lt. Nightingale thought that the father might hold him responsible for the accident which killed his son."

"Was Hugh?"

"Of course not. The boy was a terrible sailor. He never paid attention in practice. Hugh told me all about it. He had actually thought of taking the boy off the team because he thought he was a danger to the other team members. And then the boy's own carelessness cost him his life."

"And Lt. Nightingale believes that his father came to the party yesterday in the disguise of a waiter to murder Hugh?"

"Isn't it preposterous? After all these years. I'm sure there's no connection with this waiter and that boy. The accident must have happened over ten years ago. And now the police are going to waste time hunting for him when they should be looking to see who wanted me dead."

"Imogen, are you sure of this? Who would want you dead?"

"Marilyn Hansen for one. She hated me for taking Hugh away from her."

"Did you see her near the glass of wine yesterday? Between the time you put it on the plant stand and Hugh drank it."

"I might have," Imogen said, screwing up her brow in a pensive frown. "I've been trying to remember, and I think she might have been nearby. I thought I saw her talking to Cousin George. Although why on earth George March would waste his time on a tiresome woman like that, I can't imagine."

"I was standing near you, and I don't remember seeing her. I thought George was talking to Claudine."

"I said I wasn't sure." Imogen paused, then looked away and spoke. "There is one other person I suspect."

"Who?" Caroline asked. There was something ominous in the way Imogen spoke.

"My niece Claudine."

"Claudine? No. I can't believe it."

"Don't be fooled by her, Caroline. There's something not right with my niece. I've seen it the whole time she was growing up. Claude never had a son. Pamela had two miscarriages before Claudine was born. Claude knew that she would be his only child, and from the beginning he's treated Claudine with kid gloves. She's always been protected from failure."

"But what does that have to do with you?"

"I've spoken out about it. I didn't want her to be brought into Syndicat Revel. Claudine was furious. I can't help but think she's the one who tried to kill me yesterday. And I think she will try again."

"It can't be."

"I'm trusting you with this information, Caroline. You're the only one I can trust. Please help me. The police don't believe me. They're off on some wild goose chase for a waiter. You've got to help me find out who tried to murder me. I know you can. They got Hugh instead. But whoever it is will try again."

"I don't know, Imogen. I can't make sense of it all now."

"You were right there when it happened. You must have seen something, Caroline. Do you understand? You hold the key to solving this mystery."

11

Her daughter-in-law's decision to pay a visit to Imogen Revel had not pleased Louise Kent, but she had said nothing to Caroline on the previous evening. The next morning, however, as she lay in bed, Louise wondered how to advise her daughter-in-law against becoming close to Imogen. The events of Saturday had certainly been confusing. First the death of Hugh Dockings, then the appearance of Hank Nightingale back in their lives. Now Imogen's reaching out to Caroline for support which her mother-in-law believed she was too fragile to provide.

"Good morning, darling," Caroline's voice sang as she kicked open the bedroom door. "I've brought your tea."

Louise smiled as Caroline gently deposited the tray on the soft cream of the duvet cover. Without missing a beat, her daughter-in-law's hands settled the pillows into the small of Louise's back.

"Thank you, dear," Louise said.

Caroline went to the windows and began opening the draperies to let in the morning light. The room's shades of mauve and pink came alive. Caroline returned to the bedside and kissed her mother-in-law tenderly on the cheek. The bedroom was part of the three room suite in the east wing which the two Kent women shared.

"You look rested," Caroline said approvingly. "I do believe being back at Kenwood is doing you a world of good."

"I will agree with you," Louise admitted. "I'm finally pleased with the way the rose garden is coming back. I've been eyeing the old perennial bed next to the gazebo. I think, with George's help, I can bring it back. I see some of the old roots have pushed up leaves this spring."

"Oh, this sounds expensive," Caroline laughed. How much it should cost to employ George Anderson as part-time gardener was a question over which Louise and Caroline agreed to have differing responses.

"I promise to stay within the budget we agreed on," Louise said. During the time of the Texas tenants' stay a service had been engaged to maintain the grounds. Their work was cursory at best. Many of the flower gardens had been mowed over and much of the ornamental shrubbery had been allowed to grow wild. Whenever it was possible, Louise liked to spend her time in the garden, returning the grounds to their former glory.

Caroline sat down on the bed. She took Louise's small pink hand, and the old grey diamonds of her engagement and wedding rings sparkled in the light against their platinum settings. They had belonged to her husband's grandmother, the first Mrs. Frederick Kent.

"Why did you say on Saturday that Imogen was the one the wine was meant to kill?" Louise shook her head. "I saw her last night, you know. She's worried about her life."

"Why?"

"Imogen believes the killer meant to get her, and that she, or he, will try again. You said on Saturday --"

"I know what I said, Caroline, but why does it concern you?"

"Imogen is afraid. I think I can help her."

Louise felt her heart begin to hurry its beat. "Caroline, you must be careful. You have only recovered from a difficult experience in your own life. I don't think you are ready to help someone else cope with a loss just yet."

"But, don't you see, Louise? I understand how Imogen feels. I'm the one person who can help her."

"No." Louise was vehement. "I won't let you do it to yourself, Caroline. Especially for Imogen Revel."

"Reed worked for the Revels. Don't you think he would want me to help?"

"No," she repeated. "I do not. Imogen is no concern of yours."

"Not even if her life is in danger?"

"There are two issues. One is that I don't want you going back to relive what happened to Reed. Comforting Imogen is bound to bring all that back." She saw from the look in Caroline's eyes that she had forecasted right. "And, secondly is Imogen herself. You won't be appreciated from that quarter."

"She's asked for my help."

"That surprises me. She is a difficult person in the best of times. I've never known her to ask anyone for anything."

"Her fiancé has been murdered."

Louise sighed. "The police are investigating, Caroline. Leave all this to them. I know you proved yourself a good detective with the murders here, but it's not your job to help the police." She paused and looked at the younger woman with concern. "You haven't mentioned Hank Nightingale at all."

"What's there to say? He's in charge of the case. I had to give a statement."

"You know that I came to like Hank, Caroline. I wouldn't have thought it in the beginning when it was obvious he was becoming interested in you. I'm not a snob, but a policeman, I thought. What would people say?" She put up her hand to stop Caroline's open lips from beginning to respond. "But he was, is a good man. I thought it was a good thing that you spent time with him. I was sorry when you stopped. But I respected your decision."

"Thank you. It was my decision."

"What did he say to you? At Mon Plaisir."

"We were cordial. Hank's a gentleman, as you have just pointed out."

"Hmmn" Louise sighed. She patted Caroline's hand. "He was a good friend to you."

"We're becoming friendly again. I think he knows the terms of our friendship."

"And he accepts them?"Louise looked unconvinced. She knew love when she saw it, and Hank had been in love with Caroline.

"Yes," Caroline said emphatically. "He does."

"Good."

"What do you know about Imogen Revel? Why don't you like her, Louise?"

"You know Frederick had been close to their father."

"Yes, of course. That's why they were so kind to Reed."

"He deserved whatever position they offered him."

"And Imogen? What was she like when she was young?"

"Difficult. I can never think of any other word to describe her. Physically she was always bigger, stronger than Claude. She used to bully him when they were young." The image of it made Caroline laugh, and Louise relaxed.

"Reed said she was smart."

"Oh, yes, that was true, Caroline. She did well in school. Her record was head and shoulders above Claude's."

"Yet Claude got the prize."

"I don't understand."

"Syndicat Revel. He was groomed for the chairmanship. Not Imogen."

"Women, especially in society, weren't thought of as being suited to the business world."

"So Imogen became a teacher. The only profession for a woman!"

"She didn't have to become anything. She didn't have to work."

"Perhaps she wanted to earn her own money."

"Teaching wouldn't give her much of that." Louise opened the teapot to check if there was any tea left. She poured herself a dark, grainy last cup from the pot. "Anyway, she got her living expenses from her allowance."

"Allowance? She doesn't have her own trust fund to draw from?"

"No. The Revels are very patriarchal. Nothing would have been put in Imogen's name. First her father, old Henri, and now her brother Claude have overseen her money. None of it is considered hers, you see."

"How medieval. And yet Claudine has been spared that fate."

"Yes. I thought that was decent of Claude. Not the kind of thing a young woman of today wants to put up with. Besides, there's no son."

"What about Claudine? Would she have any reason to hate Imogen?"

"Hate? Is that something else Imogen told you?"

"In a roundabout way."

"She's exaggerating, and it's upset you. You see? I'm right. Please don't become involved with Imogen. Will you promise me?"

"I can't, Louise. She came to me for help."

"You'll be hurt, my dear. I can see it coming."

"I'm stronger than you think."

Louise was unwilling to say she disagreed, and the conversation ended as Mattie appeared in the doorway, carrying a large breakfast tray. The aroma from under the covers of the dishes announced the contents before the cook could get the words from her mouth. Sausages, if Louise was any judge of the scent.

"Since you hardly ate a thing for your dinner last night," Mattie announced, "I thought I'd better get a good hot breakfast into you before you got up. There's pancakes and sausages." She cast a disgruntled look at Caroline. Her thin lips curved in a disapproving attitude. "Same as for the guests in the dining room."

Mattie's hard stare pushed Caroline into a standing position, and the tray was put in front of Louise as Caroline expertly drew the small tea one aside.

"Them two old sisters from Boston is in the dining room, Mrs. Caroline, with all their papers and folders, asking for you. I believe they need some of your tour advice today. Cheryl's getting their breakfast to them." Cheryl Tyson was the second of the maids, a young Navy wife from the Newport base who worked week days. "I don't know when that couple you put in the corner bedroom in the west wing will be down. Seem to be late risers."

"We'll leave the chafing dishes out on the sideboard, Mattie. Guests have from 7:30 until ten to eat."

"Ten o'clock for breakfast! I don't know how anyone can wait until the middle of the day to have their first meal."

"Thank you, Mattie," Louise interrupted, as she chewed determinedly on a sausage. "This is delicious."

"Thank you, Missus."

"I'll be going, Louise," Caroline said. Louise saw the look of wariness she gave Mattie as she disappeared through the door. She was reminded of two house cats she once had who didn't get along. They always walked wide tracks around each other.

"Why don't you go and help her downstairs, Mattie?" Louise said.

"I'll run your bath and get you settled in it before I go back to the kitchen."

"Yes," Louise agreed with resignation. "That will be very helpful of you." She cut into the tall stack of pancakes. Butter dribbled out into the sea of maple syrup swimming on her plate. The second sausage floated downstream.

"Afterwards I can set you up on a nice longue chair in the conservatory and keep the guests out of there so you can get a proper rest."

"I don't mind sharing the house with the guests, Mattie. I wish you would believe that."

"I know you just say that for Mrs. Caroline's benefit. Of course, if it means that much to you, you can count on me to keep your secret."

"Thank you, Mattie," Louise said. She took the opportunity to push her half-eaten breakfast aside. Her mind was too preoccupied with her worries about Caroline to match wits with the cook. "Now, if you'll just draw my bath, please."

"It's a pleasure," the cook replied.

As the tall, thin woman went through the door to the bathroom, she was humming. Louise listened for the familiar rush of the water into the tub and the sounds made by the opening of the jars which housed her array of bath preparations.

"We're all ready for you," Mattie called.

"I'm coming," Louise answered loudly. To herself, she murmured, "I need a good soak to sort things out. I won't have Caroline upset."

"What is that you said about Mrs. Caroline?" came the voice from the bathroom.

"I don't know what you're talking about," Louise said firmly as she reached the bath. "You ought to get your hearing checked."

Mattie didn't answer, an action for which Louise was profoundly grateful.

"Now," Louise said as she stepped out of her slippers. "I won't have you helping me into the tub like an invalid. Go downstairs and give Caroline a hand. That you did hear me say."

Mattie nodded and left. It felt good to Louise to have the last word with someone at Kenwood for a change. Now if she could only convince Caroline not to get involved in Hugh Dockings's murder. It would be difficult, Louise thought, as she felt the warm water in the tub seep up to her shoulders. *Difficult*. There was that word again.

12

"I shall go mad, Claude. I absolutely shall go mad if your Uncle Dorsey doesn't go home. He's getting on my nerves, and what's more, he knows it."

"I think you're exaggerating, Pamela."

"Everyone else in the family agreed to go home and return on Friday for the service. But not Dorsey. No, Claude, he's the perennial guest." Her voice carried a mocking tone which he found unpleasant when directed toward a member of his family.

The banker had been making telephone calls in his study when his wife had interrupted him. Claudine, with her youthful energy to get back to business, had returned on Sunday to the office in New York for the beginning of the work week. Realizing how little his physical presence was needed nowadays in the merchant bank itself, Claude had been conducting his affairs and making money here in what had been -- until five minutes ago -- a pleasant country retreat.

"He's lonely," he explained patiently to his wife. "Uncle Dorsey only wants someone to listen to him."

"Then you listen, Claude. Or get Aunt Grace back. She's been listening to his stories for years despite the fact that she already knows all of them. I'm tired of hearing all about the history of the Revels, their rise in fortune, their acceptance by society. Generations of success outwitting their banking rivals. God! It's like a damned television show. The Revels! Tune in every week. The problem is that Dorsey's series is one big re-run."

"Can't you ignore him?" Claude asked gently. "The house is big enough for you to avoid him."

Claude hated to see his wife becoming upset. Pamela upset translated into his having to do something about the cause of her distress. Always that pressure to take care of everything. Would he ever be free of it?

He sighed and looked up at the pinched face of his wife. She was showing her age this morning. Perhaps she hadn't taken as much care as usual with her hair and make-up. He couldn't recall seeing her ever look so haggard.

"Are you feeling all right, Pamela? You do look tired. You might be coming down with something. Aches and pains can put a person in a disagreeable mood."

"Disagreeable? Disagreeable's hardly the word for how I feel. And I'm not 'coming down with something,' as you say. And further more, I'll be a damn sight more than *disagreeable* if you don't do something about Uncle Dorsey."

"All right," Claude said, rising from his desk. He took one last look at his notes and mentally tallied the telephone calls left to be made that day. He liked catching people early, and so far he had cornered three important quarries and accomplished several key objectives. It was a good business day. And that is what he enjoyed: productive financial days.

"Thank you, Claude," Pamela said. Her gratitude sounded genuine. "I'm sorry to interrupt your work, but I do need you."

"What can I do? I will be happy to sound Uncle Dorsey out on his plans, but I doubt I can get him to leave immediately. Perhaps if I took him out for lunch, that would get him out of your hair for today. Yes," he said, pleased with himself, "why don't I take him away for the afternoon?"

It would give him the rest of the morning for his work.

"And you will suggest that he cannot stay here at our house indefinitely?"

"He enjoys Newport in the summer. He always has. My father treated Mon Plaisir as if it belonged to everyone in the family. His brothers and sisters were always welcome to stay with their families. My father felt strongly about it. You know that, Pamela. And you've always accepted that I want to continue that same hospitality."

"I have always welcomed your family. It's that this week... I thought Imogen would be on her way to Greece today. And now. Claude? What's going to happen? Do you think she'll return to Camden?"

"I'm not sure." He knew that was not the answer she wanted, and he took her by her slim shoulder and nudged closer to her. She accepted the half-embrace and waited. "You must give her time. Look at how she's acted over this service on Friday."

"It's going to be horrible."

"No, no. I can handle Father Halloran. I have an appointment to see him tomorrow morning. We'll have a prayer service in the chapel on Friday that Father Halloran will lead. Ostensibly he will do it to offer prayers for the family. I'll make it seem to Imogen that it is all being done for Hugh. She won't understand the difference."

"Are you sure? She wants the casket brought into the chapel."

"The body is not going to be available in time. I've checked with the police. We will go ahead with the prayer service and do all the trimmings. We can pray for Hugh, say some type of thing that comes across as a eulogy. I'll be happy to speak myself."

"And you think this will pacify Imogen?"

"Once we're all in the chapel, there's nothing Imogen can do. She will be too busy moaning over Hugh, if I'm any judge of the situation. Let her do her crying and get it over with."

"Oh, I dread it."

"We must get through it. And I know I can count on you, Pamela, when the chips are down."

"Yes." She sighed again and looked up at him. "Claude, who do you think killed Hugh Dockings?"

"Why, he killed himself. I think that's perfectly clear."

"He committed suicide? I don't believe it."

"Not suicide. The poison was meant for Imogen. That part of the story she did get right."

"Wait, let me understand this. You think Hugh put the poison in Imogen's drink?"

"It's the only logical explanation."

"But why?"

"Surely you can see that from the beginning, going back to last Christmas when we first met him, that he didn't give a fig for Imogen. It was the Revel money he was after."

"I did believe that."

"Of course. He was marrying the Revel millions."

"But Imogen doesn't have money of her own."

"I'm sure he didn't understand that. Perhaps Imogen hadn't made that clear to him."

"It would be like her. She would be so clever."

"Remember that they made their wills in April, in anticipation of being married. I think that's important, don't you see? Hugh was to inherit whatever Imogen had, as naturally she would from him. He must have thought that he would be rich if she died."

"What about Des Arbres? I thought no one outside the family could inherit Revel property?"

"And Hugh couldn't. I made sure of that when Imogen consulted Ned Babson, our family's lawyer, to do the wills. The way her will is written, Hugh received only a life interest in Des Arbres. He could have continued to live there past her death, but that's all."

"So what did he think he was getting if she died?"

"No doubt being able to live in Newport rent-free was attractive to him. He only needed the pavilion for his own lifetime. And, of course, he did believe he would inherit Imogen's money. Don't forget that she had promised to buy him that sailboat. I'm sure he didn't realize where she was getting the money."

"From you."

"Yes. I know you didn't approve, but I was pleased to make her a gift of whatever she would need for the purchase. She's entitled to the money. We have plenty, Pamela, and I couldn't begrudge my sister that request."

"And there would have been others. Hugh Dockings was going to be expensive to keep."

"I'm sorry, but I would have paid the bills."

"I suppose it's because of Claudine."

"Yes. She's going to have the life Imogen would have liked to have had. Freedom to pursue her career, being in control of her own money. It's too late for Imogen, and I'm sorry about that."

"Don't be. Imogen was born at the wrong time. We women all have had to accept things like that." She smiled ruefully, and he wondered what private grievance she bore. "I'm curious, Claude. What does Imogen inherit from Hugh?"

"I don't know exactly. Apparently he owned the cottage in Waterville where he lived. He may have some money saved, but not much I suspect. Imogen can't receive his pension from the school because they were never married. Ned will tell us about that soon enough."

His wife looked somber as she considered what he had said. Finally she spoke in a resolute voice. "It would be good if the police could prove that Hugh poisoned the wine. It would make everything go away."

"I'm not sure how they will prove it. This may be one of those cases which is never solved."

"What about this mysterious waiter? The one who's supposed to be some man who hated Hugh."

"I wouldn't put too much stock in that suggestion. The police are chasing clouds, if you want my opinion. It sounds good, but I believe my solution is the right one. Hugh tried to kill Imogen. He didn't care for her, and he could do away with her without feeling any remorse. He'd be free to live his life in retirement the way he had always lived it. Concentrating only on number one."

"Himself?"

"Exactly. And who had access to cyanide? We must remember that the man was a science teacher."

"But why would Hugh drink the wine if he knew it was poisoned? I was standing near him and Imogen when he began to choke. He looked so surprised."

"That's an easy one. Remember the glass had been sitting on the plant stand for several minutes. Possibly five minutes, or even longer. The man was drunk. He wanted a drink so badly that when Imogen put the glass in his hand, he drank it. Don't you see? In his drunkenness he had forgotten that he had poisoned the wine."

"It does make sense."

"I'm right," he said firmly. "I know that's how it happened."

The telephone call from Caroline had come to Hank the first thing that same morning. He had been surprised, pleasantly so, to hear her voice at the other end of the instrument. She wanted to talk to him. *Urgently*, she said.

Hank wanted to see her again and was glad for the opportunity, but there was something in the sound of her voice that also interested him. "It's about Imogen Revel," she had explained. "I'm worried about her."

The earliest time available to meet with her was after lunch, and it was at half past two that he turned the unmarked black police car into the gates of Kenwood. The stone marker which had the estate's name etched into the grey rock pillar was unobtrusive. There was no sign that the property was an inn and guests were welcome. He had always liked that touch. The setting was bucolic. A grove of beechwood trees, their young spring leaves vigorous in the sunshine, stood along the front of the property, bordering the winding drive on one side. On the drive's other side, an old stone gate house stood guarding the entrance.

Hank let his gaze take in the house slowly as it came into his view. There were two compact wings on either side of the main wing. The Palladian windows with their graceful topping curves were trimmed in white against a simple grey facade. He had admired the house from the first time he had come there.

Caroline met him at the door and led him through the large foyer, past an imposing staircase, and toward a hall which ran down the east wing. There was no reception desk for guests. Checking in at the Inn at Kenwood Court was no different than arriving at a private home where one was immediately shown to a waiting guest bedroom. Bills and other financial matters were handled discreetly.

"Do you have many guests at present?"

"Only a few. It's mostly week-end business still, although we do have good bookings for the end of this month and through July and August."

She took him back to her office, the familiar old, dark paneled room.

A massive oak desk dominated the room, which also contained the required modern office machines to run the inn's business. A large number of framed black and white photographs lined the walls. Hank knew from past experience that they told the history of the Kent family.

"Thank you for coming, Hank. I went to see Imogen Revel last evening. I hate to interfere with your investigation, but I am very worried about her as I told you on the telephone."

Hank listened patiently as Caroline recounted her conversation with Imogen Revel. He did not interrupt because, although he was strongly of the mind that Dockings was the victim and the waiter could well be his killer, he had no proof as yet.

When Caroline was finished, he remained silent for several seconds.

"You ought to know that we do have a promising lead. This missing waiter may be a man called Donald Montgomery whose son died while sailing with Hugh Dockings. Unfortunately we haven't been able to locate him." The Pennsylvania address provided for the Montgomery family from the boarding school had turned out to be an old one, with no forwarding address. Keisha McAndrews was checking DMV records for a lead on a newer address.

"But suppose Hugh was not the intended victim? That would make that old business unimportant."

"We can't discount that until we find Montgomery and see if he can be positively identified as being the missing waiter at the Revels' reception."

"What if the killer, not Donald Montgomery, tries to kill Imogen again?"

"You want a promise that she will be safe. You know I can't give you that."

"Surely the Revels are an important family in Newport." She stopped and looked embarrassed. "I'm sorry. I didn't mean that the way it came out. Everyone's life should be important."

"Look, Caroline," he said. "I will talk to Imogen Revel about this myself. You're right in one respect. We don't want any more deaths. That I can assure you."

"I understand that, Hank. And I do thank you for listening. It would be a load off my mind if you could see that Imogen is protected."

"You can count on me to do my best."

13

It was late that same afternoon when Ben came into Hank's office with the report on the autopsy done on Hugh Dockings. As the medical examiner, Daniel Peters, had predicted, the cause of death was asphyxia due to ingestion of a lethal dose of cyanide.

"Hydrocyanic acid," Hank said, reading out loud, "also known as prussic acid. Dr. Peters was right on the money."

"Interesting, isn't it? I can't think of another case like it in all my years with the department."

"No food in the victim's stomach," Hank said, his eyes on the page in front of him. "That, combined with the large amount of alcohol he had consumed, made the poison fast-acting."

"There's a note at the end." While Hank found the last page, Ben continued. "It says you can find hydrocyanic acid in peach pits, apple seeds, and some other fruits."

"I see. Did you note any fruit trees growing on the Revels' estate?"

"Anybody can buy apples at the supermarket."

"But how many people know you can get prussic acid from the seeds? Besides, you'd need quite a bit."

"You think it came from The Camden School science labs?"

"We'll have to confirm the substance is kept there. I may as well tell you now. I'm driving over to Waterville tomorrow."

"Do you want me to come with you?"

"No. Actually I'm taking Caroline Kent with me."

"Oh?"

"I suppose I have to explain."

"I am a little curious."

"I want to take a look at Hugh Dockings's cottage. We've already learned about this sailing death. There might be other clues there to the man's life and why someone might want him dead. Miss Revel inherits the house upon the death. It turns out they had made reciprocating wills in the spring."

"That's very interesting, Lieutenant."

"Yes. And we'll get to that in a bit. I just got back from seeing Miss Revel. When I told her I would be going to the cottage, she said she wanted her representative to accompany me. I'll have a search warrant for Connecticut, of course. I don't want any trouble down the road on this."

"And Mrs. Kent is her representative?"

"Imogen Revel telephoned her while I was there, and she has agreed to go. We're leaving first thing tomorrow morning. It also gives me an opportunity to nose around at the school, as well. It's a little unorthodox, but I think it will be all right. Caroline has taken on some kind of caretaker role with Imogen Revel. I'm afraid that Miss Revel has convinced her that the killer was after her and that he or she will try again."

"And what do you think about that?"

"As I see things, everything hinges on whether the wine was served with the poison already in it or was the cyanide put in while the glass was on the plant stand?"

"Did you read my interview notes with George March?"

"I see that he confirms seeing Imogen put the glass on the plant stand."

"Yes, but he doesn't remembering seeing Imogen pick it up again. He did say there were several people in the vicinity. He noticed the discussion between Hugh and Imogen over who should drink the wine. He's sure others could have heard that also."

"And the wine was on the plant stand for several minutes."

"Unfortunately he isn't sure who was near enough to the glass to touch it. But he said he doesn't see why it wasn't possible, given the activity there. Any number of people were standing there by one of the French windows which was open to the terrace."

"I noted he was talking to Claudine Revel during this time."

"Talking shop, he says. They work together at the family's bank."

"Damn," Hank said suddenly. "I wish we could find that waiter." He had listened earlier as Imogen had described why she feared for her life, and he couldn't yet rule out that she was supposed to die instead of Hugh.

"Keisha's checking. She ought to have something soon."

"And what about the Block Island P.D.? What do they have on the death of Dennis Montgomery?"

"I spoke to them this morning. They have to get the file together and fax us their paperwork. It should be coming tomorrow morning."

"Tomorrow I'll be in Connecticut. Why can't they get it to us tonight?"

"It's not that big of a department, sir."

"All right. I'm impatient, that's all."

"You mentioned something about wills earlier, Lieutenant."

"They were drawn up by the Revel family's attorney in April."

"Is that usual to do so far in advance of your wedding?"

"I don't know. I've never been married. But, I suppose people like the Revels think of these financial matters more than people like us do, Ben."

"I was thinking more of Hugh Dockings. A bit presumptuous, I'd say, on his part."

"When I look through his papers tomorrow, I'll get some idea of his financial situation."

"And what about the Revels?"

"What about the Revels?"

"I've been thinking about that sailboat Imogen Revel was going to buy Dockings. You know. The one that was going to cost two hundred and fifty thousand bucks." Hank nodded. "Well, she hasn't bought it yet. I get the idea that the family money is controlled by that Claude Revel. Now suppose he killed Dockings because he didn't want his sister spending all that money on her new husband. They think about doing the wills in April. But the sailboat isn't purchased, and here it is June already. You're a sailor, Lieutenant. If someone was buying you a fancy sailboat, wouldn't you want it all ready for the water now, not later in the summer?"

"It's a point well-taken."

"I think we ought to look at the brother as a possible suspect."

"Claude Revel?" Ben nodded. "Oh, the chief will have a field day with that one."

"I don't suppose you've thought of looking into the finances of that family bank of theirs?"

"You mean that the Revels may not be as rich as we think they are?"

"Lots of people put up a good front."

"It's not a publicly held company. It may be hard to get the information."

"I can start digging."

"All right," Hank said. He was reluctant to let the Revels know he was looking into their family's money, but he trusted Ben to do the work carefully.

Could it be that Imogen Revel's marriage was unpopular with her family? Was another strain on the Revel family purse so unwelcome that someone had resorted to murder? Hank thought of the grandeur he had first seen at Mon Plaisir. It had all appeared a flawless setting. And yet today he had also seen Kenwood where the Kents' family fortune had been dissipated by immoderate investments. Even bankers took risks these days.

How sound was Syndicat Revel? Could there be a thread there to lead him to the discovery of how a dose of cyanide found its way into the French wine which came from its chairman's own cellars?

The next morning's weather was sunny and pleasant, and Caroline knew she ought to be enjoying the drive from Newport to Waterville as a respite from the seven-day-a-week responsibility of being an innkeeper. Yet she found herself uncomfortable in the car. Was it the close proximity to Hank? Or was it the memory of the unpleasant argument she had had with Louise earlier that morning over her trip.

In the driver's seat, Hank tried to make pleasant conversation by introducing various innocuous topics such as a recent article in the *Newport Daily News* about the traffic situation on Memorial Boulevard and the latest winner of the annual Newport Chowder Cook-Off.

None had received more than a word or two of response.

"We should be getting off 95 soon," he said. "Then Waterville is only about fifteen miles or so north of the exit."

Caroline was lost in her own thoughts. How could she explain the trip to Louise when she wasn't sure herself of her real motives? All she knew was that when she had heard Imogen's voice on the telephone, she had quickly agreed to make the journey, even though she knew that her time today would have been far better spent working at her own business.

"A penny for your thoughts," Hank said, jolting her from her self-absorption.

"Oh, I'm sorry. I guess I haven't been good company, have I?"

"That's all right," he said congenially. "Relax."

The car had left the main highway, and the scenery had changed, becoming more green, less commercial. Caroline looked out of the window at the horizon, trimmed by the blue of the river.

Hank easily found the cottage. As they approached the doorway of the spare structure, he handed her the key which Imogen had given him on the previous day.

"Here, you'd better take charge of this."

She opened the door, and they stepped inside. The house had a stale smell about it, and Caroline began opening some of the windows. Interior decoration had not been one of the late Hugh Dockings's talents, nor, all too obviously, had housekeeping. The downstairs living room and kitchen were a jumble of mismatched furniture, piles of magazines and newspapers, full ashtrays and dirty cups and glasses. The coffee maker appeared to hold the last pot of coffee it made. Caroline frowned at the mess.

"Am I allowed to clean up these dirty dishes?"

"No," he said firmly. "Not for evidence, and especially because you shouldn't have to. You're Miss Revel's representative, not her maid."

"I can't bear this disorder."

"I want to see everything as Dockings left it."

"All right."

They inspected the second floor where they found a bathroom and two small bedrooms, one of which had been turned into a study. The same clutter existed in this area, as well. They saw that Hugh had not bothered to make his bed, which was covered with the remainder of the clothes he had apparently decided not to pack.

"It almost looks as if he was planning to return," Caroline said.

"Yes," Hank said, taking a critical look at his surroundings. "I'm going to start in the study."

"What do you want me to do?"

"You were the actress," he said. "Why don't you go around this place and tell me what kind of a character you find the late Hugh Dockings to be?"

"All right."

She was intrigued by his assignment. "I'll start downstairs."

"And if you find anything that looks like it might be the motive for his murder, bring it to me immediately."

"Agreed," she said.

"And, don't," he called after her as she began to descend the staircase, "clean anything up!"

After an hour or so of browsing through the titles of the books and DVDs in the living room, inspecting the edible contents of the kitchen, finding his stash of inexpensive red wine which Dockings bought by the gallon, and turning up dust and crumbs everywhere, Caroline thought she was beginning to know her character.

The late Hugh Dockings indeed had a devotion to sailing. That had been evident in his reading material, as well as in several DVDs devoted to the more technical aspects of the subject. Caroline noted, however, that there were no decorative touches associated with sailing in the cottage. No photographs or prints, no miniature boats on display, no nautical brass work. The one token reference was the kitchen calendar featuring twelve photographs of a dozen sail boats racing especially tumultuous waters. Caroline noted there were no calendar dates marked with reminders of appointments, birthdays, or other notations, not even a mark for the Sunday of his planned marriage to Imogen Revel.

There was ice cream in the freezer, a premium brand. The expected frozen, prepared dinners were absent. The dusty cans and boxes in the pantry closet indicated their owner had owned them indefinitely.

Caroline returned to the living room and surveyed the space. Hugh's favorite chair was easily identified. It faced the television set. Beside it, a table held the remote control, an ashtray and a dirty drinking glass with the familiar pigment of dried red wine at its bottom. Caroline approached the chair gingerly. She brushed her hand across the soft cushion and felt the uneven grit of unidentifiable, old food.

"What's this?" she asked out loud. There was a corner of white paper visible between the cushion and the arm of the chair. Lifting the cushion, she saw that it was a crumpled document which had been jammed aside. She opened it and began to read the contents. It was a letter.

14

Before Hank began examining the contents of Hugh Dockings's study he took a slow walk through the bedroom and bathroom. Hank's own apartment was far from tidy, but he couldn't have abided living in these quarters. The accumulation of hair imbedded in the tufts of the bedside rug was disgusting, and he wondered how a man could plant his two bare feet on its dirty surface each morning.

The clothes which had been left behind, along with the other contents of the two rooms, offered up one interesting fact. There were no traces of a woman's presence in either room, bath or bed. Had the women removed any personal effects? Or had none ever been allowed to stow any of their belongings in this private bachelor's house?

When he had seen enough of the living spaces, Hank returned to the study. There were books and papers on a wall of shelving, and these appeared to pertain chiefly to Dockings's duties at the school. There were a variety of science texts and reference books, a cardboard box full of old final examinations, and several loose leaf binders with lab sheets for student experiments. Several notebooks held the methodical lesson plans for the various levels of students whom Hugh taught. There was no computer, and Hank surmised Dockings had made use of the school's machines.

After reading a few things at random, Hank put the rest aside and started to investigate the drawers of the small work desk. There was nothing of interest in the topmost cavities: pens, paper clips, and the usual stationery supplies. The large bottom drawer served as a small filing cabinet, and here Hank found the dead man's bank statements.

Hank opened the bank file. A study of the last two months' statements indicated that Dockings had his weekly paychecks direct-deposited into his checking account at a local bank. The paid checks suggested that the expenses were primarily those associated with the running of the cottage -- there was a mortgage on the property -- and large American Express bills. The residue cash had been allowed to accumulate in a savings account at the same bank.

Further inspection of the files revealed material relating to Hugh's health insurance and medical bills, his most recent school employment contract, and a bundle of fresh-looking legal forms stapled together. Hank leafed through the packet and identified its contents as the several papers which Hugh had signed upon his retirement from The Camden School. At first glance, the documents appeared to be the standard mix of continuation of insurance coverage and notice of the amount of pension to be paid, with date of commencement. Hank noted that the bank to which the pension checks were to be direct-deposited was in Newport.

Hank gathered up the files to take back with him. One of his colleagues at the department had trained as an accountant, and she could be called in to analyze financial documents connected with a case.

After removing all the folders from the desk, Hank saw that there was a large manilla envelope lying flat on the bottom of the drawer. The envelope looked worn and Hank thought it had been handled often.

The sheaf of yellowed newspaper clippings which he withdrew were held together with a rusted paper clip. Carefully he separated the clippings and laid them out on the desk top.

The story of the death of Dennis Montgomery peered up at him in the headlines and photographs which had been printed in the days following the boy's death in 1997. There were stories and pictures from the Block Island newspaper, as well as the local Waterville paper and the Montgomerys' hometown newspaper in Pennsylvania.

The headlines describing the event were vivid.

Tragic sailing death off Block Island

Local teenager lost in fatal boating accident

Coach suspected of negligence in death

The soft, earnest face of Dennis Montgomery stared up at Hank. The photograph had been taken for some formal occasion, the school yearbook most probably. Dennis had blond hair and pale eyes. His full lips were curved in a slight, self-conscious smile. He looked very young.

A hearing had been held, and Hank scanned the account of the proceedings. A photograph accompanied the article in the Block Island paper, and Hank read the caption under the group of figures emerging from the municipal building.

GRIEVING PARENTS of Dennis Montgomery leave yesterday's hearing on the island to determine the cause of their son's sailing fatality in May. Donald and Ruth Montgomery (shown at left) refused to talk to reporters waiting outside after their son's drowning death, which occurred in rough waters off Block Island during a Camden School team practice race last spring, was found to be accidental. The Montgomerys had sought to have the coach of The Camden School's sailing team, Hugh Dockings, charged with negligence in the accident, but yesterday's action cleared the coach of any wrongdoing in connection with the death.

The image of Donald Montgomery was small and blurry, but to Hank's eye, there were similarities between this man and the picture made of the missing waiter at the Revels' party. He went to the top of the stairs.

"Caroline," he called. "Can you come up here for a minute?"

When she heard the sound of Hank's voice, Caroline had been reading the letter she had found in Hugh's chair for the second time.

The first reading had shocked her, and she wanted to make some sense to herself of the words on the paper.

"All right," she answered slowly.

He was standing at the top of the stairs, his face bright with excitement. She wondered if her own face reflected the same intensity.

"Come, see something in the study."

She followed him to the desk and began reading the newspaper accounts of Dennis Montgomery's death. For a few minutes she forgot her own discovery downstairs.

"Do you see Donald Montgomery's picture?" He pointed to the small, oval face. She studied it carefully. "What do you think? Could he be our man?"

"I'm not sure, but it could be." The thick dots forming the photograph rendered it hazy and faint, but the demeanor of the man looked familiar, along with the shape of his head.

"It could be," he repeated. He took his cell phone from his pocket and quickly punched the buttons. Caroline watched his face while he waited for his party to answer. He looked energized, elated at their find. "Sgt. Davies, please. This is Lt. Nightingale. Is he in the station?" Again he waited, and Caroline felt the energy as his eyes looked back and forth from her to the desk to the phone. "Ben, it's me. I think we have something on the Montgomery boy." He paused to listen. "Good. What is it?" Again he waited for information, which when he heard it seemed to lift his vitality to higher heights. "No kidding. Well, well, well." He reached for a pen and made a quick notation in his pocket notebook. "325 Waterside Road... got it. Thanks. I'll be in touch." He ended the call and smiled at Caroline. "Some good news. We've got an address for the Montgomerys, and you'll never guess where it is."

"Where?" she asked weakly. She had allowed herself another look at the newspaper photograph, and what she saw saddened her. She recognized death's grief and heartbreak in the blank faces of Dennis Montgomery's parents.

"Right here in Waterville." He looked at the pad and repeated the street address to her. "We can see them this afternoon. I'll take you by there to see Donald Montgomery, and we'll see if we can't get an identification today."

"You're convinced he's the man you're looking for?"

"Let's say I've got my fingers crossed."

"He may be an innocent man."

"Caroline, I'm looking for you to positively identify him as the waiter at the Revels' house. We're not going to try him today. What's the matter? You look upset."

In answer she offered him the letter.

"What is this?"

"I found it downstairs in Hugh's chair. It's a letter from Marilyn Hansen. At least, I think it is. It's just signed *Marilyn*."

"Have you read it?"

"I'm afraid I did."

He took the paper and read it slowly, or perhaps, like her, he wanted to read it twice. She saw his face level into a frown, and she thought she could deduce most of his thoughts.

The letter was a threat to Hugh Dockings, written in the raving, bitter style of a woman scorned.

"You have taken everything from me," Hank read out loud, "and left me nothing in return. That frigid rich bitch has money, but that's all. How can you touch her? Her skin is like a toad's, and I don't believe you do touch her. Unless you're drunk, and you're numb when you try to screw..." His voice trailed off, and Caroline saw he was uncomfortable to continue reading in her presence.

"I know. It's pretty graphic," she said. At the letter's end, Marilyn had threatened to castrate her former lover.

"What do you make of it?"

"The last part, do you mean?"

"Oh," he said, slightly embarrassed. "But, surely, that last part..."

"Don't contemplate it, Hank. You look a little green." She repressed a smile while he recovered his composure.

"There's real anger there."

"It doesn't specifically mention death."

"We'll have to talk to her about this, Caroline."

"I thought we were going over to the school anyway."

"Yes, I wanted to see the science department set-up. And now when we have her give us the tour, she'll have to explain more than the labs and chemicals to us."

The headmaster of Camden was all smiles as he greeted Caroline and Hank on their arrival. Nick Pratt quickly waved away his secretary and took complete charge of his guests.

"Have you had your lunch yet?" he inquired solicitously. "I haven't had mine, and I think I can offer you something fairly decent from the dining room. We pride ourselves on our good table here."

"That's all right," Hank said without consulting Caroline. "We'll get something after we finish here."

"Fine," Nick said. He looked disappointed at not being able to entertain them. Caroline thought Pratt's gaze lingered on her longer than it needed to, but she dismissed her irritation. "What can I do for you exactly, Lieutenant?" the headmaster asked. "I believe that you said something on the telephone about wanting to see where Hugh taught."

"I want to see the science department and learn who had access to the chemicals stored there. I thought we might get Ms. Hansen to help us. I telephoned her last night to tell her we'd be here today."

"She's on campus," Nick said. "I saw her earlier." Pratt pushed a button on his desk and the capable voice of his secretary came on. "Barbara, ring Ms. Hansen. She's waiting in the science department. Tell her the police are here, and we're on our way over there."

Their walk across the quiet campus could have been the tour of two parents, in the care of the headmaster, taking a look at the school on behalf of their prospective offspring. Nick chatted amiably, directing Caroline's attention to the grounds and facilities, boasting of the school's place in the hierarchy of New England boarding schools. They passed several gardeners, working in the flower beds and trimming shrubbery.

"How long has Marilyn Hansen been teaching here?" Hank asked abruptly. His mind had been far away from Nick's commentary.

"Twenty-two years," Nick answered promptly.

"Any complaints against her?"

"I'm sorry, Lieutenant, but I wish you would be more specific."

"Is she a competent teacher? Students, parents like her? Things like that. Does she drink?"

"Her evaluations are fine, and she is, if I have to say, middle of the road in her relations with the students and their parents. As for the last question, I can't answer."

"No concerns on that score?"

"Why do you ask? If you would tell me why you want to know, that might help."

"She may have done something rash, perhaps under the influence."

"Do you mean she killed Hugh Dockings?"

"I'm not suggesting that right now. Only that drinking might explain some evidence we have."

They had reached a low, rambling brick building, and Nick took them through classrooms which connected to a rabbit warren of labs and supply rooms. Devoid of students, the hallways had an eerie stillness. A solitary teacher, cleaning out his room, gave them a curious stare. Pratt waved to him, calling him by name and wishing him a good summer. At the end of their quest they found Marilyn Hansen waiting in one of the supply rooms. A young woman, dressed in jeans and a T-shirt, was standing in the corner.

"Oh, good," Nick said when he saw the two women. "You've got Jackie here. Lieutenant, Caroline, this is Jackie Connelly. She is the lab assistant for the chemistry and biology classes."

"Thank you for coming, Ms. Connelly," Hank said. "And you, too, Ms. Hansen. You can both be most helpful. I won't waste your time. We have the autopsy report on Mr. Dockings, and the cause of his death can be traced to his ingestion of hydrocyanic acid."

Jackie flinched, and Caroline saw Marilyn give the woman a hard look.

"Hydrocyanic acid," Nick repeated. He looked square at Marilyn. "Do we keep the stuff here?" He waved his hand at the room's shelves and cabinets which contained a large assortment of bottles and canisters.

Jackie tapped the keys of a computer on the counter, scanning entries. Finally she pointed to the screen. "There. There's the entry for the last batch."

"I don't know anything about the chemistry supplies," Marilyn said. "I'm biology."

Hank read the record and looked across at the shelves. "Where is it? You are supposed to have two bottles of 250 milliliters each."

"Because it is a poison, it would be in the locked cabinet," Jackie said. She took a key from her jeans' pocket and opened a small wooden cabinet. For several seconds, she examined containers. "Here's one, but I don't see the second," she said, her back to the group. There was the clatter of bottles bumping against each other. "No, there's definitely only one here."

"Would it have been your responsibility to put the hydrocyanic acid in the cabinet when it arrived, Ms. Connelly?" Hank asked.

Jackie turned around. "Yes, I handle all supplies."

"Do you remember handling these particular bottles?"

"We don't use it much, and I'd have to think. The entry says we received some during the last school year, in October, along with several other items. I might remember putting it away. I think I did. No one else would have. The supplies are my responsibility."

"May I see the remaining bottle?" Jackie handed him the glass bottle. The container was shaped like a small Bell jar and had a stopper. The glass was thick and textured. The symbol HCN was printed in large letters on the label.

"Which teachers would use this chemical in their lab work?"

Jackie shook her head. "Chemistry, for sure. That's all I can suggest."

"Do you use it, Ms. Hansen?" Hank asked. The biology teacher was looking at the bottle as if the poison was capable of escaping on its own power.

"No, not in biology." Her reply was firm.

"Who has access to this room?"

"Everyone on the science faculty," Marilyn said. "And students can come in here."

"May I see your key, Ms. Hansen?" Without speaking she handed him a bunch of keys. Hank found the small key and tried it in the lock. It fit. "And every faculty member in the science department has a key to that cabinet?" He returned Marilyn's keys.

"Everyone?" Nick turned to Jackie. "Would you know?"

"They should, but people can't always find their keys or they don't want to be bothered digging them out of their desks or wherever they keep them."

"You're saying that you are asked to open the cabinet for other staff?" This was Caroline's question. She had been following the conversation closely.

"A few times," Jackie admitted. "The faculty is often in a hurry. Sometimes they send a student to find me to fill a request."

"Do you remember if you handled such an order to produce hydrocyanic acid for a teacher or student?" Hank asked.

"Oh, students would never be given anything which is poison. I would deliver that myself, in person."

"And did you... since October?" Nick asked.

"No, I'm positive I did not," Jackie answered.

"Then someone with their own key took the missing bottle," Caroline said.

"It would seem that way," Hank said. He looked at Marilyn. "Would you agree with me, Ms. Hansen?"

"I might."

"Do you have a key, Mr. Pratt?"

"Why would I have a key?" He looked shocked. "No, I don't."

"Who else is on the science faculty?"

"There are two more members, Tom Silva who teaches physics and Jon Murphy who teaches earth science."

"If you don't need me any further," Marilyn said, "I'll go back home." She was grasping her keys tightly in her left hand. "This is supposed to be my summer vacation."

"I'm afraid we do need you a bit longer, Ms. Hansen," Hank said. Caroline shifted uncomfortably. Was he going to bring up the letter in front of Nick and Jackie? "Thank you, Ms. Connelly. You've been most helpful. You, too, Mr. Pratt." He handed Jackie the bottle, and she replaced it in the cabinet, taking care as she locked the small door with her own key.

"Come with me, Jackie," Nick said. "Can I offer you some lunch to make up for bringing you out today?"

Marilyn stood taut, and Caroline looked away from the woman's apprehensive eyes.

"And now, Ms. Hansen," Hank said. "I have something else with which only you can help me... in the matter of the death of Mr. Hugh Dockings."

15

His first interview with Marilyn Hansen had not gone well, and Hank was determined to keep the upper hand in this second one. He wasn't encouraged by the look of defiance with which the biology teacher favored him. He knew her attitude was masking fear, and it was up to him to tear off her shield.

"How long did you and Hugh Dockings have a relationship, Ms. Hansen?" he began.

"You mean how long were we screwing?"

"If you wish to put it that way," he said evenly.

"Eleven years."

"I see. And Mr. Dockings was happy with this arrangement?"

"I thought so." The words came from her lips in a sneer.

"What, typically, would have been a week's activities? How did you spend your time together?"

"When the weather was cooperative we went sailing most weekends. Hugh could take out the school's boats, and we would go overnight usually."

"Friday and Saturday?"

"Yes."

"Where did you go in the boat?"

"Sometimes we went up the river, sometimes out to the Sound. In the summer, when we had the free time, Hugh liked to sail to

Martha's Vineyard and Nantucket." She paused, as if the recollection of some particular trip was remembered fondly.

"Were you a good sailor, Ms. Hansen?"

"I'm prone to seasickness. Hugh could sail the boat single-handedly."

"Perhaps you served as the cook onboard?"

"Oh, no. I'm a lousy cook. We always ate out. We'd dock somewhere... Hugh had several favorite places... we'd always go to a restaurant."

"Did you often eat out here in Waterville during the week?" She nodded. It began to explain the large American Express bills he had found in the cottage. "Sounds like a nice, cozy arrangement."

"It was," she said.

"And then it ended at Christmas. Did you have any inkling of that coming?"

"No." The syllable was clipped.

"You were upset?"

Marilyn Hansen expelled a breath, which sounded like the entire air contents of both her lungs. Her lips reformed the sneer, and she reached for a packet of cigarettes.

"I don't think you can smoke in here," Hank said. She ignored him and lit up, putting her keys on the counter so she could ignite her lighter. "So you did nothing," he said, going back to his questioning, "and they were to be married last week-end."

Marilyn shrugged, the cigarette smoke re-filling her lungs, giving her back her nerve. Hank waited for several seconds before taking the letter from his breast pocket. While she followed his hands with her eyes, he unfolded the paper and smoothed it into a flat plane on the counter top.

"Someone wrinkled up your letter. This is your letter, isn't it?"

"I was angry," she conceded. Her voice had a conciliatory tone. "He forgot about me as soon as that bitch dangled that boat and a house in Newport in front of him." She was speaking to Caroline exclusively, and Hank let her go on. "He wanted security for his old age. He hadn't saved much money. God, I still can't believe it."

"He was comfortable with you, and you let him take advantage."

"I thought that's what he wanted." She took a long drag on the cigarette.

"Until he found someone better."

"Yes," Marilyn spit out bitterly. "I just didn't know it would be Imogen."

Caroline watched the other woman carefully.

"And what did you want to do to Imogen?" Caroline asked.

"Did you send her letters, too?" Hank asked. Marilyn shook her head.

"He wouldn't talk to me or return my telephone calls. He humiliated me in front of the faculty. That's why I had to write that letter."

"So you took the cyanide from the cabinet in this room and brought it with you to his wedding party."

"No! No, I didn't. I told you before, and I meant what I said. I wouldn't kill Hugh. That was not my revenge. Imogen Revel was my revenge."

Hank pushed the letter close to her face again. "But you threatened him? This is the proof."

"Oh, I would have done that." She tried to grasp the letter from his hand. "I would have cut his damn dick off." Hank pulled the letter away from her reach. "You've got me on that, Lieutenant. The problem is, that wasn't the thing that was done to him last Saturday. Now was it?"

"Well," Caroline said to him, as Hank pulled out of the school's parking lot, "that was interesting."

"Yes," Hank admitted. "It certainly was."

"And do you think she's guilty?"

Hank shrugged. "Evidence is what we need, and we still don't have it. I wonder where that second bottle of hydrocyanic acid is. I'm thinking of getting a search warrant for her house, but I know she would have gotten rid of it by now."

"She wouldn't have needed to use the whole bottle to kill Hugh."

"No, but I'm sure if she had it, she would have discarded it, and it's probably already on its way to the local landfill."

"A needle in the haystack, would you say?"

"Yes."

"Have you ever suspected Nick Pratt, Hank?"

"Pratt? Why?"

"I don't know. Something about him. He's so... oily."

"You can't arrest a man for that."

"I know, but could he have any reason for wanting Hugh dead?"

"Look, the man's a lecher, I can see that. But, so far there's no link to Dockings that looks suspicious."

"What about those two other science teachers? They both had keys to the cabinet."

"Neither was at the Revels' party."

"That's odd. Hugh didn't invite them, or they didn't want to come? I did see two men at the party whom I thought were from Camden."

"One of the two men was the other physical education teacher who taught with Imogen and the second was a history teacher. He was going to be Hugh's best man."

"Well, I'm still going with the theory that Imogen was the intended victim. Marilyn could have lied to us back there." She paused. "Perhaps Nick wanted Imogen gone so he could hire someone younger and sexier to take her place."

"He did, but you're joking, I hope."

"And so you're still counting on Donald Montgomery to be your suspect?"

"It looks good so far. You saw those newspaper clippings. How would you feel? The Montgomerys believe Hugh killed their son."

"I know," she said softly. "Blame can be hard to live with."

"Look," he said. "There's a nice-looking restaurant coming up on the right. I bet you could do with some lunch. Let's get something to eat before we tackle Donald Montgomery." He was pleased that she smiled at the suggestion. "You were good back there with Marilyn Hansen, Caroline."

"Thank you," she said.

The Montgomerys' house was a short drive from the restaurant where Hank and Caroline shared a pleasant lunch, their conversation staying on the case.

"Should I be quiet during your interrogation?" she asked as they walked up the steps to the front door of the Montgomerys' unimposing house.

"Oh, no," he answered. "Be yourself. If you want to ask any question, do it. The important thing is to make the I.D.. I want this to be a calm meeting."

The door was answered by a small woman about fifty years of age. Her cheerless face looked leery as Hank introduced himself.

"The police," she said, recoiling from the doorway. "What do you want? Has something happened?"

"Is your husband at home, Mrs. Montgomery?" She nodded. "We've come to speak with him. This is Caroline Kent."

"Hello, Mrs. Montgomery," Caroline said. Whether Ruth Montgomery thought Caroline was another police officer was a point Hank ignored.

"Come inside," Ruth said.

They followed her through a dimly lit hallway into the kitchen. A man was sitting, drinking black coffee at the kitchen table. He looked up as they entered, his expression remaining wooden.

"Don, here's some people to see you."

Donald Montgomery got up from the chair. Hank saw immediately the resemblance to the newspaper photograph. Age had taken its toll, but it hadn't changed the hollow look of misery in the pale eyes.

"Good afternoon, Mr. Montgomery," Hank began. He offered his card, but the man didn't take it. "I'm here to see you in connection with a case I'm working on in Newport, Rhode Island."

Behind him Ruth Montgomery sucked in her breath.

"Why don't we go into the living room, Don?" his wife suggested.

"I'm fine here," her husband said.

"All right, sir. I'll get right to the point. We have reason to believe that you were in Newport on Saturday, the fifth of June." He looked at Caroline for agreement, and she gave him a slight nod of her head. "Were you, sir?"

"What is this about?" Ruth asked. "What has he done?"

Hank turned toward her. "What makes you think he's done anything, Mrs. Montgomery? Because you know that Hugh Dockings was murdered that day... in Newport? Were you at the home of Claude Revel on the afternoon in question, Mr. Montgomery?"

"Did this lady see me?" he asked, pointing to Caroline. Hank thought Donald must have remembered seeing Caroline.

"You were a waiter, I believe," Hank continued. "Is that your usual occupation?"

"He doesn't work... he can't work... not since..." His wife's voice trailed off.

"Since when, Mr. Montgomery?"

"Since our boy was killed. Since that bastard killed our Dennis."

"*That bastard* as you call him, is dead himself now. What can you tell me about that? You were there when he died. Mrs. Kent saw you looking at the body while it was lying on the floor."

"I wanted to see it with my own eyes. They said in the kitchen that someone at the party had died. I rushed out there, and it was Dockings."

"Did you bring him the last glass of wine?"

"Yes," he said weakly.

"No, Don, don't say anything without a lawyer." Ruth rushed to her husband's side and gathered his frail body into her arms. "Can't you see he's sick, Lieutenant? The doctor said he has to be kept quiet."

"Perhaps you should call a lawyer, Mrs. Montgomery," Hank said. "I have some more questions to put to your husband. We can wait." He looked across the room to the telephone hanging on the wall.

Ruth had helped Donald back into the chair. He reached for the coffee, but she pushed his hand away. "You've had enough. Remember what the doctor said."

"I don't care what the doctor said. And I don't want any lawyer."

"How did you get hired for the Revels' party?" Caroline asked. Her voice had the gentle tone of a friend.

"I didn't," Donald answered. "I just showed up."

"But you were dressed for the part," she encouraged. "How did you do that?"

"I found out who the caterers were to be. It wasn't hard. I knew what their staff would be wearing. It wasn't hard to find a duplicate uniform."

"That was very clever," Hank said.

"I've had practice," Donald said.

"You've followed Hugh Dockings before?" Caroline asked. Donald nodded.

"How long have you been following Hugh Dockings?" Hank asked. When Montgomery didn't answer, Hank turned to his wife. "How long has this been going on?"

"For the last four years," she answered. "I told him not to do it. I knew he was going to get into trouble someday."

"You've been stalking Hugh Dockings. For what purpose?"

"I... I wanted to see him, to see the man who did that horrible thing to Dennis."

"How could that help you, Mr. Montgomery?" Caroline asked. "What would you gain?"

"I don't know," Donald answered.

"He wouldn't stop," Ruth said. Her face was pitiful, and she was holding back tears. "He was obsessed with him. That's why we moved here. So he could see him at the school."

"You followed him at the school?"

"I saw him everywhere. At the school, at the boat dock, at the liquor store. All his favorite places." He moaned. "Everywhere he went... except sailing on that boat, the same boat where Dennis died."

"Did you ever go into his classroom?" Donald nodded. "When he was there?"

Donald shook his head. "Early in the morning, before he got there."

"But why?" Caroline asked. "I still can't understand why you would want to be near him."

"He can't explain it," his wife said. "All I know, is that is what our life has been these last three years. His compulsion to see Hugh Dockings."

"Did you kill him?" Hank asked. For an instant he forgot about the lawyer and the rights of a suspect. He was almost relieved when Donald shook his head. "Have you ever been in the chemistry supply room at the school?"

"I don't know," Donald answered. "Maybe, I'm not sure."

"Don't say any more until I get a lawyer."

"It's all right, Ruth. They can know."

"Know what?"

"I didn't kill him, Lieutenant. I thought I would denounce him at that fancy party in front of all those people. It's true. I had been following him for three years, trying to decide how to make him pay for killing Dennis. When I saw in the school paper that he was going to be married, I thought I would go there to this party and tell everybody what a monster he was, that he killed my son. And he was drunk at that party. Just like when Dennis died. You only had to look at him. He was always drunk."

"Why didn't you denounce him?" Caroline asked.

"I kept waiting," Donald said slowly. "I wanted to... I don't know, I couldn't say the words. I did stay near him and offer him drinks. He took six glasses of wine from me. Six!" He paused, and his head leaned back. "I was a coward. I never did it, did I, Ruth? I couldn't even scream his name as a murderer to all those people." His head flopped forward, and Ruth grabbed at his chin and held it firmly.

"That's enough," she said, turning to Hank.

"And then he was dead," Donald said sadly. His voice was hardly strong enough to be heard. "Dead," he repeated.

16

When Louise had first come to Kenwood as a young bride, she had taken for granted the staff of servants who kept the estate running. Meals appeared, clothing was cleaned, flowers were grown. She never worried about who had polished the silver or even who had set the dining table. Now all these household responsibilities fell to her and Caroline. The small hired staff helped, but while the business was young, Louise was constantly aware that she and Caroline had to economize by doing all that they could themselves. With her daughter-in-law away for the day with Hank Nightingale in Connecticut, Louise was kept busy not only with her own chores, but those which Caroline normally performed.

By early afternoon Louise had attended to the serving of breakfast and lunch and helped Cheryl tidy the upstairs guest rooms and the downstairs reception rooms. The telephone had rung several times for requests for information about the inn, and Louise suspected there were e-mail messages waiting, as well. In the middle of the afternoon she paused to look longingly at the sunny outdoors, but accepted the fact that her project to reconstruct the perennial garden must be ignored today.

When the front doorbell rang at exactly 4:30, Louise was in the kitchen with Mattie, beginning the preparations for dinner. Minna Whitten and her sister, Abby Benton, took their evening meal at

Kenwood. While most guests enjoyed venturing out to one of the city's inexhaustible selection of restaurants, the two Boston ladies preferred the comfort -- and Louise suspected, the security -- of the inn's dining room. Caroline had insisted that offering a full dinner would be a feature at Kenwood, and should guests wish to take advantage of this service, they only had to make arrangements in advance.

"Good afternoon, Louise," Dorsey Revel greeted her. "Bet you are surprised to see this old traveler at your door."

"A bit," Louise answered. "Why don't you come inside?"

"Pamela's on the warpath at Mon Plaisir. Claude says I have to get out of the house during the day." His black eyes danced with delight. "So I've come to pay a call. Are you *at home* this afternoon?"

"I'm always home in the afternoons, Dorsey. I work here."

"Oh, my dear," he said, taking her arm. "I did forget you were a working girl. I've come to take a look at the place since you've changed Kenwood into a hotel. I can recommend this place. I have lots of friends who like to come to Newport. Why don't you show me around?"

She gave him the complete tour, upstairs and down. Dorsey, as usual, was curious about everything. She had shown him the empty guest rooms, and he had chafed to be able to peek into those which were occupied.

"I couldn't possibly," she had said firmly.

"Well," he said as they descended the front staircase at the end of his inspection, "the old place still looks the same in many ways. I'm glad Caroline didn't see fit to change it. Many's the night my brother Henri and I sat in that library with Frederick and discussed the fate of mankind over our cognac."

"Yes, I remember."

"Ah, those were the days, Louise. I remember them well. And you were as lovely then as you are now."

"Dorsey, your silver tongue is one thing that never changes." She had meant to chastise him, but the truth was, after her long work day, she enjoyed the compliment.

"Now," he said. "What about giving me a drink?" He looked at his watch. "The sun is well over the yard arm."

"Come into the library. Caroline keeps a drinks' cabinet for the guests, and we will treat ourselves."

He took her arm, and they went into the library, which was where Caroline found them, chatting over martinis, half an hour later.

"Well, this is how the help performs when the boss is away," she said, laughing.

"Oh, Caroline, dear. Dorsey surprised me with a visit." Her body was warm with the glow of the alcohol in her drink. "Come, join us."

Caroline paused in the doorway, and gestured back to someone in the hallway. "Come on in here. I've found Louise. She's got a visitor."

Hank Nightingale came slowly into the room. "Hello, Mrs. Kent. I hope I'm not intruding."

"Nonsense," Caroline answered for her. "I promised Hank a drink, Louise. We've had a long day and got into commuter traffic on the way home."

"Of course," Louise answered. "Good evening, Lieutenant. Are you acquainted with Mr. Dorsey Revel?" For an instant, it seemed to Louise that the house was their private residence again, with no paying guests on the premises. "This is Hank Nightingale, Dorsey, who is in charge of investigating Hugh's death."

Dorsey was instantly on his feet and took the detective's hand. "How do you do, my boy? You've been naughty. You've been promising to come to see me, and you haven't."

"I know, and I apologize, Mr. Revel. You are at the top of my list. At the beginning, these investigations are so hectic. How is your niece, Miss Revel?"

"Imogen? Fine, don't you worry. She's strong as a horse, and she'll get through this. Between you and me, I don't think she's lost all that much." He winked at Caroline. "Remember, Caroline, you are my alibi. Have you told our detective that?"

"No, Dorsey, I really haven't yet. Let me get Hank a drink first. What will you have?" Louise caught the easy familiarity with which Caroline addressed him.

Hank looked at his watch. "I guess I'm off duty now. I'll have a vodka on the rocks, with about an inch of water."

Louise motioned for him to sit down on the empty sofa. She was wondering what her social duty was as the hostess of this impromptu gathering. Dorsey, as she might have expected, relieved her of this obligation.

"Now, tell me, Lt. Nightingale, how are you doing catching the murderer? Do you have any leads?"

"Several," Nightingale answered.

"Claude told me about this waiter business. Amazing, isn't it? Fellow comes to our house, bold as brass, and starts poisoning people."

"I don't think he did it," Caroline said. She handed Hank his drink and helped herself to the martini pitcher.

"Oh? Did you give him an alibi, also?" Dorsey tittered.

"No, but I've met him, and he's a broken man. He couldn't kill anyone."

"Perhaps Lt. Nightingale would rather not have us discuss his case," Louise broke in.

"That's all right, Mrs. Kent. Your daughter-in-law and I have been discussing it all day."

"Yes, we learned so much on our trip," Caroline said. She took a seat next to Hank and turned to him brightly. Louise hadn't wanted Caroline to start detecting again, but it was evident she had enjoyed herself. "My head is spinning with possibilities," she added.

"Then it's time you took a break."

"I rather hoped Mr. Revel might tell me something about his family, if that doesn't bore you, Mrs. Kent. Caroline tells me he is the unofficial family historian."

"Then let me start at the beginning," Dorsey said with enthusiasm. He settled back in his chair and picked up the long-stemmed martini glass from the table. He took a long sip and sighed. "Heaven. There's nothing like the taste of the cold, dry gin martini. I don't know how you can drink that tasteless stuff, Lieutenant." He pointed at Hank's glass. "This is the goods." He finished the drink, and Caroline rose to refill his glass. "Now where was I? Oh, yes the start of the Revel family."

"That may be going back too far," Louise said.

"Not at all," the lieutenant said. "Let me hear the story, Mr. Revel."

"The first Claude Revel came to this country in 1874. He was a young commoner. No money, no title, no family connections. The American Civil War had ended in 1865, but Claude didn't know the significance of that. He was from France, you see, and his destination was for New Orleans, which was a former French colony. The young man had worked for a merchant bank in Paris -- family legend has that it was the Rothschilds' own bank, but I've always been skeptical of that story -- and so he knew something about the cotton trade. He was sure America would welcome a bright young man. What he didn't understand, of course, is that without the slaves, the New Orleans economy was dead."

"Claude thought he would get work in the cotton business?" Caroline asked, sitting back down next to Hank.

"Yes, but as I've said. There was nothing in New Orleans after the war except gambling and loose women. He met his future father-in-law in one of the brothels."

"Dorsey!" Louise said. "You don't know that."

"Oh, it's true enough. One of his daughters kept a diary, and old Dorsey Bishop had told her. Claude has her journal in the library at Mon Plaisir with the family papers."

"It was a long time ago," Caroline said. "Keep on with the story, Dorsey. We're riveted."

"As I said, Claude met Dorsey Bishop in a brothel where they were both enjoying the charms of the city's more talented women... don't you think it's fitting that I'm named for him, Louise?" She waved her hand at him, as if she could discourage him after all these years. "Dorsey had struck it rich in the Nevada silver mines. His wife, her name was Hannah, didn't want to bring up their daughter Violet in the rough atmosphere of the camps, so Dorsey had brought them all to New Orleans. Now you can imagine that Hannah would be unhappy there, also. Gambling, fancy houses, what kind of place was that for their daughter? How would she ever find a suitable husband?" He winked at the detective. "Are you following me, Lt. Nightingale? Do you know what's coming next?"

"Your grandfather married Violet Bishop."

"Bingo. He was the elegant young Parisian, and Hannah Bishop grabbed him up for her daughter before you could say *parlez-vous francais*. Not that I expect he struggled too much. Always good to have silver in the family, don't you agree?"

"Or a bank," Nightingale responded.

"Eventually, they had both. Dorsey gave part of his stake to Violet, and Claude used it to capitalize a merchant bank."

"In New Orleans?" Caroline asked.

"No, in New York City. By then Claude recognized there was no future in the south, and I imagine Hannah Bishop was glad to get out of New Orleans. The whole family came north. The young couple already had their first son, my great uncle Claude. He died of pneumonia when he was only nineteen years of age."

"You have an excellent memory, Mr. Revel."

"It was important. It made Claude's second son, my grandfather Henri, his heir. Violet and Claude had six children, as did my own parents. I'm the only male left from my generation, you know. My brother Henri died in 1991, and my older brother Claude was killed at Anzio in World War II." He shook his head sadly, then said, "Imogen died in 1997."

"Imogen?" the detective asked. He looked perplexed.

"My sister Imogen. Family tradition gives us all the names of our ancestors."

"Your sister Grace is still alive," Hank said.

"Yes, and Violet, also. Although she is past it, I'm afraid. Talks to the cat, but not to us humans."

"Who is Grace named after?" Caroline asked. She was clearly enjoying the narrative.

"Violet Bishop had an older sister who died in infancy. She was Grace."

"And who was Imogen?" Hank asked.

"Ah," Dorsey said, smiling. "She was Claude Revel's mother. Imogen Dupuis, before she married Henri Revel in France."

"Which members of the family are employed at the family's bank now?" Hank asked.

"My nephew Claude, of course, as the chairman. My sister Violet has her two sons in the bank. They are Henri and Claude. There's George March who had the good fortune to be named after his father. And also the son of my late sister Imogen. He's another Claude. We're like one of those old children's toys where you open the hollow figurine and you keep getting smaller and smaller versions, all one inside the other. When you get to the end, there is a tiny version of the original. You might say that one is Claudine."

"And the bank is prosperous?" the detective asked. He waited for an answer while Dorsey sipped his drink. Caroline got up to give Hank a refill.

"It keeps providing for us. Four generations, and now a fifth beginning."

"And you of course worked there, Mr. Revel?"

"Certainly."

"Everyone must be quite proud of Claudine," Caroline said.

"I suppose so," Dorsey answered with a hesitation in his voice that was unmistakable.

"Imogen isn't happy, is she?" Caroline asked.

"You must realize, Caroline, that she never forgave Claude for being the boy while she had to be the girl. Growing up, they were very competitive. Claudine's coming along and being a girl, too... well, Claude's given her advantges Imogen never had. Imogen was furious when Claude arranged for Claudine to intern in London two years ago with a banker he knew over there."

"And what about Claudine? How does she feel about Imogen, Dorsey?" Caroline asked.

"Claudine hasn't learned to have patience dealing with her, as we have all learned to do. My sister-in-law insisted Imogen see a doctor when she was young. The girl was so unhappy."

"I can see why," Caroline said.

"That's when she decided to take up the teaching profession. But, all those years she spent in Waterville teaching physical education. You don't need a brain for that."

"She was always very athletic," Louise said. "I remember her as a good horsewoman. Didn't she win trophies as a youngster?"

"Frankly, I remember her as a gawky child, all arms and legs. Never a beauty."

Dorsey laughed and put down his empty martini glass. "Now, dear ladies, I think I've leaned on your hospitality enough for one evening. Lieutenant, if you need more of this kind of thing, call on me at Mon Plaisir. Or better yet, why don't you invite me down to the police station? I have to be out and about these days, as Louise can tell you, and I would appreciate seeing the inside of the local jailhouse."

17

The prayer service to mark the occasion of the death of Hugh Dockings was held three days later in the chapel at Mon Plaisir. Louise and Caroline arrived a few minutes before eleven and were met by Dorsey Revel, who gossiped as they walked along the hallway.

"Imogen wanted a Mass for Hugh. Can you believe it? Father Halloran was adamant against it."

"Was Mr. Dockings Catholic?" Louise asked.

"Of course not," Dorsey grinned. "Worshiped that god of wine, don't you think?" Louise frowned. "No, Imogen was only being difficult, Louise. Father Halloran made it clear to Claude that he is here to offer a prayer service for the family in our time of need. In Imogen's case, her need is to memorialize Hugh, of course. She put up a fuss, but Claude finally had to tell her just seconds before you arrived that she must conduct herself properly. As a Revel. And the only reason he was so forceful with her is because Pamela is livid that anything to do with Dockings is taking place here in the house. She's had to organize the funereal repast. Imogen insisted on a proper meal afterwards in the dining room."

The threesome entered the empty chapel. Caroline had never been inside the room before. The carved rosewood walls were decorated with a series of oil paintings portraying scenes from the life of Jesus Christ. A magnificent panel of stained glass behind the altar depicted the Resurrection. The high, vaulted ceiling had heavy beams and a single French wrought iron chandelier which matched the Renaissance-style ones in the ballroom. Persian carpets covered the oak floor. There were plain wooden chairs for seating. Caroline sat down, bowed her head and prayed.

When she looked up, Imogen was coming into the room. Walking alone, she was followed by Claude and Pamela. Behind them came the rest of the Revels, all formally dressed and with somber faces. Caroline was surprised to see that Claudine was absent, and, as she looked further into the family group, she realized that George March was missing as well.

Imogen took her place in the front row of chairs nearest to Father Halloran, who had appeared from a small anteroom next to the altar simultaneously with the family.

The priest began with prayers spoken with due respect for the occasion, but Caroline sensed little of the feeling which would be offered to a grieving family.

Then Claude Revel rose to speak, and Caroline could not help thinking of theatrical productions she had been in where stage entrances and exits were skillfully executed.

The speech was dignified. Claude began with a tribute to Hugh Dockings which, in his deep rich voice, sounded honest and sincere. He described the late chemistry teacher as *respected* by his students and *valued* by his colleagues. She thought of Marilyn Hansen and Hugh's *value* to her.

Finally, after extolling Hugh's prowess and courage at sea -- Claude had educated himself on Hugh's several ocean sailing journeys -- he looked straight at his sister.

"But it is my sister Imogen who will bear the real brunt of Hugh's passing. He has left her before their true happiness could begin. There is life hereafter, and that is where Imogen and Hugh will be joined in eternity. Our prayers are with you, Imogen, today."

Imogen started sobbing. No one from the family reached an arm to comfort her. Caroline felt the sharp tug of Dorsey's hand on her sleeve.

"Give him the hook. Right, Caroline? Start the music."

She frowned at him to behave himself, but he was smiling, looking directly at Claude.

"Father Halloran will conclude the service with the blessing," Claude said. He had seen his uncle's gay expression and was displeased. "Then we will all move into the dining room where we will drink a toast to Hugh and celebrate his life over a meal."

Considering the circumstances of his death, Caroline thought the idea of drinking a toast to Hugh Dockings an ironic touch. But she remembered that during her visit to Des Arbres on the day after his murder, Imogen had asked her to do the very same thing.

In the dining room, Caroline was seated next to Pamela Revel. Louise was further away, placed next to Grace March. Clearly Caroline's seating had been done to give the mistress of Mon Plaisir a respite from her Revel relations. Once again, Caroline understood her social duty. After Claude's toast to Hugh -- the wine served was white -- Pamela talked continually while she jabbed impatiently at the salad greens which cradled the cold lobster on her plate.

"You wouldn't believe the melodramatic things Imogen's come out with, Caroline," Pamela said in an unusual display of camaraderie. The two women had known each other through their husbands' business connection, but Caroline had never considered herself a real friend of Claude's wife. "She talks about her life's being over, which of course it isn't. Until last Christmas the man didn't mean a thing to her. Suddenly he wants to get married, and she brings him to New York and presents him to the family. Claude was sure he was after the money. And I have to say that I do agree with him."

"They were both middle-aged, Pamela. Perhaps their feelings for one another were rooted in their need for companionship."

"He allowed himself to be led around by her, that I'll say. Let her do whatever she wanted at Des Arbres. Always agreeable about that, oh yes. Of course, it was the boat he was after."

The conversation paused as their salad plates were exchanged for the main course. Sole almondine. It was Friday, and the Revels were observing the old church constraints against eating meat.

"Well, I'm glad Claude didn't have to go through with that," Pamela declared. "I don't resent Imogen's having the family's money, but to spend it on that man." Her voice had become loud. Pamela was drinking the wine, an agreeable Sancerre, as if it were water.

"Now I think she plans to stay here in Newport all year-round. Everything now is *what Hugh and I were going to do together*."

"Perhaps she finds that a comfort," Caroline answered in a low voice, which she wished Pamela would match.

"I wouldn't know," Pamela answered as she waved to a servant to fill her wine glass. "She doesn't confide in me."

"Why should I?" came a harsh voice from the head of the table. Imogen had been seated next to her brother, and Caroline realized that she must have been following their conversation all along. Claude laid a restraining hand on his sister's arm, but the damage had been done. Imogen rose from the table. The look of hostility in her eyes, as she surveyed her sister-in-law who was choosing at this moment to eat her fish with delicate pleasure, surprised Caroline. "I shall go to my home, Claude. I need to be alone."

"Please stay, Imogen," her brother implored. "The family is here to see you, and you have an obligation to remain at the table with us."

"I will not remain where I am attacked and demeaned."

"Pamela didn't mean --"

"I think she did, Claude."

"Pamela," Claude now implored his wife. "Please say something." Everyone around the table waited.

Pamela looked at her husband and his sister. Both were standing, and she appeared to be taking in their full measure, the tall woman and the shorter man. Suddenly Pamela laughed.

"There," Imogen said. "I cannot remain under these circumstances. This is your and Pamela's house. I am going to mine."

"Please," Claude said weakly, and Caroline was unsure to whom the entreaty had been addressed.

In any event, both women who were candidates for his appeal were ignoring him. Imogen strode grandly from the room, and Pamela reached for her wine glass and drank the contents.

"Well," Dorsey said, from somewhere to Caroline's right. "That was a grand gesture." She turned to see him lift his wine from the table. "I say we drink to them both, Imogen and Hugh. What a team they would have made. The Dockings... a whole new chapter in Revel history."

Claude resumed his place at the table. No one else lifted their glass in tribute to the two absent guests, and Caroline wondered how much each were actually missed.

After lunch was concluded, Caroline decided to visit Imogen at Des Arbres. Pamela had retired to her bedroom, and Claude was seeing to the formalities of bidding guests good-by and attending to the few who remained. Louise had reluctantly accepted Dorsey's offer to drive her home.

"I appreciate your wanting to check on Imogen, Caroline," Claude said gratefully. "She doesn't seem to want to have anything to do with the rest of us. You mustn't blame Pamela, either. I'm afraid it is my daughter who occasioned Imogen's outburst. She insisted on going to London, and taking George March with her. You may have read in the news last week that one of the highest Russian central bank officials has resigned, throwing the credit markets there into turmoil. There was a meeting of the banks who have loans out to the Russian government in London this morning. Claudine believed she needed to be there to protect Syndicat Revel's position."

He said the last with evident pride, and Caroline murmured her assurances that Claudine surely made the decision that was right for her.

"I don't know what comfort Claudine would have been to Imogen today," Claude said sadly. "They have never been close. George ought to have stayed behind. But... well, Claudine insisted, and I have encouraged her to begin making these kinds of decisions."

And so Caroline presented herself at the door of Des Arbres. Imogen seemed happy to see her.

"How are you, Imogen? Can I make you a cup of tea?"

"I was thinking of having some cognac. Will you join me?"

It was early in the afternoon to be drinking brandy, but Caroline nodded as she followed Imogen into the living room. She accepted a glass from the bottle on a side table.

"It was kind of you to come to see me, Caroline," Imogen said. "You are becoming the one friend I can count on. Do you know what I was thinking just before you came?" Caroline shook her head. "That I no longer want to live."

"You know that's not the answer."

"Didn't you feel you might want to die after Reed was killed?"

"No," Caroline said. "Do you know why?" Imogen shook her head. "Because of Louise. I wouldn't have put her through a second tragedy. My own family would have been devastated as well."

"I didn't know your parents were living."

"They're in Arizona now. I can't see them that often, but I wouldn't hurt my family by taking my own life."

"I have no one who cares for me. I have no parents, no mother-in-law. Hugh's parents are both dead. He was an only child. No one in his family ever knew how much I loved him."

"You must find a reason for living."

"I can't think of one." She drank the cognac and sniffed in tears. "You saw how the rest of my own family treats me."

"Pamela had too much wine. I'm sure she didn't mean --"

"What about Claudine? She couldn't be bothered to be here. She's in London, playing the important banker. Oh, I'm so sick of her anyway. I'm glad she wasn't here after all."

While Imogen poured herself a second glass of cognac, Caroline looked around the room. The furnishings looked unfinished. She realized there were no personal touches, no photographs or small objects which would give the room something of the presence of its owner. She was reminded of Hugh's cottage in Waterville and its lack of personality.

"Do you know what would make me happy, Caroline?" Imogen asked suddenly. Before she could reply, Imogen answered her own question. "To find Hugh's murderer."

"The police have several leads," Caroline said.

"If you mean that waiter, that's all wrong. The killer was out to get me. Why won't they find who wanted me dead? I told that Lt. Nightingale when he was here, but he's ignored me. He probably thinks I'm some middle-aged woman in the change of life. I ought to speak to Claude. Perhaps he can have him taken off the case and someone who will listen to me brought in."

"Oh, no, you're wrong, Imogen. Hank is a good policeman."

"*Hank?*"

"Lt. Nightingale." Caroline saw the look of surprise on Imogen's face at the suggestion of familiarity between her and the detective. "We did spend the day together in Waterville. I'm afraid it became easier to use first names." Why did she lie? She and Hank had been on a first-name basis prior to their trip.

"How long has it been since Reed died? Which month was it?"

"November," Caroline answered. Immediately her mind filled with the familiar vision of the blue black rainy evening. She thought of how she had insisted that Reed come home from Albany, not spend the night at a hotel if he could be home to sleep in his own bed with her. She opened her eyes which she hadn't comprehended she had closed. Imogen was staring at her. Caroline swallowed, and the back of her tongue felt thick and raw. She reached for the snifter of cognac to swab her aching throat.

"I admire the way you have remained loyal to Reed," Imogen said. "I could never love another man ever again. I'm sure you feel that way, too."

"I think that's a normal reaction to have. But, time does heal. At least that is what is said."

"Do you feel yourself being healed, Caroline?"

"Being in Newport at Kenwood has helped."

"But that's because you feel that Reed is there, don't you see?"

"I'm not sure."

"Of course. He's everywhere in that house. And Louise must speak of him. That comforts you and keeps him alive."

"Perhaps," Caroline admitted. She had come to console Imogen, but the effort was draining her. How long must she stay before making an excuse that she was needed at the inn?

"If only you could remember seeing someone near the glass of wine while it was on the plant stand," Imogen said. "I know that's when the drink was poisoned. Everyone near me saw me rest it there. You were watching the glass, Caroline. Don't you remember? While you were talking to Dorsey? I saw you were restless. Your eyes were on me, on the glass. Think."

Caroline closed her eyes again, trying to conjure up the scene in the ballroom. She had been talking to Dorsey, and his comments had certainly caused her concentration to wander. He had been saying how much Reed was missed at Syndicat Revel. And Caroline had felt the familiar pangs of loss, how she thought of Reed the last thing in the evening and the first thing in the morning. Now in Imogen's living room, Caroline fought back the tears. For it was at that moment that she understood that she had come to Kenwood to sleep in a bed which she and Reed had never shared.

18

"What have we got? I think it's time to take stock of our case so far."

While the Revels gathered in the chapel at Mon Plaisir to conclude their acquaintance with the late Hugh Dockings, Hank Nightingale had called in his two sergeants to judge how far along they were to solving the late teacher's murder. Hearing Hank's question, Ben Davies and Keisha McAndrews both put down their coffee and reached for their notes.

"Shall we start with the family, Lieutenant?" Ben asked. They had been the subject of his interrogations.

"I think let's start with the school," Hank said. "Keisha, what are your impressions of the staff who came to the party?"

"Well, Doug Fleming, the history teacher, was to be best man. He didn't seem close to Mr. Dockings, thought he had been asked for convenience, Mr. Dockings's lacking any close relatives. I don't see him as a suspect. He's about the same age, plans on retiring himself next year. No motive." She put a pencil mark on her pad. "The other faculty guests included Marie Verdoux, the French teacher, Sally Kornfield and Gail Nolan, English department, Joan Freemont, an art teacher, you questioned Marilyn Hansen, and Henry Benedetto, who taught with Ms. Revel in the physical education department."

"Why were those particular people invited?" Hank asked.

"It was my understanding, sir, that all the faculty were issued invitations. These were the ones who chose to come."

"I see," Hank said. "Any particular reason you can see why these individuals came?"

Keisha shrugged. "I couldn't see any, sir. Honestly, if you ask me, they all wanted to see the Revels' house. Except for Ms. Hansen, none of them had particular friendships with either Dockings or Ms. Revel."

"You didn't pick up anything? No animosity, no jealousy? Did anyone suggest that Ms. Hansen might take strong actions against the engaged couple?"

"Well," Keisha drew out the word into two syllables, "not in so many words. But, they all knew how she hated Imogen. As far as Hugh Dockings goes, they all agreed that Marilyn had taken his engagement hard. But I don't think it occurred to them to think she might have killed him. At that point, everyone was still saying he'd had a heart attack."

"What was their opinion of Imogen?" Ben asked. "Did they like her?"

"No, not at all. Benedetto told me some stories about Imogen and the students that frankly made me angry. She was insensitive to the kids and belittled them. She embarrassed one girl so bad during a varsity game that her mother shouted at Imogen. Imogen retaliated by pulling the girl from the game."

"Did you get a name?"

"No, sir. Do you think that's important?"

"Not really. The headmaster said no parents or students were invited to the pre-nuptial party."

"That waiter was a parent," Ben said.

"Not a current one. That reminds me. Keisha, I want you to go back to Waterville. It's too late today, but you can go on Monday."

"I could go tomorrow. I don't mind working on Saturday."

"Few staff will be working at the school on the week-end. Monday."

"Yes, sir. What am I looking for?"

"Take the photograph of Donald Montgomery. I want you to show it around to the faculty and other employees. I hope nobody's left town for vacation yet. See if you can get anyone to identify that Montgomery was seen at any time in the vicinity of that science supply room where the poisons are locked up."

"Right." Keisha was hastily making notes as Hank spoke.

"Maybe a custodian saw Montgomery. Get their names from Nick Pratt and interview all of them."

"Anything else?"

"When I visited the school, I was told the faculty kept their keys to that poison cabinet in accessible places. See what you can find out about that. Did anybody lose their keys, find them missing, that kind of thing? I want to zero in on who could get at that cabinet."

"Sounds like a wide field," Ben said.

"Unfortunately, yes. Any member of the faculty could have picked up the keys at practically any time. Find out, Keisha, if any of the teachers at the party had friendships with the science staff."

"What do you think of Donald Montgomery, Lieutenant? Could he be our man?" Keisha looked intent, waiting for his reply.

"He's still very much a possible, and, yes, I like him for our suspect. But he's pretty beaten down. I don't know if he had the nerve."

"He managed to get himself down to Newport for that party," Ben said. "All dressed up in the correct waiter's rig. That took some brains, and some nerve. Maybe he was playacting when you interviewed him."

"You're right about the impersonation, Ben. It took guts to carry it off. I'd like to bring Montgomery down here for questioning, but before that I'd like to have some evidence that he was in that supply room or somewhere where he could have helped himself to those keys."

"I'll get it if it's there, sir," Keisha said.

"Good. Now, Ben, what about the Revel family?"

"I talked to all of them. Do you know there are a couple more named Claude?" Hank explained why that was. Ben shook his head. "Anyway, there were several of the relations near Imogen at the crucial time. I count the cousin George March, Claudine Revel, her mother Pamela, Dorsey Revel, and I think even Mr. Claude Revel himself. March remembers him pausing to say something to his wife about then."

"Where do you think they might have gotten the poison?" Keisha asked.

"They're rich, and I think they could get their hands on anything they want. There must be plenty of places in New York City where you could obtain cyanide without calling attention to yourself."

"And what do you see as motives, Ben?" Hank asked.

"I'm still looking into the money angle, but so far nothing's turned up that seems questionable at the bank. But, I'm not finished. I told you I think Claude Revel didn't want to foot the bill for a new brother-in-law, and I suppose his wife and daughter might also share his aversion to parting with the family's money."

"There seems to be some hint of trouble between Claudine and her aunt."

"Yes, that, as they say, is common knowledge. George March said it was a shame, given that Claudine is so brilliant, etc., etc.. I think he overdid it, sir, but he does seem that type of person. A little gushy. The idea that Claudine would kill Hugh to get at Imogen... well, I guess that's possible." His doubtful tone contradicted his words.

"You don't believe it."

"I think the crime's more complicated than that. Something specific, not just a simple act of revenge."

"As would be the motive if Donald Montgomery were our killer."

"That is not an uncomplicated situation," Ben said. "It's a very specific motive. Dockings killed his son, or so Montgomery believes. In the case of Claudine and Imogen Revel, you're talking about --"

"Hatred?" Keisha interjected.

"That's a strong word," Hank said.

"Those are two strong women," Keisha responded.

Mention of strong women brought Hank's mind back to Marilyn. Strong women were peppered all over this case. He remembered Grace March's proud figure in the library at Mon Plaisir as she attended on Imogen following the murder. Even Pamela, a Revel by marriage, had a steely quality which had kept him alert during their interview.

"I'd like to talk to some of the Revels again," Hank said.

"Which ones?" Ben asked.

"The women. Claudine and Pamela, first. Then I think it's time for another visit to Imogen. You can come with me, Ben. Two minds are going to be better on this."

"When do you want to go? Tomorrow?"

"No, we'll take the week-end off. Let this case percolate in our minds for a few days. Something clever might come to us. Nobody is going anywhere."

"What about Donald Montgomery?"

"I don't think he'll skip, but I could be wrong. Why don't you telephone the department in Waterville. Let's keep them up to date."

Ben and Keisha sat while Hank reviewed his thoughts.

"One last thing," he said. "Miss Revel seems convinced that the poisoned wine was meant for her. Any ideas on that?"

Keisha was the first to speak. "It could be Marilyn Hansen. The teachers indicated she was as angry with Imogen as she was with Hugh."

"What about that letter she wrote Dockings?" Ben asked.

"The letter mentions a physical retribution on Hugh Docking. Specific, as you would say, Ben."

"Very specific, Lieutenant," Ben agreed.

"All right," Hank said. "Hansen has to be considered for a suspect."

"If we have to look at who would want Imogen dead, we've got to start with motive," Ben said. "I say it's money. If Imogen were dead, she couldn't spend the family's money on Hugh."

"That seems pretty drastic," Keisha said. "Killing a member of their own family. I don't know. That motive fits more with the attempt being directed at Dockings. Why kill your family when you can kill a stranger? Nobody knew or cared about Dockings."

"I agree," Hank said. "If the killer wanted Imogen Revel out of the way, we need to dig for another motive."

"Look," Ben said. "Money, position, prestige all mean a lot to that family. Dockings didn't fit in. They thought he was crude; he drank cheap wine. I think I can see one of the Revels trying to keep Imogen from bringing him into the family."

"I wonder," Hank said. "What you are saying sounds disturbed to me. Can you think of anybody in the family who would kill Imogen?"

"Maybe they were all in on it," Ben said.

"Each one took a turn at putting a drop of cyanide into the wine? They would have had to form a line at the plant stand." Hank was growing impatient with this line of thinking. Sometimes Ben went a little too far with his theories. "What we need is evidence. That means locating that bottle or someone who remembers seeing something happen at the plant stand. Or, if Montgomery's our man, we need someone to have noticed him tamper with the wine before he served it."

"He would have gotten the wine from the barmen at the service bar in the dining room," Keisha said.

"What have we got from the barmen?"

Keisha rifled through her notes. Hank waited. He was ready for a day off. Tomorrow he would get outdoors and take a breather from the case. He had already checked the weather forecast, and the two days promised to be clear and breezy. The opportunity to do some sailing would be welcome. If it wasn't too late, he could offer to crew on *Fancy Boy*, whose image bobbing at her berth in the harbor brought a flush of pleasure to his chest.

"Here it is, sir." Keisha had found her paper. "Let me see what I have. Two of the barmen remembered the waiter who couldn't be found at the end of the party."

"Did we ever show them the photograph we have?" Keisha shook her head. "O.K., that's got to be done. Ben, let's see. Can you do that first thing Monday while Keisha goes to Waterville?" Ben nodded. "Let's get them on record with the positive I.D.." He gestured for Keisha to continue.

"One barman thinks he remembers the last tray of drinks he filled for Montgomery posing as the waiter."

"Was that last tray the one that had the glass in question?"

"There's no way of knowing, sir. The waiters kept coming back to be re-stocked. They all got the same selection of white and red wine, plus champagne and sparkling mineral water. Champagne seemed to be the most popular drink, by the way." She glanced at her notes. "Then white, the sparkling water. Hardly anyone wanted red."

"A sunny afternoon in June is not the place I connect up with drinking a glass of heavy red burgundy," Hank commented. "Claude Revel indicated that red was the future groom's favorite drink, and he honored that. Montgomery would know Dockings drank only red wine. He followed him to the liquor store."

"I'm afraid I didn't ask specifically if the barman saw Montgomery put anything in one of the glasses. At that point it all didn't connect up yet. I didn't know what the cause of death was going to come out as."

"Well, we know now, and I think you'd better ask about that, too, Ben. It seems unlikely that the tampering would have taken place in full view of that service bar, but you never know. I've been doing some thinking about that."

"How it was done?" Ben asked.

"Yeah, the vessel containing the cyanide would have been small. No one would have carried around that 250 ml. glass bottle from the school, assuming that's where it came from. I was thinking the stuff would have been transferred into another bottle. Small enough to fit in a pocket, or maybe a purse. The cyanide would be emptied out quickly into the wine, and the killer would have to move swiftly."

"Also some sleight of hand," Ben pointed out.

"Yes, the container would have had to be easily opened, probably while it was in the killer's pocket. Then, one fast motion to eject it into the drink."

"You can buy stuff like that at the drug store," Keisha said.

"Cyanide?" Hank asked.

"No, no. Those little bottles you were talking about. They sell them in all the discount stores. Little containers to make your own travel-size packages of lotion and shampoo. They come in all kinds of shapes and sizes. Some of them even have those pop tops you can lift up with your thumb."

"I see it," Hank said.

There would be no way to trace such a purchase if every discount outlet in Rhode Island, Connecticut and New York sold these containers. It would seem a woman, but plenty of men shopped in discount stores. He couldn't picture Claude Revel pushing a cart through the aisles of his local Wal-Mart, but when Hank imaged in the figure of Donald Montgomery, he saw the scene quite clearly.

19

Hank Nightingale's apartment was located in a quiet street off upper Bellevue Avenue in an old, pink stone Victorian villa. When he had first seen the place, Hank had been attracted to the eccentric look of the exterior. The inside of the apartment had high ceilings and tall old-fashioned windows. He had expanded comfortably into the three rooms which were his to inhabit.

On Saturday morning the detective was enjoying a rare, leisurely second cup of coffee outdoors on the porch, which wrapped around two sides of the villa. None of his fellow residents were stirring. A neighborhood cat was sunning herself on the wall behind the house. With eyes half-closed, the feline was exhibiting a serenity that made the detective jealous. Hank had scheduled two whole days to recharge his batteries, and already he was feeling that he had frittered away half the morning in unproductive daydreaming.

"Well, Delilah," he said to the cat. Her name wasn't Delilah; in fact he didn't know what her gender was, let alone her name. But she looked to him like a she and very much like a black cat who ought to be called Delilah. "What are your plans today?" The cat yawned on cue and Hank smiled. "A lazy Saturday. I see. Perhaps a bird or two will tempt you." He had often seen the bodies of dead birds in the yard, their bloodied, matted feathers scattered over their mutilated corpses. The sight displeased him, he who had seen a few human corpses in his day. At work, he had to display an unemotional reaction toward a victim, but inside the confines of his home space he wanted to see nothing of violent death.

His cell phone rang. For an instant he hoped it was Ben or Keisha with some news about the Dockings's case. Then when he remembered that he had left messages to set up a sailing date for the week-end, he wished that the call might be an answer to his longing to be out on the water.

"Nightingale," he said crisply into the phone.

"Hank, it's Dave. Don't you ever go off duty?"

"No. What's up? Are you racing this week-end?"

"I can't. I'm going up to Maine for a reunion at my college. I didn't sign *Fancy Boy* up for any racing today or tomorrow."

"Oh," Hank answered. He didn't try to conceal his disappointment.

"Hey, sorry. You're usually up in the air so much on week-ends. Lately I never count on you for crew."

"Oh, I know. Don't apologize. It's just that this week-end I'm taking some time off."

"Why don't you take the boat out yourself? You know the combination to get into the cabin. I don't think Jake's doing anything. Call him and go for a cruise. It's not racing, but you can get in some practice. I bet you're getting rusty, old man."

"Yeah, yeah. I can sail rings around you, Dave. Who taught you how to use the GPS you bought and couldn't make work?"

"Do you want to use my boat or not this week-end?" His tone was a friendly, mocking one, and Hank knew it was a signal to ease the tightness he heard in his own voice. He inhaled deeply, picking up the drifting smell of salt water which was never far from any spot on the island. "How about it?" Dave asked. "It's a shame for you to lose such a great sailing week-end just because I have to see how much hair all my classmates have lost in five years."

"Thanks, Dave. I think I will. That's really good of you to offer."

He concluded the call by asking Dave for news of the last several races and wishing him a good time at his reunion. They would talk again next week. Hank punched in the numbers for Jake Halloway and waited. After five rings the voice mail told him that Jake was unavailable. Hank spoke briefly of his desire to make an impromptu sailing date for the current week-end and hung up.

Delilah had jumped off the wall and was sauntering along the line of the fence, sniffing the air and looking up at the tall trees for any sign of her favorite feathered prey. Hank got up, too, and took his coffee cup back into the apartment. He was restless and suddenly had the idea to go for a run. His exercise schedule, like everything else in his life, had grown erratic and dependent on his job. He enjoyed running and knew it was important to keep in shape. He hadn't had to chase any bad guys for a few years. But one never knew when the job would call for it, and today would be a good day for a run.

When he returned, sweaty and hot, he showered and dressed in khaki pants and a navy blue T shirt. Looking in the mirror as he dried his dark curly hair with the blow dryer, he examined the lines around his eyes. They looked deeper than he remembered their being on the last idle day when he had studied them. He had always been called handsome, and he guessed he was. But he was no longer youthful. Forty was fast approaching.

His phone still had not rung, and Hank took his car keys from the hook by the kitchen sink and left the apartment.

The maid, a cheerful young woman with a blond pony tail, showed him into the office and told him to wait there while she found Mrs. Kent. Hank had shown her his credentials by way of introduction, and the young woman had unquestioningly admitted him to the house.

Kenwood had not been his intentional destination when he left his apartment. He had driven down Bellevue Avenue toward Ocean Drive with the vague idea that he would park on the drive and walk down among the cliffs at the ocean's edge. It was a popular spot for sightseers and picnickers, and when he arrived he saw the hot June day had brought out hundreds. Instead of parking, he stayed in his car and drove to the end of the drive where he turned and doubled back to Bellevue Avenue.

After he made the turn he realized he was only a few minutes from Caroline's house, and when he reached the side road which led to the Inn at Kenwood Court, he turned off onto it.

The pictures lining the walls of the old smoking room went back several generations in the Kent family. During his previous times at the house, when he had investigated the inn murders, Hank had examined them all. They fascinated him with their happy scenes of garden parties and croquet matches. What Hank had decided must have been somebody's first automobile was commemorated with a shot of three smiling young men, dressed in white jackets and straw hats, crowded into the open car.

There was a picture of Louise, looking young and happy, cradling a fat baby tight against her breast. The young Reed Kent was a pleasant looking infant, with wisps of fine blond hair framing his round face. Hank looked at the other pictures as Kent grew from babe in arms to a lean, confident adult.

A photo of Reed taking the helm of a large sailboat was occupying his attention when the door opened and Caroline came in. He turned quickly.

"Oh," he said. "I was just looking at the sailboat. It looks like a Pearson I once crewed on."

She came wordlessly toward the picture and stared at it. Why did he have to draw her attention to it? He saw that she was preoccupied. What had he been thinking to interrupt her in the middle of the day on a week-end? She had told him that most of her guests this time of the year only stayed there for the week-end.

"I really don't have any excuse for coming. I was in the neighborhood, and I decided to drop by. Perhaps this isn't the best time."

"You're not working on the case today?"

"Sometimes a day off aids the thought processes. I'm trying to get a brainstorm. I went for a run, then a drive."

"And?"

"Nothing. I thought you might have remembered something."

"And that's why you came?"

"No," he said honestly. "I'm so unused to having a day off, I don't know what to do with myself."

She looked at her watch. "Have you had lunch yet?" He shook his head. "Well, if you can wait about half an hour, I can give you some."

"Thank you. That's the best offer I've had so far today."

"You can wait in here, but it's pretty dreary on such a sunny day. The back terrace gets the sun, or the conservatory is pleasant this time of the day."

He chose the conservatory where he found some magazines to read, and at ten minutes before two, Caroline appeared with a tray of sandwiches and a tall carafe of iced tea. She sat the food down on one of the low tables and began fussing with the plates.

"Here," he said, jumping up. "You've served the paying guests. This freeloader will help himself."

They served themselves and settled down on one of the Bentwood sofas to enjoy their meal. The scent of her perfume was strong, and he realized that she had been perspiring from the exertion of her work.

For several minutes they ate in silence. He was hungry; this was the first solid food he'd had all day. The room was cool, with a stone floor and tall, airy windows. The Bentwood furniture was old, but of good quality, and the worn green cushions were extremely comfortable. Plants and potted flowers of all shapes and sizes were placed around the room. Hank had the sensation that he was sitting in a garden.

It was Caroline who spoke first.

"What are your plans the rest of the day?"

His pent-up frustrations at not being able to race that week-end spilled out, and he concluded with his complaint that his work schedule these days often conflicted with the racing calendar.

"It's been two years since I've been able to do the race to Block Island."

"Have you thought of getting your own boat?" Caroline asked. "Then you could take it out on your off-days. I know it's not racing, but you could be on the boat whenever you wanted."

"You know I couldn't afford the expenses. Besides, I guess I would miss the racing. I want to be part of a crew."

"Would you like to come sailing with me?" he asked suddenly. He knew that it was his heart which had pushed the words out of his mouth. His brain would never have allowed him to make the suggestion.

"Racing, you mean?" She looked surprised.

"Oh, no. I mean today. Just a day sail."

"Today is half-gone, and we have some guests arriving. That's always hectic."

"Then tomorrow?"

"Sunday? I'm afraid that's a difficult day also. And where are you getting a boat anyway?"

He explained about Dave's offer to use *Fancy Boy*, and he knew by the look in her eyes that she was falling for the self-sorry way in which he had portrayed himself, adrift this week-end without sailing companions.

"I wish I could, but I took the whole day last week to go with you to Connecticut and then I was away from the inn several hours to attend the memorial service yesterday. I've got too much catching up to do." Her voice was firm, but he saw in her eyes some contradiction. He thought she wanted to go, and that was almost as good to him as if she had said she would go.

"How about next week-end? I'm sure I could talk Dave into letting me borrow the boat again?" He was thinking he would rent one if she said yes.

"I don't know. I'd have to check the bookings. We're starting to get busy."

"But you will go sometime," he pressed. "Perhaps a day during the week. That's actually better for Dave because he doesn't use the boat himself while he's --"

"Oh, there you are, Caroline. I almost couldn't find my way back here." The dissonant sound of Imogen Revel's unmistakable voice broke into his appeal. For several seconds he could not find her in the room with them, his line of sight hidden by a huge Ficus tree. "The maid said you were having your lunch in the conservatory, and I said I knew you wouldn't mind if I disturbed you --"

She stopped in the middle of her sentence as she came around the tree and saw Caroline sitting with him on the settee. The look of confusion on Imogen's face was unmistakable. She stared open-mouthed, first at them, then at the used lunch tray set for two, and then back at them both. Caroline was quickly to her feet.

"Imogen, hello. I didn't expect you today." Hank could have sworn that the word *obviously* was forming on Imogen's lips, but he knew that was his own jealousy. This interruption appeared especially cruel to him.

"I couldn't be alone today," Imogen said slowly, her black eyes locked on Hank, who had risen in the instant after Caroline. "It's one week today."

"Week?" Caroline's mind was blank, but he knew to what Imogen referred. It was the one week anniversary of Hugh Dockings's death.

"Hugh," Imogen explained. "He died a week ago today." She suddenly collapsed into a chair and began to cry. Caroline was immediately at her side, taking the woman's long, bony hands in her own.

When Imogen was finally able to control herself, she looked at Caroline and said, "Oh, what you must think of me. To break down like this."

"I understand," Caroline said.

"I knew you would. I knew you would be kind when no one else is."

Hank caught Caroline's eye and signaled that he would be going. She nodded and turned back to Imogen.

Hank walked across the stone floor tiles, his heels clicking rhythmically as he went. Near the doorway he paused to look back. He wanted to see her smile at him, but Caroline's concentration was completely on the older woman now. Her arm rested companionably on Imogen's shoulder.

He had managed to be first in Caroline's thoughts for a brief time. He told himself he ought to be content with that. But he was disappointed that any desire on Caroline's part to sail with him had disintegrated so easily when Imogen's needs were made known to her. At this moment, Hank knew he was the furthest person from Caroline Kent's thoughts.

20

L ouise had been putting dishes away in the pantry when the maid Karen informed her that Imogen Revel had come, looking for Caroline. Hurrying across the house to the west wing, Louise contemplated what she was going to say when she encountered this unwelcome caller.

When Louise arrived at the hallway which led into the conservatory, she was surprised to see Hank Nightingale standing outside the doorway to the room. She had been pleased when Caroline had invited him to stay for lunch. As she had told her daughter-in-law recently, she genuinely encouraged their friendship. It was Imogen, and her preoccupation with death, which Louise wished her daughter-in-law to avoid.

"Karen told me Imogen Revel is here. Is she in there?" she asked. He nodded and gestured toward the open door. "Oh, dear. And you left them alone?"

"They seemed to want to be alone, Mrs. Kent."

Louise shook her head and eased her small frame into the doorway. She was well aware that the plants camouflaged the space, and she made no pretense that she was not listening to the conversation inside the conservatory. Louise saw Hank watching her carefully, and she motioned for him to be quiet.

"-- doing here?" Louise caught the end of Imogen's question.

"We were having lunch, Imogen," Caroline answered.

"That seems inappropriate, Caroline."

"I don't know what you mean."

Louise shot a look at the policeman and saw that he could hear the dialog as well as she. He looked uncomfortable, but she motioned him closer to the doorway to show that she wanted him to remain.

"I saw the way he was looking at you," Imogen said. Her voice was aggrieved. "You have to be careful, Caroline. You're such a nice person, and you can't see it, but I know he's taking your familiarity as encouragement."

Louise stepped back into the passageway and now wordlessly indicated for Hank to follow her into the library, which was across from the conservatory. Once they were inside, she closed the door.

"It's all wrong," she told him. "You've got to help me to extricate Caroline from developing this friendship with Imogen Revel."

"What can I do about it? Surely you have more influence with Caroline than I do."

"You're a policeman. Use your authority to tell her to stay out of this business entirely. I think she'll listen to you."

"I don't think our history proves that, Mrs. Kent."

"And when are you going to start calling me Louise?" she asked kindly.

"Thank you, Louise. I appreciate that. But I'm afraid, because Caroline was a witness at the murder scene, it's not going to be possible to keep her out of this. Between you and me, I'm not happy that she seems intent on helping Imogen through her bereavement, either."

"Caroline had to deal with her own grief. I know you think you know about that, but you can't imagine how abandoned she felt, how we both felt." He opened his mouth to speak, but she held up her hand to silence him. "Now, this spring, I've seen her finally beginning to come out of herself. She smiles now most of the time, and I didn't think a year ago that was going to be possible."

"I'm sorry I haven't been part of that."

"Yes, well, I let Caroline do what she wanted about that. I hope you understand that I didn't interfere in her decision to stop seeing you. She is free to do whatever she wants. I put no restraints on her."

"I appreciate your saying that," he said. "Now tell me exactly what it is about Imogen that makes you want Caroline to stay away from her."

"Imogen can be manipulative. She's like all the rest of the Revels in that regard."

"Are you sure Caroline can't handle this? Perhaps she needs to counsel someone like Imogen during a time of similar difficulty. Maybe this effort is another sign that she is healing from her loss."

"No," Louise said firmly. "You don't know the Revel family like I do. I've always regarded them as a selfish, insular family. They're proud of their tradition, but to me that's always been an excuse to use other people and then discard them."

"I see," Hank said.

"My husband was friendly with Henri, although, to tell you the truth, that friendship was rooted in a business relationship."

"Despite what you think, are you sure you're not being overly protective of Caroline? She's intelligent and ought to be able to see what Imogen --"

"You can't see," she interrupted him, "as Caroline can't, how Imogen is trying to take advantage of Caroline's generosity. Well, I won't let her."

"How can I help?"

"You must continue to be a friend to Caroline. I can see that you want to be." She saw him color at the observation, but she had counted on that.

"I'll try," he answered, "if you want me to."

"Good. The important thing is to protect Caroline, and we will be allies in that, if you agree."

"Of course, I agree," the policeman said forcefully, "But I still have to investigate Hugh Dockings's murder." He shook his head.

"I'm afraid Miss Revel doesn't think much of me as a detective so far."

The frosty look which Louise gave Imogen as the three women said their good-byes in the foyer half an hour later left little doubt in Caroline's mind of her mother-in-law's feelings toward Imogen.

"I have some work to do in my office," Caroline told Louise as the door shut behind Imogen. Caroline had decided to try to ignore the remorse which she felt in going expressly against her mother-in-law's wishes. "I think this would be a good time to catch up on my paperwork."

Louise had nodded, and Caroline went back to the office, spending two hours entering data into her computer's financial program. At five o'clock, still troubled by Louise's attitude, she turned off the computer and decided to take some exercise before starting her evening's tasks.

A brisk walk on the Cliff Walk could always be counted on to refresh her mind and body, and she slipped out the door at the back of the house. She walked across the lawn to where the pathway cut into the shrubbery and stepped onto the Cliff Walk.

The sun was still warm, and the wind off the ocean filled her nostrils, clearing her head almost instantly. Across the vast curving expanse of the water, on the tip of the horizon, a sailboat glided majestically between the blue of the sky and the crystal aquamarine of the ocean. She thought of Hank and his offer to take her sailing. She had almost made up her mind, during Imogen's visit, to refuse him should the offer again be made. It was an activity she only connected to Reed, and Imogen's disapproval had hit its mark. But now, seeing the sea and feeling the exhilaration of the force of the air on her face, she reconsidered that she might well want to sail again.

The Cliff Walk was crowded with people, most of whom were tourists who always could easily be identified. They often slowed or stopped their walking completely, staring curiously at the large houses which fronted the water. The visitors pointed at the elegant facades of the estates and snapped photographic mementos of their trip to Newport. She circumvented several groups, some posing with the mansions in the background, others with the broad expanse of the ocean in their lenses's frame.

Dogs and baby strollers also obstructed the footpath for the serious walkers like herself, who strode at a steady gait. Runners also used the Cliff Walk for exercise, and from time to time the panting of one came up behind her or confronted her as she made the winding turns along the narrow, twisting trail which threaded its way over the cliffs, high above the ocean.

Caroline glanced at her watch and realized that Louise and Mattie were probably in the kitchen, beginning their daily discussion of dinner and dividing up the tasks preparing the meal entailed. She hurried her pace to return to do her share of the work.

As Caroline rounded the curve where The Breakers sat grandly on its flat green lawn and descended the stone steps which evened out the path there, she was surprised to see Claudine Revel, attired in shorts and a T-shirt, jogging toward her. Caroline paused as Claudine ran up the steps and stopped, the look of startled recognition on her face.

"Claudine," Caroline said pleasantly. "Hello."

Claudine was sweating, but barely out of breath as she smiled at Caroline. "Well, hello, Caroline."

"I thought you were in London."

"I just got back. I came up from New York to report on my trip to my father, and I was so stiff from the plane and then the car ride that I decided to take a run first."

"Oh, well, don't let me detain you."

"No trouble. My father's out actually. Apparently Mother is in a state, and Uncle Dorsey's staying on at Mon Plaisir isn't helping. So Father takes him out for the afternoon. They drove up to Bristol for lunch and aren't back yet."

They were standing in the middle of the steps, and several people had to make their way awkwardly around them. Caroline sensed Claudine was eager to talk.

"Have you finished your run?" She was quite sure, given the perspiration dripping from Claudine, that the young woman had. Her thick, wiry black hair was stuck to her forehead, and she looked well-exerted.

"Yes, I'm heading back home. I can take the turn up there where the street is open to the path. The house is just beyond there."

"I know," Caroline said, "but, do you have some time to visit? I'm on my way back to the inn. I could give you a cool drink."

Claudine was surprised, but interested. Caroline thought she knew how the young banker felt at the prospect of returning home to encounter Pamela's crossness. "Sure. Why not?"

The two women walked down the steps and in a few minutes they were at the pathway to Kenwood. Claudine had been quiet, and Caroline had also kept silent. Once they were on the grounds of Kenwood, Caroline spoke.

"I was at Mr. Dockings's memorial service yesterday."

"Oh, I see. You had to go to that."

"I wanted to. Imogen specifically asked me to be there."

They had reached the kitchen entrance, and Caroline opened the door. As she expected, Mattie was busy at the stove and Louise was chopping vegetables for the salad. Both looked up as Caroline entered, and she saw Louise's troubled face as Claudine followed.

"Hello, Claudine," Louise said, recovering herself upon seeing the second surprise Revel guest in the same afternoon. "This is a pleasant surprise."

"I ran into Claudine on the Cliff Walk and invited her back for a cold drink." She went to the refrigerator and took out a large pitcher of iced tea. "Can I pour you some, Louise?" Louise shook her head. "Mattie?" Caroline asked, with a nod toward the stove where the cook shrugged her shoulders in response. Caroline poured a glass for Claudine and one for herself.

Claudine drained her glass and Caroline refilled it.

"This hits the spot, Caroline, but I wonder. Could I use your bathroom?" She looked juvenile at having to ask.

"Of course," Caroline responded. "Here. Follow me."

She led Claudine to the powder room off the foyer and waited for her at the front door.

"Thanks," Claudine said as she joined Caroline. "Now I'd better be going home."

"Do you want a ride?" Claudine shook her head. "Seriously, it's no trouble, and you've got to be careful now. You've cooled down. You don't want your muscles to get stiff."

"You don't have to. Honestly, I can run home."

"I'd like to talk to you, Claudine," Caroline said suddenly. "Why don't you let me drive you home?"

Claudine hesitated, but she agreed. Caroline fetched her purse and car keys from her office. They walked toward the garages.

"What is this all about, Caroline? It sounds super mysterious."

"It's about your aunt."

"Imogen?" Claudine's manner immediately stiffened, and Caroline realized she ought to have better prepared her before launching into the subject.

"She visited me today."

"I wasn't aware that you two were friends."

"We weren't until recently." They had reached the car, and Caroline unlocked her old BMW convertible. Claudine got in the passenger side.

"I love these cars," Claudine said. "I've got a new one, but sometimes I wish I had one of these old classic ones."

Caroline started the engine and backed out of the garage bay.

"Imogen seems very vulnerable to me now, Claudine. And I think I know how Imogen feels. It's a terrible loss, the loss of a husband."

"They weren't even married yet," Claudine said, the petulance strong in her voice. "It's not the same as you and Reed."

"No, but they were going to be the next day, and in some ways, that's a bigger tragedy to have to experience than my own."

Claudine turned to her, and her face was red with anger. "You loved Reed, Caroline. She didn't love Hugh. She was just using him to escape my father's control. Can't you see that? My aunt hates that my father controls her life."

"There may be some truth in that, but I think she cared for Hugh."

"You didn't see them together. She led him around like a dog, and he was happy about it. My mother said he was after the money, you know."

"Claudine," Caroline said, sighing. "We can't know all the reasons why two people want to be a couple. Some are selfish... on both sides."

"Well, I'm not planning to establish my marriage on such a basis."

"You don't have to. You have your own money and a job, one with a position of importance with Syndicat Revel."

"So?" Her voice sounded young and impertinent.

"Imogen was denied all that. I don't think your family realizes what that's meant to her. She's angry, deep inside. She feels cheated. Can you even try to understand how she feels?"

"No. And I'll tell you why. Because I *was* given that chance. Why couldn't she be happy for me? Couldn't she support my father when he broke with tradition? You must know how strong that has been. It's the way things have been in the bank for over a hundred years. Reed worked for Syndicat Revel. He knew how hidebound every male has been. My father has been fantastic to me. I like to think I am grateful."

"And I'm sure you are, but --"

"But, nothing, Caroline. Imogen hates me because I'm young. She wants to see me fail. She tells our cousin George March all the time what a failure I'll be and that he should have been designated the next chairman."

They had reached Mon Plaisir and Caroline stopped the car on the drive in front of the main door.

"I'm sure George doesn't listen to her."

"No, he doesn't," Claudine said proudly. "But that hasn't stopped her. And I'm sure she's saying the same thing to Claude and Henri Cort and Claude McCauley. According to Imogen, each one of them should expect me to make a mess of things."

"You don't know that."

"You weren't there. Christmas two years ago in London. Father was entertaining two of the directors of the bank where I was interning. Imogen was there because we had to take her along with us because she had no other place to go for the holidays. And do you know how she paid us back? Right there at the table, she started saying ugly things about me. My father was appalled, and I thought my mother would have a stroke."

"No."

"Yes. She dismissed my abilities, my education... my God, my brain! Right in front of the people for whom I was working and trying to prove myself."

"Claudine, I'm sorry," Caroline said. "I didn't realize it had gone that far."

"Well, it has, and you can thank Aunt Imogen for getting it there." She opened the car door, speaking without turning back. "Thanks for the ride."

Caroline watched as she ran up the steps and into the house.

"She wants me dead," Imogen had said of Claudine that afternoon while she sat with Caroline in the conservatory. "She was the one who killed Hugh. I'm convinced of it now. You have to help me, Caroline, to get the proof." The words echoed now in her brain. "Claudine wants me dead. She hates me."

Was Claudine's assertion that Imogen hated her a blind to cover that it was Claudine herself who bore her aunt malice, strong enough to wish her death?

21

M onday dawned rainy and grey, and Hank's spirits as he came back to work matched the weather's damp gloom. His much anticipated week-end was a bomb. The two days off had given him neither the pleasures of sailing nor the answers to his murder case. Looking at the pile of paper in his in-box, he cursed the folly of being an optimist. A clean desk would have been his reward had he spent the week-end at the office.

He flipped through the last several additions to the in-box. Nothing caught his eye. He turned on his computer to check his e-mail. Janet Dawson, the accountant turned police officer, had a message for him, and he quickly clicked the computer's mouse to read it. Finally, some information concerning Hugh Dockings's financial files.

The message spilled out on the screen, and Hank mumbled a few profanities. Janet had been assigned to go to a training session in Providence the previous week, and she had promised to take the files with her. Her e-mail apologized for the fact that she had not had the opportunity to delve into the material, and she assured Hank that she would make time for it at the beginning of this week. He sent back a message to ask that her report become a priority, as much as that was humanly possible given her other responsibilities.

He was overwhelmed suddenly with the desire to talk with someone live about the case. Keisha was on her way to Waterville to do the follow-up at The Camden School, and Ben had been sent to show the photograph of Donald Montgomery to the barmen from the Revels' party. Hank thought of Caroline and how easy it had been to fall into the familiar pattern, established the previous autumn, of talking his case over with her. Their day trip to Connecticut lingered in his mind, and he realized what a source of pleasure the memory of it had become to him, carrying him through the frustrations of the last several days. He reached for the telephone and punched the number of the Inn at Kenwood Court.

The telephone was answered by Louise. Caroline was busy with one of the guests, and Louise, her voice sounding encouraging, asked Hank to leave a message. There was no message, he said. He would try again at a more convenient time.

"Let her call me, if she wants to," he said to himself as he replaced the telephone receiver. Despite the enthusiasm in Louise's voice and his promise to her, the memory of his last look at Caroline, sitting with Imogen in the conservatory, was vaguely unpleasant. He was beginning to dislike Imogen Revel far more than was good for him to do on a case. When he considered Imogen's situation, she ought to have been an object of his pity. The death of her fiancé on the day before the wedding was a tragedy. He doubted whether another chance at marriage would present itself. Hadn't Imogen's brother said as much during their first meeting?

Deep within her, did Imogen understand this truth? And did that explain Imogen's sudden interest in Caroline? Was she to fill the void left by Hugh? Now that the pavilion belonged to Imogen, Hank realized that she could remain in Newport all year round. And if Caroline reciprocated her friendship, Hank couldn't shake the feeling that Imogen was going to pose a giant roadblock to re-establishing a relationship between him and Caroline.

Hank reached for the telephone again. This time he called Mon Plaisir and asked to be put through to Pamela Revel. He couldn't wait for Ben to return to the station. Hank wanted to be moving on the investigation, and he decided an interview with Imogen's sister-in-law was in order.

"You seem quite at home here, Imogen," Claude said amiably to his sister. They were sitting at the small dining table in the room at Des Arbres which had been made into the dining room during the renovation work. Their lunch was finished, and Imogen was serving coffee in the dainty cream-colored porcelain cups which had been part of the family table service ordered for Mon Plaisir by their grandmother. Each piece in the service bore a gold monogram, IMR, for Isabelle Monroe Revel. By an interesting coincidence, the initials matched his sister's: Imogen Madeleine Revel. When they had fitted out the pavilion, his sister had been insistent that she be given the service, and Pamela had acquiesced, mainly because she preferred the Wedgewood she had acquired for her own family's everyday use.

"Are you happy here?" he asked.

"Happy is hardly the word I would use for my present state, Claude."

"Of course, of course," he said quickly. "I had really meant to inquire if you are content to live here in the pavilion."

"It is my home now, Claude."

"Of course it is, but I wondered if it wasn't perhaps lonely. After all, the idea of living here was to make it a home for two." Dancing around the subject of Hugh's death was becoming a talent of Claude's.

"That has been denied me."

"Yes. I wish I could make things up to you, but I don't know how."

"I'm managing on my own, Claude. You needn't concern yourself with me. You've got your wife and your daughter to worry about."

"You're still upset with Pamela and Claudine, aren't you? Because of the memorial service."

"I've forgotten that. It's a triviality as far as I'm concerned that your daughter didn't come to Hugh's service or that your wife made a fool of herself afterwards."

Claude swallowed hard. The words fell back in his throat, and he shook his head gravely. He filled the gap in the conversation by cutting a piece of the Stilton from the cheese board and putting the crumbling wedge on his plate. Carefully he spread a thin slice of crusty bread with the cheese.

"I'm glad you're not upset then, Imogen." He dared not look at her face while he spoke the next words. "It makes what I want to discuss with you that much easier."

"Well, I guess I'm not surprised that this luncheon has a purpose. You didn't come to see me out of a desire to spend time with me. Is this about money?"

He was amazed at her conclusion because it was accurate. There would have to be caution exercised here. He had to handle her carefully.

"Ned Babson called me this morning. Hugh's will has to be probated. Do you understand what that means?"

"I'm not an idiot, despite the manner in which I've been treated by the men in this family. I understand probate."

"Good. I wasn't sure. Well, you know that Hugh's cottage will have to be sold. There is a mortgage, and Ned has --"

"What makes you think I want to sell Hugh's house?"

"I just thought... really, Imogen, you have Des Arbres. What would you do with a cottage in the middle of nowhere?" He had a sudden happy thought. "You're not thinking of returning to Camden, are you?"

"No, I've finished with that part of my life."

"Then you ought to sell the house there," he said, glumly. "Besides it's not free and clear. You would have to pay off the mortgage. How would you expect to do that?"

"Hugh left me some money."

"Ned said there isn't enough in Hugh's bank accounts to settle the mortgage. Apparently the man lived month to month."

"I could rent the cottage for the income."

"Don't be ridiculous. It's not worth bothering with. You should sell it and realize whatever profit the sale brings in after the mortgage and taxes are paid."

"I wish you wouldn't interest yourself in this, Claude. I find it insulting that you are making financial decisions for me with my money and my property."

"Yes, things are different now. And I have something to say about that, also."

"Yes?" Her tone was acrid.

"I've discussed this with Ned, and I want to settle some money on you."

"Money?" She was definitely surprised.

"Yes. I realize the events of the last two weeks have changed things. You didn't expect to be still a single woman, and I want to treat you as if you were married."

"That's ridiculous. I'm not married, and I never will be."

"You're not an old woman, Imogen. You don't know what lies in the future. But, nevertheless, I think the right thing to do is to give you some money of your own. I should have done this years ago. You'll have your own income --"

"I don't want it."

"I beg your pardon."

"I said I don't want your money, Claude. Give it to Claudine. I've got my own money now."

"I don't understand. What money?"

"I told you. Hugh left me money."

"Oh, Imogen, let me try again to make you understand. The estate Hugh left doesn't amount to much. You can't live on what Hugh left you."

"I don't want to talk about this any more." The look on her face was the one he remembered her having as a child when she tried to get the better of him in some dispute and had been thwarted.

Claude was puzzled. He had expected his announcement would bring his sister pleasure. He had also anticipated that she would be grateful to him for suggesting it. What was she thinking? Hugh's money didn't add up to a month's living expenses, and she no longer had her salary from Camden.

Imogen didn't understand the first thing about money. It was his fault, and his father's. They both should have seen that Imogen of all people needed to be financially independent. Her mental health would have been a lot stronger if his father had accepted that, and Claude had been foolish to carry on the tradition. So many problems would have been avoided.

"All right," he said. He and Ned could work things out on their own. It would take some time to set up a trust for Imogen, which she could use during her lifetime, as that was the device Ned had suggested in case any more fortune hunters appeared to court Imogen.

"Oh, there you are, Claude." The sound of relief in Dorsey Revel's voice was evident as he met his nephew on the steps of the pavilion. The banker had just said good-by to Imogen, who was now standing in the front doorway, watching him depart. The mulish expression on her face reflected her continuing resolve to be stubborn on the subject of her financial situation, and he was leaving Des Arbres with grave reservations on his part as to the course of their future relations.

"Hello, Uncle Dorsey," Claude said. "Is anything the matter?"

"Plenty, my boy. I'm glad I found you. Big trouble at the house. You're needed."

"What's wrong?"

"Our detective friend has telephoned."

"Yes, I know. I saw the message he left for Pamela this morning. One of the servants took the message while I was on my private line.

159

I would have spoken to Lt. Nightingale myself, if I had known. But, I thought if it were anything important he would have asked to speak to me in the first place."

"He wants to interview Pamela again. She just came back from her luncheon engagement and returned his call. You'd better come, Claude. She's not happy." He grimaced as if Claude certainly understood all that descriptive entailed.

"What is it, Claude?" Imogen's voice was harsh. She walked toward them. He and Dorsey were standing on the narrow stone path which led away from the front steps of the pavilion.

"Oh, it's nothing, Imogen. I'll take care of it."

"I heard Uncle Dorsey mention the police."

"They want to interview Pamela," Dorsey said. His grin was irritating to Claude. He realized his wife had been right to want his uncle out of their midst. A murder investigation combined with Uncle Dorsey's high-spirited nature was a disaster waiting to happen.

"It's that detective, isn't it?" Imogen asked. "Claude, you must do something about him."

"Lt. Nightingale?"

"I want him off the case."

"Imogen, please." Claude assumed his best conciliatory voice. "Don't excite yourself. There is nothing --"

"I don't want him on the case, I said." Her voice was shrill. "Call someone. You can call someone in the city and have him taken off the case."

"Why?" Dorsey asked. "Don't you want to learn who the murderer is?"

"He's not doing anything to solve the case. He ignores everything I say."

"Imogen," Claude began carefully. "Now don't do this. The police must be left alone to conduct their investigation. The less we interfere with them the better. Pamela and I will see Lt. Nightingale together. I'm sure it's some small detail he wants clarified. These policemen need their reports in order. When is he coming, Dorsey?" He was still controlling his voice to underscore the unconcern he wanted to project but certainly wasn't feeling. What did the damn man want anyway? Claude had felt uneasy since he had seen the message for his wife on the pad by the telephone.

"Pamela told him she couldn't see him until tomorrow. Stalling for time, don't you see?" Dorsey's black eyes were big and bright.

"Well, that's fine then. It means whatever it is can wait."

"Claude, you should tell Imogen who you and Pamela think the murderer is. It will make her feel so much better to know."

"Uncle Dorsey, this isn't the time." Claude felt himself losing control of the situation.

"Claude." Imogen had grabbed him by the arm and was squeezing it with all her might. She was hurting him, and he wrestled from her grasp.

"Imogen, please. I think I had better call Dr. Stanton. You need something to help you relax." How he wished Aunt Grace had stayed on after the memorial service. She could handle Imogen better than anyone else in the family.

"I don't want Martin Stanton. He's a quack who'll just make me swallow some pills. I don't want pills. I want --"

"Yes," he said, again searching for the right tone of voice to use. "I know, I know. This will all be over soon, and we can get back to normal."

"Tell her, Claude. Once she knows, she'll feel better."

"What?" Imogen asked, staring at her brother. "Feel better about what, Claude?"

Dorsey filled in the void before Claude could frame his reply. "Hugh."

"Hugh?" Imogen repeated.

"Is the murderer," Dorsey said.

"Uncle Dorsey," Claude said. Now it was his turn to grab the other man's arm and twist it with all his might.

"What is he talking about, Claude?"

"Nothing, Imogen. Just something we had been discussing, it's nothing." Dorsey squealed in pain.

"You said Hugh is the murderer."

"No, Imogen."

"Yes, he did," Dorsey exclaimed, freeing himself from his nephew's hold. "And it's a damned clever solution. Don't you see, Imogen? He was trying to poison you."

Dorsey's voice and face were triumphant. Imogen looked at her uncle for several seconds, her face becoming pink and flushed. Then she turned her mounting fury on Claude. Weakly he could only offer his hand to her.

"Kill me?" she shouted. She pulled away from Claude, who felt he knew neither what to say or to do. "You believe that my Hugh tried to kill me. Oh, Claude." She began weeping, and Claude wished with all his being that he could close his eyes and will her out of his life.

"How, how," she cried. He closed his eyes to her tears.

"He was no good, Imogen," he heard Uncle Dorsey say. "Be glad he's gone."

Claude opened his eyes in time to see his sister fall to the ground in a dead faint. Dorsey was shaking his head over her.

"Now, look what you've done, Claude."

22

Twenty-four hours had passed since Hank had telephoned Caroline, and there had been no return call. Hank was determined not to let his mind create reasons for the slight. Caroline's failure to call him back could have any number of simple explanations. The summer season was beginning in Newport; days at the inn were bound to be busy. He resolved to concentrate on the case. Caroline was within his grasp. He was convinced he had a foothold back in her life, and he was determined to keep it.

In the meantime, it was back to his inquiry. Keisha had returned from Connecticut late the previous day, and now she sat before him.

"I don't know, Lieutenant," Keisha had said, "if this is what you want --"

"I want what you have found out, Sergeant."

"Well, then, it doesn't look good for evidence of Montgomery's guilt. I found the custodian who is responsible for cleaning the science wing. He identified Donald Montgomery right away from the photograph, said he saw him regularly."

"How regularly?"

"Once a week at least lately. The custodian, Jerry Santos, said he'd often see Montgomery early in the morning walking in the hall, and then in Mr. Dockings's classroom."

"Did Santos ever talk to Montgomery? He wasn't concerned that a stranger was always around the building?"

"Santos got the impression that Montgomery was a friend of Hugh Dockings. He isn't sure if Donald said so, or something else put the idea in his mind."

"Did Jerry Santos ever see Montgomery speak to Dockings?" Hank asked.

"No, but his duties got him out of the science wing before school started, and Dockings didn't come in until after Santos left."

"What about the supply room? Did Santos ever see Montgomery in there?"

Keisha shook her head. "No, the custodian seemed to understand because the chemicals were in there, he had to be careful cleaning the place. I guess that was drilled in to him by someone. So my guess is that Santos would have remembered, if Montgomery had been hanging around in there."

"Damn," Hank said. "And nobody else saw Donald Montgomery in the supply room?"

"No, Santos was the only one who recognized him from the photograph, and that has to be because he was around so early in the morning to open up the classrooms."

"And what did Montgomery do in the classroom?"

"That's the part I think you'll be disappointed to hear, Lieutenant. The custodian said that Montgomery just sat in one of the chairs... at one of the student's desks. Do you think it was his son's?"

"I don't know how he'd have any way of knowing that."

"Montgomery wasn't furtive, Lieutenant. I think that's important. He didn't seem to care whether the custodian saw him waiting there or not. I don't know, sir. I think it's a dead end."

"Ruth Montgomery said her husband just wanted to keep seeing Dockings," Hank admitted. "So we don't have anything?"

"Not on Montgomery, sir. None of the other teachers or custodians recognized his picture."

"Did you see Marilyn Hansen?" Keisha nodded. "And she couldn't make an identification from the photograph?" Keisha shook her head. "She must have been involved with Dockings when the accident happened; according to her, 1997 was after the time she started seeing him."

"She said she never saw the man in the photograph."

"All right. What about keys?"

"I know you wanted to find someone who missed their keys or lost their keys, but nobody came up on that, either." Keisha opened her notebook. "Ms. Hansen said she kept hers in her purse in her desk. The drawer locks, and she carried the key with her in her lab coat pocket. She wore that during the school day. The physics teacher, Tom Silva, said he always kept his keys, including the one to the supply cabinet, in his pants pocket. I believed him, sir. He looks like a very systematic man; he's the department chairman. The other science teacher, Jon Murphy, didn't have a key to that cabinet and said he was pretty sure he'd never been given one. Wouldn't have any reason to use it, he said."

"Oh? That's interesting."

"Here's actually what's the most interesting thing. Marilyn Hansen said that Hugh Dockings kept his keys in his top desk drawer. He had a set with only the keys he needed for school: his classroom key, some special computer lab key, the poison cabinet key, and the key to the faculty mail room, which apparently is kept locked so that students can't get in there. She said his habit was to put the keys in the top drawer of his desk so he could grab them... mostly, to go to the mail room during the day."

"Top drawer, huh? That's pretty accessible."

"You think somebody stole his keys?"

"Who? Donald Montgomery? Dockings didn't put the keys in there until school started in the morning."

"Yeah, Montgomery wouldn't have found Dockings's keys in the desk if he was nosing around the classroom early in the morning, before Dockings could put them there."

Hank spun his chair around and looked out the window. He had come across no keys that he could remember at Hugh's cottage in Waterville. He made a mental note to check the report on the contents of Hugh's pockets at the time of his death.

The rain had stopped, but the sky remained misty and desolate. Hank turned back to Keisha.

"What else can I do?" she asked. She saw he was frustrated.

"Here's a question: where do you buy hydrocyanic acid if you're an ordinary person? Why don't you try to buy some and see how difficult it is to do."

"Great," Keisha said. "I'd love to figure that one out."

"O.K., get started on it."

She had nodded and left him alone in the room where he had sat, re-reading Ben's notes on the interviews with the two barmen. Both had positively identified Montgomery as being a waiter at the Revels' party. That needed to be done, but it only confirmed a fact they'd already known. Donald Montgomery could not be eliminated completely from their investigation, and neither could Marilyn Hansen. But what evidence was going to link either to the crime? Everything so far was circumstantial. He needed some evidence that either suspect had been in possession of cyanide and had tampered with Hugh Dockings's red wine. He pulled out his file on the witnesses' interviews and spent some time with a yellow legal pad making a drawing of the section of the Revels' ballroom near the French doors and the infamous plant stand. He tried to place people in the area based on each other's recollection of who was standing near Hugh when he collapsed.

Dockings had joined Imogen and Claudine. Caroline had been standing with Dorsey, she facing the threesome. Claudine moved to talk to George March. Caroline saw Pamela; somebody remembered seeing Pamela talk to Claude. He rifled through the notes to find that reference. It had been March. Nobody remembered the waiter at this point, but Montgomery had admitted serving the last drink to Imogen.

As Hank studied the drawing once again this morning, he decided that the time had come to have everyone tell their versions of the murder scene again. Their first attempts had been soon after the death. The shock and excitement would hinder clear recollections. It was ten days since the event. Someone, in the retelling, could easily add something to the story not present in their original version. The detective had known this to happen before. A second account could be gotten from a witness with infinitely more detail than the first. Time had a way of doing that to the mind. The details would fill in as the witnesses' minds churned around what they had seen happen.

Ben was waiting in the squad room, drinking his coffee and eating an Egg McMuffin. Hank spied Janet Dawson across the room.

"Sergeant," he called. "Got anything for me?"

She crossed the room. Dawson was about his age, dark-haired and slim. She had forsaken the financial career for which she had trained to join the department. She was all business, frowning as she came to Ben's desk where he was in the act of draining the last of his coffee and pitching the fast food wrapping into the trash can

"Two points," she said to Ben. Hank was surprised she had a sense of humor.

"Have you looked at my files yet on the Dockings's case?" he asked.

"I'm getting ready to do it right now. I'll have something for you by the afternoon. I'm sorry about the delay, but time got away from me in Providence."

"That's O.K.. Today's good. I'm going out on some interviews, but I'll be back later. Leave everything on my desk, if I'm not back before you're ready to check out."

Ben was wiping his hands together and now he rubbed his fingers on his lips.

"Are you ready, Ben? I told Pamela Revel we'd be at Mon Plaisir at ten? Do you want to wash up, make yourself presentable? I'll be outside in the car."

Ben took the hint, and several minutes later they were in the car, winding their way across town to Bellevue Avenue. As they drove past the Tennis Hall of Fame, Hank thought he was beginning to detect the surging of the population which usually hit Newport this time of the year. The Friday of Memorial Day week-end was the traditional beginning of the summer season, but early weekdays in June were still calm compared to July and August, when the streets were mobbed morning, noon and night with vacationers.

The tourists in the crosswalk in front of the Newport Casino building were mostly middle-aged and older, in town to see the mansions, have lunch and to do some shopping.

The police car reached the Revels' green wrought iron gates, which had been left open. There was some kind of crest in the stone pillars to which the Mon Plaisir gates were attached, but Hank couldn't make out the details on the design. A small black sign at the base of the pillar announced that the house was Private Property. He followed the drive up to the front steps. There was no portico, only a simple, but large, oak front door, surrounded by carved stone. Hank parked the black unmarked car to the left of the steps and both policemen got out.

Mon Plaisir's yellow exterior looked pallid without the sun's rays to light it. Eight chimneys towered up from the green mansard roof. As he and Ben walked up the short flight of steps to the door, it was opened by Claude Revel. He must have been watching for them to arrive.

"Pamela's waiting for you, Lt. Nightingale," he said without greeting. He turned and they followed him through the house to the study.

Mon Plaisir was quiet this morning. Hank expected to see the figures of servants going about their duties in that noiseless way good domestics have, which makes them anonymous to the household's residents. But none seemed to be in this quarter of the house. Perhaps the Revels did not employ that many full-time staff.

In the study, Pamela was sitting in a tall, blue wingback chair. Behind her a large oil portrait of an eighteenth century nobleman watched the room. The bearded man's hard black eyes and black hair suggested one of the Revels, but Hank doubted that this was a genuine ancestor. Dorsey had said the original Claude had arrived in America penniless.

Pamela started as they entered the room, and Hank realized that by having a 24-hour period to contemplate the police visit, the couple had over-prepared themselves. He dismissed making the usual opening pleasantries and began.

"I need to ask you, Mrs. Revel, if you will go over with me what you remember of the afternoon of June fifth."

"I've already done that," Pamela said, as her husband was saying, "But, she's done that."

"Yes," he explained to both of them, "but I need to fill in some blanks. It would help me to clear things up if you could describe the day's events to me again."

"But, Claude," she said, turning to her husband. "If you tell him what we've worked out, I'm sure we don't have to bother doing this."

"Worked out?" Hank asked.

"Why that Dockings is the murderer." Pamela looked pleased with herself. Hank was reminded of Delilah the cat after she'd finished her hunting.

The banker did not look as smug as his wife, and Hank was curious why. Nevertheless he prompted Claude for the explanation. Claude reluctantly outlined his theory to Hank, ending by pointing out that Hugh, being drunk, would have very well accepted the glass of poisoned wine from Imogen.

"He had forgotten he had even poisoned it," Pamela announced triumphantly. "I don't suppose you can get any evidence, however."

"No, I suppose I can't," Hank said thoughtfully.

The possibility that Hugh had tried to kill Imogen had briefly crossed his mind at the beginning of the case. This was when he had first heard of the insistence by Imogen that her fiancé drink her wine and he had refused. Dockings had expected the waiter to return with a glass for him, and Hank had surmised that the time lapse could have given Hugh the opportunity to poison Imogen's wine.

"Why would Mr. Dockings want to kill your sister, Mr. Revel? What is your theory on his motive?"

"I don't know exactly," Claude said uneasily. "I suppose because he realized he couldn't go through the ceremony on the following day."

"Did you notice Mr. Dockings tamper with the wine, Mrs. Revel? You were standing nearby, I believe, at the time."

"Well... no, but I wasn't watching him and Imogen all the time."

"Is your daughter at home this morning?"

"No," Claude answered. "She's gone back to New York. Do you need to speak with her?"

"I would like to get her recollections of the time in question, also."

"Claudine was talking to me and George March," Pamela said testily. "She wasn't paying attention to Imogen or Hugh. But, I'll tell you who was. Caroline Kent. She was trapped with Uncle Dorsey, and it had been my intention to go over to rescue her. If Hugh hadn't fallen on the floor, I was just about to do that. Caroline was so bored. You could see it on her face. She kept looking around, and I'm sure she saw Hugh very well. He was right behind Uncle Dorsey."

"That's right," Claude said. "Will you need to interview my sister further, Lt. Nightingale?"

"Yes. I'm hoping one of the witnesses will remember something. Details often come back after time passes."

"I'm not sure that interviewing my sister at this time is a good idea, Lieutenant. My sister is not handling things well. Losing her fiancé, not being married after all, it's all taking its toll on her. She's not been herself, and I'm frankly worried about her. I've been trying to get her to have Dr. Stanton examine her."

"She doesn't want to see the doctor?"

"No. She can't see how Hugh's death is affecting her mental state. I'm not sure, in fact, that she ought to remain here on the estate. The memory of Hugh's death here is so strong."

"Where would your sister go?" Hank asked.

Claude sighed. Hank thought he looked genuinely worried. Was it for his sister? Or for some other member of his family?

"Personally," Claude said, "I would prefer if she took a rest cure. Martin Stanton has recommended some possibilities."

A rest cure. What was that a euphemism for? A sanitarium. A clinic in Switzerland. How far away would she be sent? Hank shifted his eyes to Pamela Revel. She was watching her husband and smiling. Once again he was reminded of Delilah. He had seen the same look on the cat's face as she had stood over her dead prey.

23

"I need to see you, Caroline."

The pleading voice at the other end of the telephone was an unhappy intrusion into what for Caroline Kent was already a perfectly horrible day.

The week-day maid Cheryl, feeling ill, had gone home after breakfast had been served. Louise had been unavailable indoors since mid-morning, gardening with George Anderson who was spending one of his half-days on the estate. The work inside the house had fallen to Caroline and Mattie, who was at this moment sulking at the kitchen sink and grumbling that "the Missus shouldn't be outdoors on such a cold, damp day."

Imogen's telephone call couldn't have come at a worse moment. Caroline gritted her teeth and tried to summon up concern for her friend. Her argument with Mattie was only on hold until Caroline returned to help with the baking, which Mattie had stubbornly insisted needed to be done today on top of everything else. Every counter surface was covered with bowls and pans. A dense haze of flour hung in the air.

"What's wrong, Imogen? You sound distressed." Caroline had no idea of what else to say. Imogen's moods continued to confound her.

"It's Claude," she cried out. Caroline felt the sting in her ear, caused by the loudness of Imogen's voice. "He said the most horrible thing to me yesterday at lunch. I couldn't sleep last night."

"How can I help, Imogen?"

"Please come over here. I need you."

"I can't leave the inn just now. I wish I could, but I can't."

"What about Louise? Can't she manage things for you?"

"Louise isn't here," Caroline said. It seemed an easier explanation than the exact truth.

"Oh," Imogen said, sounding surprised. "Where is she?"

"Can't you tell me what's the matter over the telephone, Imogen?"

"I said that Claude has told me something awful."

"Is anything wrong? Has something new happened?" Caroline tried to think of what her brother could say that would be *awful*. "Did you have an argument?" Caroline glanced at Mattie's unforgiving thin profile.

"No. Oh, I don't think I can even say the words."

"Do you want me to talk to Claude?"

"No, Caroline, that wouldn't be a good idea. Can't I see you? I could come to Kenwood."

"I'm very busy now, Imogen, and I have someone coming to see me in half an hour."

"I see," Imogen said, her voice growing cold and bitter. "I suppose you are seeing that policeman again."

"As a matter of fact, I'm expecting someone to look at our facilities because they want to have a private party in one of the mansions." Caroline felt herself becoming angry. The judgmental quality in Imogen's voice was upsetting. She wondered how Imogen would feel to know that Caroline had risked her mother-in-law's displeasure by seeing Imogen.

"Oh, very well. I'm sorry that I've bothered you."

Caroline suspected that the tone in Imogen's voice was affected, but she gave in. "You haven't bothered me at all," she said calmly. "I'm having a bad day, that's all. Things around here have gotten more hectic than normal today. One of the maids is sick, and I --"

"I said I'm sorry I bothered you, Caroline. Good-by."

"Wait, Imogen. I've an idea. Why don't you come for a late lunch tomorrow?"

The dial tone began to buzz, and Caroline knew that her caller hadn't heard her invitation. Slowly she walked back to the wall next to the sink and replaced the telephone receiver in its cradle. Mattie had begun slicing apples for the pies. She looked up petulantly as Caroline expelled a deep breath and compressed her lips. She was undecided as to whether she should call Claude or not. After another sigh, Caroline decided against it. Interfering was not something she judged that Claude would appreciate. It was all right with him when Caroline attended on Imogen. That kept her away from the rest of the Revels. Louise had said the Revels were selfish people, and that was a fact about them that Caroline was learning, also.

She heard Mattie grunting and looked up to see the cook pushing her rolling pin into an enormous mound of pie crust dough.

"Here, Mattie," Caroline said. "Let me help you."

"If you have the time, Mrs. Caroline," Mattie said. "If you're not too busy chatting on the telephone."

"No, Mattie, I'm finished on the phone for a while." She suddenly thought of Hank's call on the previous day. No message, he had said. It couldn't have been important, she thought as she reached for the stack of pie pans. Otherwise he'd have told Louise that he wanted her to call him back.

Despite his misgivings over Hank's talking to his sister, Claude Revel had declined to accompany him and Ben during their visit to the pavilion. After telephoning from the main house to announce their presence, Hank and Ben took the short walk across the estate and knocked on the door of Des Arbres. There was a long interval before Imogen opened the door. Her face was angry, and he knew he faced a difficult interview.

"This is inconvenient, Lt. Nightingale," she said. "I don't feel well."

Her face did not appear to be the face of a woman who was physically ill, but Hank remembered her brother's concerns about the state of her mind.

"It won't take long. I'm only here because of my need to speak to you concerning the investigation of Mr. Dockings's death." He tried to appear non-threatening. Above all he didn't want her to sense his growing personal antagonism toward her.

"Come in then." She went into the living room and took a seat on one of the upholstered chairs and stared ahead. Ben sat down on the high-backed sofa and took out his notebook. Hank remained standing and took the opportunity to look at the interior of the residence. It was an awkward room, and he found his attention drawn to the window where the view on this side was of a formal garden planted with a series of symmetrical flower beds.

"This is a lovely view, Miss Revel," he said pleasantly.

"Hugh didn't try to kill me," she said.

"I know that," he answered, turning back to the center of the room. "It doesn't make any sense."

"It doesn't?" she asked. He thought she looked surprised.

"I don't see a motive."

"Thank you," she said. "Hugh wouldn't kill me. He loved me."

Hank didn't think that was the reason, but he didn't share his conclusions with her. Let her go on thinking she was the attraction, not the money.

"You'll be pleased to learn that I am also close to eliminating the waiter from my list of suspects." He saw Ben look up in surprise. Hank hadn't known until he had said it that he didn't believe Donald Montgomery was the killer.

"Then you accept that he wasn't trying to kill Hugh?" Hank nodded. "Do you think now that someone was trying to kill me?"

175

"I am considering it," he said. Again, Ben looked askance, but Hank continued. "The poison, it seems to me, was introduced into the glass of wine while it sat on the plant stand. I'm asking everyone who could have seen the glass to remember exactly what and who they saw near it at the key time. I wonder... could you give us an account of what you did from the time you took the glass of red wine from the waiter's tray? It's very important."

"Yes," she said, "I can see that."

"Sergeant," Hank said. "Make sure you use the tape recorder for this."

Ben nodded and took the small, portable machine from his pocket. Hank waited until the tape was running.

"All right, Miss Revel. You can begin."

Imogen stared intently ahead as she began speaking in a quiet voice. "I took the glass from the tray. It was, as I already told you, the last glass of red wine. The waiter offered the tray to me first, and then to Claudine. She took a glass of champagne. Hugh, being the man, was served last. There were no more glasses of red wine on the tray." She paused, nervously looking at the tape recorder. "Then, let me see, I... no... Hugh asked the waiter to get him another glass of the red. That's when I said for him to take mine. But, the waiter said he would be right back."

"He said that. You're sure?" Hank asked.

"Oh, yes. But, of course, he didn't come."

"How soon did you put the glass on the plant stand?"

"I was holding it, telling Hugh to take it."

"And you didn't drink from it?"

"No, I didn't."

"Why?"

"Because I wanted him to take it. I said that."

"But you expected the waiter to return."

"But he didn't."

"No," Hank said thoughtfully. Montgomery had said he hadn't come back.

"Claudine was there. I was telling her about our going sailing in Greece. She wanted to know all about it, and I didn't have time to drink the wine if I was telling her all about it. Don't you see?" He nodded. "So I decided to put the glass down. Someone had come close to my hand and almost knocked the glass from it. We were near the French doors, and lots of people were going out onto the terrace. I believe they were smoking out there."

"Who was near you when you put the glass on the plant stand?"

"Uncle Dorsey and Caroline Kent were right there. Claudine, at that point, saw George March and said she needed to speak to him."

"Was Mrs. Kent facing you?"

"Yes, and she saw me put the glass down. I'm sure. She was watching me and Hugh. I don't know why, really. Now that I think of it, she seemed awfully interested in looking over at us."

"I was told your uncle is quite a talker, but tends to repeat his stories."

"I suppose, although I don't know how Caroline could have heard that many of them. She's not been in Uncle Dorsey's company all that much." She seemed to be thinking hard. "No, I think that's curious, now that I think of it. Why did she keep staring at us?"

"Did you see your brother and his wife in the vicinity?"

"Yes."

"Why don't you pick up the story at the point where you set the glass down?"

"All right. I put the glass there. It was precarious, and I had to push it against the base of the planter. I was afraid that the palm frond would touch the wine, and I wanted to make sure it didn't. Then, well, I just walked back to Hugh."

"How many steps was that?"

"A few. He was right there, you see."

"And he didn't speak to anyone while you were putting the glass down?"

"No."

"But wouldn't you have your back to him at that point?" He was remembering the drawing he had made on the yellow pad.

"Well, yes," she admitted. "But when I turned around, no one was there."

"All right. Continue."

"I don't know that there's much else. The waiter didn't return, and Hugh began to get irritable. I didn't want him to be upset at the party, so I went back to get the wine to give it to him." She took a handkerchief from her pocket and wiped her eyes. He remembered another one like it from their first interview. Both had her monogram with the large R at the center.

"And how soon was that?"

"I think a few minutes. Two, maybe three. That's all"

"What did you and Mr. Dockings talk about in the interval?"

"I don't remember."

"Try."

"I think it was mostly about the wine, the waiter, where was he. Oh, I remember. I asked Hugh if he'd had anything to eat. He looked as if he hadn't."

"And had he?"

"No. He was probably too nervous to eat. He had to meet all the family and Claude's friends from New York he'd insisted on asking. Plus everyone we know in Newport. Hugh was intimidated by that. He wasn't used to society."

"So you gave him your drink?" She nodded. "Did the glass look any different when you picked it back up?"

"No, of course not."

"And then Mr. Dockings drank the wine?"

"Yes." She said it so quietly that Hank doubted the tape had picked up the word.

"I see," Hank said. She was looking sad, and he decided to give her some time to recover herself. Finally he asked, "Do you remember seeing Marilyn Hansen during this time frame?"

"Marilyn?" She looked startled. "Marilyn," she repeated and frowned, squinting her eyes. "I think she had been smoking on the terrace. I did see her go out. But I'm not sure when she came in. She chain smokes, and I think I saw her going out several times that afternoon to have a cigarette. It's a disgusting habit, but she's too weak to quit."

"Do you think she's strong enough to try to kill you, Miss Revel?"

"It's possible," she said slowly. "Is there evidence to suspect her?"

"I suspect several people at this point, and she is one of them."

"What about Claudine?"

"Your niece?"

"Is she one of your suspects, Lt. Nightingale?"

"What would be her motive?"

"She has always hated me."

"Do you mind telling me the reason why?"

"She has always been resentful of me. She's not very bright, you know, and I told my brother that. He never should have given her the position at Syndicat Revel."

"Was she near the plant stand while the drink was there?"

Imogen thought hard.

"I think it was when I was asking Hugh if he had eaten anything, and he said he hadn't. I reminded him that there was smoked salmon, and he loved smoked salmon. He always complained when we were at a restaurant and the portion was small." Hank nodded. Suddenly she jerked forward.

"What is it, Miss Revel?"

"That's when I saw Claudine by that palm. I'm sure of it. I did see her go right up to it."

"And George March was still speaking with her?"

"No, he had left her. She was alone." A look of amazement came over her face. "Of course, that's when she did it. She was standing there, and I wondered why she didn't move. I saw her face. Now I understand why she looked like she wanted to laugh. She thought she was finally getting rid of me."

Ben had driven him to the Kingston train station to catch the Amtrak train to New York City. Hank would arrive in Penn Station later that same evening, spend the night at a hotel, and see Claudine Revel and George March at the bank's offices first thing on the following morning.

His sergeant had been disappointed not to accompany him on the trip, but Hank was reluctant to authorize expenses in Manhattan for two. He had been shocked at the price of a second class hotel room. Meals, he knew, would be equally expensive. Besides, he preferred to travel alone. Listening to Ben's chatter on the four-hour train trip would have exhausted him. Jean had been nagging him to take a night course with her at the local adult ed program, and Ben was having none of it. Unfortunately he couldn't explain this to his wife, only to his lieutenant.

The decision to go to Manhattan had been a quick one on Hank's part. Imogen's memory of Claudine's going near the wine glass while it sat on the plant stand had to be verified. Both Claude's daughter and George March needed to be questioned on Imogen's testimony.

"I'm not satisfied by this whole business of Claudine Revel's talking to her aunt to learn all the details of her honeymoon," he had said to Ben in the car. "Doesn't it strike you as odd that this young woman can't stand her aunt, yet makes cocktail party small talk with her?"

"I agree," Ben said. "It's fishy. She could have been hanging around Imogen to wait for an opportunity to poison her drink... that is, if she is the murderer."

"You had her on your original list of suspects."

"I did. And I'm still tied to money as the motive. And she fits in with that."

"Well, I'm going to talk to our young banker. She needs to explain this very thoroughly."

"What about March?"

"He had the best view, I'm convinced, of the whole scene. I think if I can get him to re-tell his narrative, some of the missing pieces will fall into place. Did Claudine and he part company before the murder? That's the key right now."

"March told me they didn't."

"He might not have realized that Claudine had left only a minute or so before. If she left George, dropped the poison into the glass... Imogen picked it up, and Hugh drank it immediately... well, that wasn't much time. The poison took effect almost as soon as it went down Dockings's throat. Miss Revel said that Dockings hadn't eaten anything at the party. Remember Dr. Peters said that cyanide is absorbed faster on an empty stomach."

They had reached the old brown and yellow Victorian station at Kingston, and Hank was grabbing his overnight bag from the back seat. He still had to buy his ticket, and the train was due in less than five minutes.

"Thanks, Ben. I'll call you in the morning."

As he walked toward the building, the detective was thinking of Caroline and how he would come back tomorrow afternoon. He would have time to see her for an interview and ask her to tell her version of the murder scene again. It was only once Hank was in his seat in the crowded train, and it was pulling away from the station, that he remembered he'd forgotten to go to the police station to pick up Janet Dawson's report.

24

The photograph of Reed on Caroline's bedside table was the first thing she saw every morning when she opened her eyes. It was a favorite one, a snapshot taken while they were picnicking in Central Park during their last spring together. Reed's blond hair was combed back from his forehead in the way she thought made him look handsome, and his blue grey eyes held her favorite look of thoughtfulness. This morning, like most, she picked it up and held it in her hands, caressing the cold silver frame.

How she missed him still. The feeling never left her. There were days when her heart ached for his nearness. She still dreamt of him. Only two nights ago she had dreamed that he had called her on the telephone to complain that he hadn't heard from her for so long. In the dream she was touring with a play, and she had been in a strange hotel room, listening to his voice as he encouraged her to call him more frequently while she was away. She did want to call him, she had told him. And she hadn't been sure why she had been so negligent. It was a frightening dream, and she had awoke with a start, her heart pounding.

Caroline replaced the photograph on the table. She got up and reached for her robe. As always, she had to get working. There was no time to sort things out.

She had asked Molly Casey, the third of her part-time maids, to come in today to help in case Cheryl was still out sick. Two couples were arriving from Philadelphia later that afternoon, and they had requested dinner for the day of their arrival. Caroline would have to organize that order with Mattie. Perhaps Molly would help in the kitchen. She was middle-aged, and her disposition was pleasant. There was little the cook ever found to criticize about her. It would give Louise another day in the garden. She had been so enthusiastic when she had come in from her work yesterday. The perennial bed was getting in shape, and the gift of one more day to work there would be appreciated by her mother-in-law. Today's weather was expected to be sunny and warm, and gardening would do Louise a world of good. It would also take her mind away from Imogen, and Caroline could use some relief in that quarter.

The hard rush of the shower hit her shoulders. Caroline held her head back to wet her hair and felt the adrenalin flowing through her body as she massaged in the sweet-smelling shampoo. How good she felt to be alive this morning.

"Ben, it's me," Hank said when he was finally connected to the familiar voice of his sergeant. "I'm in Penn Station. The train's in fifteen minutes. Have Keisha pick me up in Kingston. We get in at 4:36."

He turned down Ben's offer to come for him. "I want to go on to Kenwood to see Caroline. You go home and have dinner with the family. Keisha can take care of me."

In answer to Ben's questions on his morning's interviews he gave a quick summary, none of it very good. Both Claudine and George March had disputed Imogen's claim that the two had parted company before Hugh's falling to the floor.

"I distinctly remember saying to Claudine, 'what is the matter with Dockings? He seems to have collapsed'." George March's rather priggish face had looked dumbfounded as he related the scene to the detective earlier that morning.

"Oh, no, Lieutenant," George protested, his black eyes disappearing into his fleshy face as he frowned. "Claudine and I were side by side at the time. She even said to me that she wasn't surprised to see Dockings staggering. She had seen him drinking a lot and thought he was drunk again." March had clicked his tongue in that way which reminded Hank of Dorsey Revel, as if everything in the world was set out for his own amusement, not because any other human being had any stake in the matter.

As she told her version of the story, Claudine's account matched her cousin's. She remembered telling George that she thought Hugh Dockings was drunk and had passed out. "He drank like a fish. The whole family noticed it."

It had been difficult to interview Claudine. She had wanted to know who had described her as going near the plant stand while the glass of wine had been placed there. Hank thought she guessed that it was her aunt.

"March alibis her, Ben," Hank concluded into his phone. "I can't break his story." He realized he had been watching the overnight bag at his feet, afraid to take his eyes from it lest it be stolen in the busy station. He suddenly felt like a rube in the big city.

"What about the fact that she was talking to Imogen Revel in the first place?" Ben asked. "How did she explain that long conversation about the honeymoon?"

"She had an answer for that, too. It seems she had promised her father she would be nice to her aunt during the party. She was asking about the sailing because she is a sailor herself and could make polite small talk about the arrangements for the holiday in Greece."

"Sounds too pat to me," Ben said. "That young woman is too clever by half."

"Well, I couldn't find an opening in her statement." He was thinking that once off his home turf, he lacked his usual cleverness to penetrate the veracity of a witness's account. He couldn't let go of the fact that both March and Claudine had handled him expertly.

Perhaps it had been a mistake to see them at the family's bank. That setting had put them one ahead of him.

"I just want to get home now. The answers to this case are in Newport. I don't know why, but that's what I've been feeling. I'm going to tackle Caroline as soon as I get back. She had a view, front and center, of Hugh, and we'll see if she remembers anything about seeing Claudine near the wine glass on the plant stand."

Hank was ready to end the call. He had forgotten to buy the newspapers, and he wanted to get some before it was time to find the gate for his train.

"Oh, one more thing, Lieutenant," Ben said. "Janet Dawson's report is still on your desk. The one about all those financial files you brought back from Hugh Docking's house in Waterville."

"Why don't you look at it when you have some time, Ben? Let me know when I get back if there's anything in it that looks promising."

Hank looked around for the closest news stand. He also wondered if he had time to pick up a sandwich. The food on the train yesterday evening had been especially unpalatable, and the least he could get out of this trip was a decent lunch. Across the concourse he spied a sign which tempted him: *New York Deli Sandwiches*. Pastrami on rye, he was thinking, with one of those big pickles that crunched when you ate it. He thought he'd even get a bag of potato chips.

"I can think better on a full stomach," he told himself. "And I've got about four and a half hours to think about this case."

With both Cheryl and Molly reporting for work, Caroline was feeling free in the middle of the day to telephone Imogen. The phone was answered on the second ring. Imogen's voice sounded trembling as she readily accepted Caroline's suggestion that she would come by the pavilion later in the afternoon.

"I don't feel at all like myself today, Caroline. Martin Stanton called this morning. He wants me to have a check-up, and I know what that means. Claude has convinced him that I should be put away. I'm so frightened. Can they take me away if I don't want to go?"

"Is that what Claude said which upset you so?"

"No, that was even worse. He said horrible things to me about Hugh."

"I'm sorry, Imogen. I will come as soon as I can finish up my work."

The guests she had been expecting arrived right after lunch, and Caroline was able to get them settled in their rooms and confirm their dinner reservations by 2:30. Molly was in the kitchen with Mattie, and Cheryl was finishing up the downstairs vacuuming. Louise was gardening, happily digging and planting. The coast was clear for Caroline to visit Imogen when the inn's telephone rang.

She took the call in her office. It was a request for a brochure and an inquiry about some dates in July. When she was finished, Caroline turned on her computer to check her e-mail. There were more requests for information about the Inn at Kenwood Court, and Caroline took about forty-five minutes logging in the names of the prospective customers on to her mailing list and making up the packets she normally sent out in answer to requests for brochures. She had no system quite yet for doing this efficiently, and she was dismayed when she looked at the clock and saw that it was almost 3:30. She would need to leave immediately if she wanted to be back to help with the supper preparation.

When Caroline arrived at the pavilion, she was stunned to see Imogen Revel. Her thick dark hair was especially untidy, and her black eyes were set in deep purple pouches. She looked in need of sleep.

"There you are, Caroline. I was afraid you weren't coming at all. You're late." She grabbed onto Caroline's arm and pulled her inside the house.

"I came as soon as I could get away, Imogen," Caroline said, gingerly releasing herself from her friend's unusually firm hold. "You need rest, Imogen. Why don't I sit with you while you lie down for a while?"

"I can't sleep. Claude has been so awful, and it's made me so afraid. He wants me to take pills." In the living room an open bottle of red wine and two glasses rested on a tray. One of the glasses had some wine in it. Caroline looked at the bottle and saw it was half full of the merlot which Imogen had purchased for the cellar she planned to start for Hugh after their marriage. "Claude wants me to go away. I know that's what he wants now."

"This is your home now. Claude gave the pavilion to you. He can't take that away from you." Could he? She hoped there weren't legal maneuvers at his disposal. Marriage to an attorney had taught her there were always avenues to be tried.

Imogen poured Caroline a glass of wine and filled her own almost to the top.

"I don't feel like I know anything anymore," she said. "It's all because of the way I have been treated my entire life. Claude is so evil toward me. And Pamela has never wanted me around. She treats Mon Plaisir as if it were her own personal property. As if it didn't belong to our family. Great-grandfather Revel built the house, as if she didn't know. It is a Revel house."

"Pamela isn't a Revel," Imogen now exclaimed, her eyes darting wildly around the room. "You know she was the one who talked Claude into giving Claudine her name. There's never been a Claudine Revel in our family."

"Yes, Imogen," Caroline murmured.

"And I am still a Revel. Now that Hugh is gone, I shall always be a Revel. And I know you're right, Caroline. Claude can't take my house from me." She paused to catch her breath. "My brother doesn't love me, not like Hugh did. Hugh wanted to take care of me. He knew how upset I was about the family's money always going to the male of the line." She picked up the glass of wine. Her eyes narrowed. "And Claude's not going to get my money, either. Now that I have some I'll be free of him." She drank greedily, swallowing half of the contents of the glass.

"What did Claude say to you, Imogen? What is it that you couldn't tell me on the telephone?" Imogen was drinking too much, and Caroline hoped that despite her protestation, Imogen had not taken any pills with the wine.

"Only that Hugh wanted *me* dead."

"That's what Claude believes happened on the day of the murder?" Imogen nodded.

"Claude and Pamela think Hugh tried to kill me with the poisoned wine. Have you ever heard of anything so ridiculous?" She laughed in a silly, nervous way.

"But, that's impossible. How could Hugh have poisoned the wine? And why? He knew *he* was going to drink it."

"That's right, Caroline. And I was with him. I would have seen him... you know I would have seen him do it."

"Well, then, it's a mistake. What Claude said, it can't be true. He must be confused." She was dismayed that Claude would introduce such an idea to his sister in her present state of distress.

"No. You would have seen him do it, Caroline. I told that policeman that Claudine did it, but he never believes me," she said in a childish tone. "But I know you didn't see Hugh touch the wine. You didn't, did you?" She looked suddenly fearful.

"I wasn't looking at you and Hugh all the time."

"But, you were. I saw you. You weren't paying any attention to Uncle Dorsey. What on earth was he talking about? Do you remember?"

"Oh, the usual stories," she answered in a vague way. She couldn't tell Imogen of the comments he had made about her and Claudine, or the sailboat purchase, which he criticized. And she couldn't bring herself to share with Imogen the things which Dorsey had said about Reed's working at Syndicat Revel.

"Stories about the family?"

"Yes."

"What stories?"

In her thoughts Caroline was beginning to see the picture of the ballroom on the day of the murder. She could make out Imogen and Hugh. They were talking, only she couldn't hear what they were saying. Only the sound of Dorsey Revel's voice was clear. Caroline concentrated her mind on Hugh's hand. There was no drink in it. She focused on Imogen's hands. They, too, were empty.

"About me, Caroline?" Imogen prodded. "What did Dorsey say about me and Hugh?" Her voice was suddenly irritating. "He was against my marrying Hugh, wasn't he?"

"I don't think... he mentioned you." Caroline's mind was seeing the party scene continue. "Dorsey was talking about my father-in-law." *Louise was such a saint through everything...such a lovely woman.* But now Caroline saw something else: that Imogen had started to walk toward her while Dorsey was talking.

No, not towards Caroline, but in the direction of a plant stand along the wall by the French doors. Dorsey was looking around for Louise. Caroline remembered seeing Imogen pass her. Caroline had intended to smile at her, but Imogen's attention was fixed on a glass of red wine sitting on the stand in the shelter under the palm. *Always so loyal to Frederick.* In the sunny ballroom, Imogen was reaching out her right hand. On her left wrist a small gold purse dangled from underneath the sleeve of the yellow silk dress she was wearing.

"Dorsey must have said something about me, Caroline. Think. Try to remember what you saw. It's important to me for you to remember. I'll feel better when I know."

Caroline turned and looked right at Imogen. She wondered whether her face was giving away the new image that was slowly coming into focus in her mind.

25

The hearty aroma of the cooking casserole of beef bourguignon greeted Louise when she opened the door to the kitchen. Molly was absorbed in scrubbing the massive wooden table in the center of the room, while Mattie was deep into the interior of the big steel refrigerator, putting away what was left from the meal preparations.

"My that is a delicious smell," Louise said. She realized how hungry her work in the outdoors had made her. A cup of tea and some food would be welcome. Mattie closed the refrigerator door and appraised her mistress with a hard eye.

"You look a proper mess, Missus. I'd best run your bath."

"I think I'll eat something first. Have you had your tea this afternoon?"

"No, Mrs. Kent," Molly answered. "Let me put the kettle on. There's some of the apple pie, and also that fruit tart. Or would you like a sandwich?" She was immediately busy, filling the kettle and placing it on the stove.

"I'll bring you up a tray," Mattie said briskly. "Molly can make it up, and I'll start the tub running --"

"I'll take a shower. I want to wash my hair."

"A bath would be better," Mattie said. "You can soak."

"Where is Caroline?" Louise asked.

190

"Oh, she went out," Molly said. "About an hour or so ago."

"Where?" Louise asked.

"Do you want the pie or the tart?" Mattie asked.

"I'll have some of the apple pie."

"I think she was stopping at Miss Revel's house."

"What?" Louise asked. She knocked into Mattie's arm as she reached for the pie safe. "Miss Revel. Did you say she was going to see Imogen Revel?"

"I think so," Molly said, conscious of the sound of alarm which had come into Louise's voice. "A woman telephoned after Mrs. Kent left and said she was Miss Revel and *where was she, she was supposed to be here already*, something like that. I thought she was expecting Mrs. Kent." Molly was eyeing Louise carefully.

"Oh, dear," Louise said. Mattie had the tea tray out and was assembling dishes for it. Louise felt leaden in her body. She was tired and hungry and wanted to be clean and fed. "And what time did Caroline leave?" She looked at Mattie, but the cook shook her head.

"I think it was about four o'clock," Molly offered cautiously. "We were making the vegetables. Remember, Mattie?"

"She went off. That's all I know, Missus. Here's your tea steeping."

Louise looked at the kitchen telephone. She briefly considered calling Caroline at Des Arbres with some excuse for her to return home. As she debated what to do, the sound of the front doorbell clanged in the kitchen.

"I'll go," Louise said. She hoped in an uncertain way that it might be Caroline returning. Perhaps her arms were full, and she couldn't open the door on her own.

"In that condition?" Mattie was taking off her apron. "I'll go."

Rather than waste time by arguing, Louise followed the cook to the front door. Hank Nightingale and the female sergeant who had been part of the murder investigation stood on the doorstep.

"Good afternoon, Louise," Hank said. "May we come in? I need to speak to Caroline." Louise stepped back, and the two police officers entered the spacious foyer. "Do you remember Sgt. McAndrews?"

"Yes, how do you do?" The sergeant nodded.

"Your tea's ready, Missus," Mattie said. "I can show them into Mrs. Caroline's office to wait for her."

"She's not at home?" Hank looked disappointed. Louise shook her head. "When do you expect her?"

"Shortly, I hope," Louise answered. "We think she may have gone to see Imogen Revel."

"Oh," Hank said. "For any particular reason?"

"I'm not sure," Louise said.

"I'd like to be sure"" Hank said as his cell phone rang.

"Yes, Ben." He listened for several seconds as his face grew grave.

"What is it, Caroline? Something's wrong. I can see it in your face." Caroline hadn't noticed her moving, but it seemed suddenly as if Imogen were sitting nearer to her on the sofa than she had been previously.

"Oh, Imogen, I'm so sorry. I was thinking... it's something I... think I saw." Her voice trailed off. She was afraid to say any more.

"You saw?" Imogen asked warily. "Saw where? Where?"

"It's the memory of the party. I thought I hadn't seen... but perhaps I was too preoccupied at the time."

"Did you see Claudine? Were you watching her?"

"No, not Claudine."

Imogen took hold of Caroline's wrist. Her grasp was strong, and Caroline put her other hand on top to loosen the older woman's grip. Imogen wouldn't let go. "You're frightening me, Caroline. Stop. Do you hear me?" Caroline disliked the sound of the grating voice. Imogen twisted her wrist tightly. Caroline was in pain, and she closed her eyes, and that was a mistake because the scene on the afternoon of Hugh's death came back into sharp focus.

Dorsey's voice again. *And Reed was still in law school.*

That's when she had seen Imogen coming straight toward her. Imogen had her right hand on her own left wrist, just as she was holding Caroline's wrist now. No, not the wrist, but opening the small gold purse hanging from her left wrist.

Caroline opened her eyes and looked at Imogen. Her face was growing purple, and her eyes were glowing now with heat and intensity.

"I ought to go, Imogen. Please." She tried to pull back her hand, but the larger, stronger one of Imogen's still held on to her like a vise. Caroline tried to stay calm. "We have guests in for dinner tonight, Imogen. There's no staff other than Louise. I'll have to do the dinner service myself."

"Hugh loved me, Caroline. He wouldn't kill me."

"I know that, Imogen," Caroline said evenly. "And I really must go now."

When Hank finished speaking with Ben, he knew he had to explain everything to Louise. He also knew that he had to go to Mon Plaisir immediately.

"It's all right here, Lieutenant," Ben had said, "in Janet's report on those files. Staring us right in the face the whole time."

"I've been very stupid, Ben."

"It's the motive all right. Just like I said."

"Hank?" Louise's voice penetrated his thoughts. "What's happened? Has anything happened to Caroline?"

"I think we'd better go over to the Revels, Sgt. McAndrews."

"Is everything all right? Please, Hank, you've got to tell me what's happening."

"Then you'd better come with us, Mrs. Kent. We can talk on the way. You'd better put a coat on. It's getting chilly, and you look as if you've just come in from the outdoors."

Keisha heard the hard steel in Nightingale's voice.

"I'll start the car, Lieutenant."

Caroline had finally managed to undo Imogen's hand from her wrist.

"I really must go, Imogen. Why don't I come back to see you tomorrow? You must try to get some rest now."

"I need some air." Imogen's voice was thick. "My head is foggy. I've had too much wine. I haven't been eating."

"Come outside. You can clear your head."

When they got to the front door, Caroline looked in the direction of the main house where she had left her car in the drive.

"Why don't I take you up to the main house? You can get something to eat there."

"I don't want to go there. Let's walk this way."

Before Caroline could answer, Imogen turned toward the path which led to the gate at the side street bordering the grounds. Caroline saw her opportunity to go the other way toward her car when she realized that she had left her purse and her car keys inside the pavilion. As she hesitated, Imogen turned back.

"Come with me, Caroline. Don't leave me. I don't feel well. Stay with me."

"I don't have time for a walk, Imogen. I must get back to Kenwood."

"We can walk on the Cliff Walk. You can go home that way."

"But, my car --"

"I'll have one of the servants return it later this evening. You won't need it. You said you have to stay in to serve the dinner tonight. You have guests at the inn."

It was still daylight, and there would be people on the Cliff Walk. Caroline looked in the direction of the wrought iron gate.

"Here, Caroline. Let me take your arm," Imogen said, and once again Caroline felt the hard clasp lock on to her wrist. She wanted to say she needed her cell phone, but something in the way Imogen was looking at her made her swallow her words.

"Claude? Whose car is that in the drive?" Pamela was looking through the tall windows of the morning room. Claude had been looking for his wife and had been surprised to find her here in the late afternoon. He joined her at the window.

"It looks like Caroline Kent's old BMW."

"What is it doing here?"

"She's undoubtedly visiting with Imogen." His wife was staring at the car with a curious expression on her face. "Caroline seems interested in befriending Imogen lately. We ought to be grateful. It takes some of the pressure off of us, my dear."

"Oh, I don't mind her seeing Imogen," Pamela said, turning from the window. "I don't suppose you've heard from Martin Stanton today."

"As a matter of fact I did." He saw the look of hope coming into her face, and he spoke quickly. "No, nothing's changed."

"She's got to go away."

"It will be tricky without her permission."

"What on earth is money for, Claude, if it can't buy us out of this?"

"Pamela, she is my sister. I've got to be careful with her. What will the rest of the family think if she just disappears one day?"

"Your precious family again. What about my sanity? You said you would do something about Uncle Dorsey, but I notice that when I come down in the morning, he's right there, staring at me across the breakfast table. Now, you say that Imogen is not going to be under this roof, and I want you to keep your promise."

"She's in the pavilion."

"She won't go back to teaching. I don't like it, Claude. She can't live here all the time. You promised you'd do something," she repeated.

"I need more time. You've seen the state she's in. It won't be long before she'll break down. It's been coming for years."

"And this murder? The police won't leave us alone."

Claude shook his head. "That lieutenant is no fool. He's going to keep digging until he finds something."

"And what will he find, Claude?"

Claude stroked the back of his own neck. He was feeling the tension, and he rubbed the tight muscles vigorously. "Please, Pamela," he implored. "We mustn't panic. We've got to wait things out. Everything will go smoothly, if we stay in control of the situation."

"That damned Hugh Dockings!" Pamela exclaimed. "I knew when I first saw him he was trouble. I told you, Claude. Last Christmas. I told you that it was a mistake to encourage Imogen's attachment to him."

"I thought... I thought at the time it would be good for her."

"To have a man? She didn't know what to do with a man."

"I know. I see it was a mistake."

"A mistake? The man is dead, Claude, and the police want to know who killed him."

"I know, I know," he said. He straightened his back and moved toward her. He felt her stiffen as he touched her arm.

"Claudine called a little while ago."

"She did?" He was surprised his daughter had not asked to speak with him.

"The police questioned her this morning. And George, also."

"In New York City? Who?"

"Your clever lieutenant."

"He went down to New York? Why? Why wasn't I told about all this earlier?"

"When he interviewed her yesterday, Imogen told Lt. Nightingale that she saw Claudine poison the glass of wine which killed Hugh Dockings." Her voice was surprisingly calm.

"No! No!" Now Claude was in a rage. He dropped his hand from his wife's shoulder and started toward the door. He must do something. "I'll speak to Imogen at once. She can't say those things. I'll stop her. By God, I'll stop her now. She's gone too far."

"Wait, Claude," he heard Pamela say in a cold voice. "It may be too late."

"What?" he asked, turning back. She was staring out the window again, her interest in the front drive returning. "What's out there?"

"The police, Claude. They're back."

He rushed to the window as the white and black patrol car pulled to a stop. He saw the tall figure of Hank Nightingale emerge from the front passenger side. He was looking at Caroline Kent's car. Claude put his head in his hands. He had a feeling that he couldn't prevent what was coming. No amount of Revel money would cover that up.

26

The wind off the ocean was strong, and Caroline shivered when she and Imogen reached the Cliff Walk. The sound of the lapping ocean waves was constant, a heavy pull of the surf onto the rocks below. Caroline looked out at the angry waves and wondered if a storm was coming up. The sky was blue, but clouds were forming in the easterly direction.

There were only a few people taking their exercise on the path. Almost no tourists were in evidence; it was becoming the dinner hour. Caroline looked among the people they passed, wondering if any of them noticed the two women marching along, the tall, older one holding onto the younger one with a firm grasp. It was almost as if Imogen had forgotten that Caroline was by her side, being pulled along by the other woman's determined gait.

They had passed The Breakers, navigating the steps which evened out the contour of the pathway there. They continued on, beyond The Breakers, passing the path which led to Kenwood. The house looked far away and quiet to Caroline. Imogen took no notice of it. Soon the Cliff Walk became uneven where the restoration had not yet reached the southern leg of the walk. Here the path was mainly dirt, and the rain of the previous day had left mud and puddles in their route. Few visitors to the Cliff Walk decided to venture past this point.

Imogen ignored the mud and strode into it. How far was she going? Caroline tried stepping around a puddle, and she felt her left ankle miss its footing in a low spot hidden under the brown water. A sudden hitch caused her foot to fall down deeper than she had anticipated. Stumbling, she would have fallen had not Imogen been holding on to her.

"What's the matter, Caroline?"

"Can we stop for a minute?"

There was a narrow sandy stretch of beach below, under the rocks. Imogen started toward the edge of the path, as if to descend to the sand.

"Please, Imogen. Let's stop right here. I think I've hurt my ankle. I can't climb over those rocks. Let me stop."

Imogen turned and Caroline could feel her breath on her cheek. There was the scent of the wine mixed with an old, sour smell.

"Let's sit then," Imogen said. There were some large rocks, worn flat by the water of centuries, beyond the muddy path. Imogen pulled Caroline down onto one, and she felt the hard wet of the slippery surface as it touched the back of her pants.

Caroline flexed her ankle gingerly. She felt it tweak, but there was no pain. They were all alone. Caroline wondered, as she studied their position, what was best to do next. The turn-off to Kenwood was on the other side of these rocks. She thought of the muddy path and the treacherous rocks which needed to be navigated to get there.

"Hugh loved me, Caroline. Why doesn't anyone believe that?"

"I believe it." Caroline took some deep breaths of the ocean air to rejuvenate herself.

"No one else did. The whole family thought he married me for the Revel money."

"But he didn't," Caroline said firmly. "He did love you, Imogen."

"And he loved me," Imogen said stubbornly. "When I said it was his duty as my husband to provide for me in case anything happened to him, he said, of course he would. He wanted me to be taken care of."

"And he did, didn't he, Imogen?"

"Yes," she said proudly. "It was so easy for him to do. He hadn't thought of the way, but I had."

"How did he do it?"

"It's a million dollars, you know. A whole million. That's what I wanted."

"Was it insurance on his life?"

"Claude is a millionaire. And Claudine will be one, too. She's getting all the Revel money from her father. I wanted to have the same."

"Did Hugh insure his life for a million dollars, Imogen?" Imogen didn't answer. She was crying small tears, which dripped down her cheek. "He insured his life and made you the beneficiary, didn't he?"

"I never thought I'd have any money that was just mine. I wanted the Revel money to be mine, but I was the girl, and Revels didn't leave money to girls. That's what they told me."

"And then you found out that Claudine was going to inherit."

"It wasn't fair! No Revel woman had ever gotten their own money. Claude made his will and was giving everything to Claudine. She would get Mon Plaisir and everything." Imogen grabbed Caroline's shoulders. "I deserved some of my family's money, too. I wanted to be a banker like Claude. I asked my father to let me go to college to study to be a banker."

"He said you couldn't," Caroline murmured.

"He said girls didn't do such things. That's when my mother talked him into letting me train to be a teacher. That's what she said proper girls did!"

Imogen shook Caroline, all her rage diverted to her friend.

"I was always smarter than Claude. I could do anything better than he could!" She was shouting now, and Caroline looked in vain for someone to notice the commotion.

"My father wouldn't leave me any money, and Claude is leaving Claudine money. It isn't fair," she cried out.

"Hugh was fair to you, Imogen, wasn't he?" Caroline slowly tried to put weight on her ankle, pressing it against a rock to test its agility. Imogen was pushing against Caroline's body now with all her might. "Hugh left you his money," she said as she tried to absorb the hard thrust of Imogen's strength.

"We made our wills," Imogen said, a glint of light coming into her eyes. "Claude said we should. Funny, isn't it? Claude wanting me to make my will. He made Ned help us. What do you suppose he thought? I don't have any money of my own."

"But Hugh would."

"Yes, but not at the beginning. It was the fact that he was retiring. That was important, don't you see?"

The dampness under the rock had seeped into the fabric of Caroline's pants and felt cold against her flesh.

"When he retired he could take care of everything I wanted. It wouldn't cost him much. The school offered him the option of converting his group policy. Hugh was so grateful when Claude gave me Des Arbres and I told him we could have a boat, too, that he knew it was only fair for him to do something for me."

"Where is Mrs. Kent?" Hank shouted as he met Claude and Pamela Revel on the steps of the mansion. During the quick drive over, Louise had repeatedly tried to reach Caroline's cell phone, but there was no answer.

"Visiting Imogen," Claude answered. "I haven't --"

His words were lost as Hank raced around the house and toward the pavilion. He was barely aware of Louise's voice calling after him and Claude's attempts to speak to her.

Hank reached the open door of Des Arbres two steps ahead of Keisha, who dashed past him and into the house. A quick search of both floors revealed that the house was empty. Hank came back outside and met Claude and his wife, along with Louise Kent, about to enter the pavilion. Keisha was scanning the lawn.

"No one's here," Hank said sharply. "Do you have any idea where they went?"

"I can't imagine," Claude began.

"Caroline may have taken the path on the Cliff Walk to return to Kenwood," Louise said.

"But she left her car," Pamela said.

Hank took the phone from his jacket pocket and punched in the telephone number of Kenwood. He tapped his foot impatiently while he waited for an answer. Finally he heard the cook's querulous voice.

"Hello," she said. "This is Kenwood."

"Is Mrs. Kent there? Caroline Kent I want. This is Lt. Nightingale. It's very important."

"No," came the answer.

"Are you sure?"

Mattie was, and Hank began giving instructions that he was to be called back immediately if she came in. After he gave the cook his number, Louise grabbed the instrument from his hands.

"Mattie, this is Louise speaking. Can you hear me?" She paused, and then said loudly, "Did you write down that telephone number?" She waited for the answer. "You must call it as soon as Caroline comes in. Go to the back window and watch for her. She's coming up the path from the Cliff Walk." She paused again, listening, and then said, "Thank you, Mattie. I know you will do it. It's a matter of life and death."

Claude began speaking again, sputtering questions, but Hank ignored him. He looked at Keisha.

"We'll go to the Cliff Walk. How do we reach it from here, Mr. Revel?"

Claude pointed to the gate. He looked frightened now. "The street there runs into the Cliff Walk." Hank began running as

Claude shouted after them, "I need to know what is happening, Lieutenant."

Keisha was in terrific shape, and he was trying to keep up with her. They couldn't stop. Time was precious.

They ran down the sidewalk, onto the road. At the Cliff Walk intersection, they turned right, jostling a couple with two small children and a large dog being led on a leash. Hank swerved around to avoid colliding with the dog.

"Hey, watch it," the man with the dog yelled.

Hank didn't even look back. He was clutching his phone, praying it would ring, but the phone stayed silent as they passed The Breakers.

At the path to Kenwood, Keisha began running toward the house. Hank called her back. "Wait," he said. He hit his redial button and waited for the answer.

"Mattie, it's Lt. Nightingale again. Is Caroline back?" Swearing, he ended the call. "She's not there."

Keisha came back to his side, and they looked in both directions. "Are you sure this is where they were coming? Why didn't Mrs. Kent go to her house? Do you think she's somewhere on the grounds?"

Hank thought hard. The right answer to that question was more important than any hunch he'd ever had in his life. He looked ahead. The Cliff Walk path seemed deserted.

"I think they went this way," he said.

They sat in silence on the rock. Imogen's plain face looked miserable. Caroline tried to look at her while she continued to flex her ankle and move her arms. She needed to feel that her body was strong again. The cold air was going right through the thin T-shirt which she had put on earlier when the day was warm.

"Did you enjoy being married, Caroline?" Imogen asked.

"Yes. I was happy."

"I wasn't sure if I would like it. I wondered how it would be to see Hugh... well, you know." Imogen's face reddened. "I never have had... a man's love."

"I'm sorry, Imogen. You've missed a lot of happiness in your life." Caroline put her palms on the rock. They slid. She needed something to help with her balance if she were to be able to stand up.

"I'm sorry about Hugh," Imogen said. "After he was dead, I missed him. I was getting used to having him near me. Perhaps I could have..." She looked at Caroline and saw the movement of her hands. Her eyes flared. "Don't leave me."

"No, Imogen," Caroline said. "I'm cold. That's all. I have to move around to keep warm. Why don't we go back to Kenwood? You could stay there with me for a while. I could put you up in one of the guest bedrooms."

"No. Louise wouldn't like that."

"I'll talk to her. You can stay." She positioned her hands again to facilitate her standing.

"But I couldn't have the money if he didn't die."

Imogen turned to Caroline and grabbed her around the shoulders just as Caroline had gotten the momentum to plant her two feet on a level spot and pull herself up from the rock.

"No, I said," Imogen shouted, lurching against Caroline's legs.

"Imogen," Caroline cried as she pulled away. "Let me get up."

Caroline was on her feet. The bad ankle continued to twinge, but she felt she could put her weight on it. Imogen fell against the slippery surface of the boulder where she had been left and tumbled onto the path. She was struggling to regain her balance. Mud smeared her arms and face.

"Help me," she said. Caroline stood, momentarily frozen.

Imogen suddenly recovered her footing, and she was on her feet like a large cat. She stared angrily at Caroline.

"You can't tell them. You can't or I won't get the money."

"I won't, Imogen." She turned and moved her good foot sideways to step away from the other woman. Imogen lunged for her.

"I know you saw me when I was walking to the plant stand to get Hugh's wine for him. At first I couldn't get my purse open, and I looked at you, and you were watching me. I know you saw me."

Caroline swirled around, desperately hoping to find firm footing. Imogen was grabbing for her arm, somehow finding a way to move forward. She was wearing leather loafers, which clawed for stability on the rocks. Caroline wheeled again, moving backwards now, toward the edge of the path where it dropped off to the ocean. Her ankle caught in the crevice between two rocks and she swayed. Out of the corner of her eye she saw the beach below. Imogen threw her whole body at her. Caroline fell to the ground in a dead drop. She felt the force of Imogen's body hit her side. Being on the ground was the only place where Caroline could be safe from being propelled over the rocks.

Looking up she saw the blur of Imogen's feet kicking wildly to stay on the path. Caroline heard Imogen scream, and she pulled herself up on her elbows.

"I can't hold on," Imogen yelled. Her feet were sliding down the side of the rocks. "Help me, Caroline."

She was past Caroline now, her head leaning precariously over the edge of the rocks. Imogen's hands reached across the slimy stones. Caroline reached for one of her arms, but it was beyond her grasp. She crawled forward, the ankle burning with pain each time she moved it.

"Grab my hand, Imogen." She stretched out her hand. "I'm right here." Caroline dragged her body forward as fast as she could.

"I'm falling," Imogen said in an astonished voice.

Caroline looked in horror as the flailing figure of Imogen Revel disappeared over the side of the rocks. Caroline closed her eyes. Her vision was crystal clear now.

They were in the Revels' ballroom, and Imogen was passing her side as Dorsey Revel's voice covered all her thoughts.

Reed was still in law school. Caroline had thought she had seen Reed's face in her mind, but her eyes had been looking at Imogen all the time. Caroline had seen her take the small container from her purse.

Caroline remembered everything now. The look on Imogen's face had perplexed her. It had been sly and furtive, and Caroline hadn't understood why a woman about to be married didn't look happy about it.

27

When Hank made out the figure of the woman in the distance he didn't believe it was Caroline. The shape was crawling on all fours, and Hank couldn't process the reason why.

"There's someone up there, by the rocks," Keisha called to him. She ran through the mud and reached Caroline several seconds before Hank was able to navigate the uneven stretch. Keisha tried to pull Caroline up, but she winced in pain.

Hank was at her side, and he and Keisha each took one of Caroline's arms. He felt her sagging, and he grabbed Caroline around the shoulders in a big bear hug.

"Are you hurt?" he asked. "What hurts?"

"My ankle," she said. "The left one."

"Lean on me," he said. "I won't let you go." He positioned one hand around her waist and the other across her shoulders. As she rested against him, he felt the wetness of her clothes. He was aware that she was shivering. "You're cold." He wondered how he could take his jacket off. "Keisha, help me get my coat off. I want to put it on Mrs. Kent."

While the two police officers performed the intricate dance of holding up Caroline, taking off Hank's jacket, and re-clothing her in it, Hank kept talking. "Where is Imogen Revel, Caroline?"

Caroline shivered again and nodded in the direction of the edge of the rocks.

"Keisha, take a look," Hank said as he finished enveloping the folds of the jacket in a double layer across Caroline's chest. She snuggled into it gratefully. Her damp hair brushed across his cheek, and he held her as tight as he dared.

Keisha looked over the rocks. "She's down among the rocks, Lieutenant. She isn't moving."

"Do you think you can get down there?"

"I'll try," she said, as she turned with her back facing to the water and began to swing herself over the side.

Hank took out his radio and called for the ambulance. He saw Keisha disappear from his view.

"What happened, Caroline? Can you tell me?" She nodded. "Are you getting warm now?" She swallowed and nodded her head again. She was looking away from the spot where Keisha had gone over the rocks.

"The paramedics are coming. We'll get you taken care of very soon. They'll bring a stretcher for you and for Imogen."

"I can walk."

"No, you can't. I'll carry you if I have to."

"Is Imogen all right?"

"I don't think so."

"You ought to go with Keisha. Maybe you can help her."

"I'm taking care of you right now." She had stopped arguing. He could feel the tiredness in her body. "How did Imogen fall?"

"She tried to push me, I think. It all was happening so fast. I caught my ankle on the rocks, and we stopped here. Then I twisted it again."

"What were you doing here in the first place?"

"She wanted to come for a walk. She made me come with her. She was upset, but I thought I could manage her."

"And she tried to kill you, too?"

She turned her face up to his. "You know?" He nodded. "All right then. You know how it happened... that day in the Revels' ballroom."

"I don't know exactly what happened, but I think you do, Caroline. You saw everything?"

"Almost everything. It all came back to me this afternoon. I don't know why I didn't know it before."

"The mind is like that. It has a lot of compartments."

"I remembered that I saw her taking a small vial from her purse. It must have been the poison, and I must have been looking right at her. She was going to put it in the wine before she brought it back to Hugh. Imogen realized I had seen her. She knew all along that I could identify her as the murderer."

"And that's why she suddenly wanted you to be her friend."

"Now I understand why Imogen kept telling me that I was the key to everything. I didn't know what she was talking about. When she said I was the only one who could help her, I thought she meant with her grief... because she had lost Hugh."

Keisha was coming up now, and Hank watched her face. She shook her head grimly.

"Imogen's dead, Caroline," Hank said. She started to cry, and he held her, not speaking. Keisha found her footing and rejoined them.

"Her neck is broken, I think."

Caroline continued to cry. Hank slowly rubbed his hand into her shoulders.

"The EMS will be here any minute." He looked back at the direction from which they came.

"The path is treacherous here," Keisha observed.

"You'll have to go to the hospital, Caroline."

"I want to go home."

"You've got to have that ankle looked at. We've got to be careful with you. We don't want you to go into shock."

She didn't put up much of a fight, and he decided to discontinue the questioning. They waited for several minutes before the familiar uniforms of the emergency medical personnel were visible coming toward them. Louise Kent was with them. She hurried toward Caroline, as soon as she realized who the wet bundle was inside Hank's coat. Keisha went to give instructions to the EMS.

"She's all right," Hank said to Louise. "She's sprained her ankle. We'll get her over to Newport Hospital." Louise's eyes asked a question, and he answered it. "She's dead, fallen over the rocks back there."

Louise made a sharp sound with her breath and looked beyond where they were standing to the empty horizon. After several seconds she reached for Caroline's hands and rubbed them vigorously.

The stretcher was ready for Caroline, and she allowed everyone to help her on to it. As the technicians were busy with Caroline, Louise spoke to Hank.

"I told Claude Revel. I hope that was all right. I thought he had a right to know."

"That's fine, Louise."

"Does Caroline know?"

"She knows Imogen killed Hugh Dockings."

"And why?"

"I don't know how much they talked about that out here." He looked around the desolate spot. Caroline could have been killed out here. It could all have ended just as easily in another way.

In the hospital, Caroline had been put in a bed for observation. Her ankle had been examined and was in a soft cast. An efficient nurses's aide had cleaned her up and replaced her wet clothes with the familiar hospital gown. Lying now asleep, she looked pale and wan.

Hank and Louise sat on opposite sides of the bed. Louise watched her daughter-in-law with a heavy heart. All the misgivings of the last two weeks which Louise had harbored concerning Imogen and Caroline's friendship were mild compared to what might have happened this afternoon. She shuddered and reached for Caroline's hand under the blanket. It felt warm and familiar. Louise clasped it and fought back tears.

"Can I get you something, Louise? You must be hungry. It's late, and you haven't had any food."

"I'm fine."

Caroline was stirring now, and Hank moved his chair closer to the bed. He reached and found her other hand.

Caroline opened her eyes and looked puzzled. "Caroline, dear," Louise said. "We're here. Hank and I are here. You're in the hospital. You hurt your ankle. How does it feel?"

"All right, I think." Caroline sounded groggy. The doctor had given her something for the pain. "Hank?" She studied him. "You're here, too?"

"Yes," he answered.

"What about Mattie?" Caroline asked.

"Mattie?" Louise frowned.

"Dinner? We have the guests from Philadelphia for dinner. Is Mattie at Kenwood alone?"

"No, dear. Molly is helping her. Everything is being taken care of. Don't worry. Try to sleep some more."

"When can I go home?"

"The doctor is coming back later. We'll see if you have to spend the night. You got awfully cold out there, and we want to make sure your temperature is stabilized."

At the mention of the cold, Caroline became downcast.

"Imogen is dead," Caroline said.

"It's better that way," Louise said. "You didn't want to see her tried for murder. It would have been a terrible thing."

"She was sick, Louise. She can't have been sane. Claude was right to think she needed care."

Louise shook her head.

"She did it for the money," Caroline said. "It twisted her, not having any all those years when all the men in the family did."

"Getting money is no excuse to kill someone," Louise said firmly.

"No," Caroline said, "but the stress she felt was real. She was sorry she killed Hugh. She said that, I think." Caroline blinked uncertainly. "I can't remember exactly, but I know she was sorry. She looked so pitiful when we were on the rocks. I... oh, and I'm so sorry, Louise. I'm sorry I didn't listen to you about Imogen. I thought I was doing the right thing by becoming her friend."

"I know, I know. But Imogen planned Hugh's death. She was cold-blooded. She talked him into taking a big policy on his life so she could kill him for it."

Caroline looked up at Hank. He nodded.

"Is there evidence?"

"We found the record of Hugh's paying the first premium in those bank account statements you and I took from the cottage. Remember? Ben Davies was able to talk to the agent who sold Hugh Dockings the new policy late this afternoon. He confirmed that the policy was in effect for one million dollars. It was term insurance. Hugh paid the first quarterly premium, which was about $900. That's all it took, and Imogen could get her pay-off."

"And she could get the money so quickly?" Louise asked.

"Despite her grief, Imogen had already contacted the insurance company to file the necessary papers for the payment. Hugh's death in suspicious circumstances was holding up the claim, and I think that's why she began insisting at the end that she had seen Claudine go near the wine, after she had supposedly left George March's company. Imogen wanted the investigation cleared up so that the proceeds of the policy would be hers free and clear. We weren't coming up with any suspects that we could charge, so she was going to provide us with Claudine."

"Very convenient," Louise said bitterly. She wasn't having any of this nonsense that the woman had been driven to kill by her unfortunate life. The suggestion was absurd. The Revels were a selfish family. She had always known so.

Back at Kenwood, they had made Caroline go straight to bed. It was late, and the house was dark. She had been told that everything at the inn was doing fine. The guests were fed and in bed. There was nothing for her to worry about. Caroline went willingly into her nightgown and slipped down in the covers. Louise wanted to turn out the light.

"Louise," Caroline asked, "is Hank still here?"

"He's downstairs in the library. I promised him a drink."

"Can you have it up here... with me?"

"You need rest, Caroline."

"I want to see him. I didn't thank him yet for coming to get me this afternoon. I forgot."

"You can do it in the morning. I'll tell him to come back to see you."

Caroline wanted to protest, but she was so tired, and the soft bed felt so warm. "Promise me you will tell him that I am grateful, and that I want him to come back to see me tomorrow."

Louise nodded and turned out the light. Caroline lay there, still. Her body wanted sleep, but her mind wanted to retrace the events of the day. So much had happened. It was faintly in her mind that she had been in real danger. Everything had happened so fast. When she had been walking with Imogen on the Cliff Walk, she had feared the journey would have no end. Yet now, here she was safe in the familiar surroundings, her pillow cradling her head.

The feel of Hank's hard shoulder against her head was there, also. The warm sensation from being inside his jacket remained with her. Caroline remembered how good it felt to have him wrapping his arms around her and pulling her tight into his body. His chest felt broad and unfamiliar, but she knew that she had felt safe there. Hank's strong arms had held her, protected her, and as she felt her eyes closing in sleep, she wanted him to be with her again.

28

The storm which had arisen during the night was over, and the following morning was sunny and clear. Caroline awoke with a start; she knew right away that it was late. The clock on her bedside table said 9:35. She sat up and immediately felt the sensation in her ankle as she moved it. Yesterday's events could have been in her dreams, but she knew in her body that yesterday had happened.

Her back felt stiff, and she was hungry. As she turned back the covers to get out of bed, her eyes rested on the picture of Reed. She looked at it for a long time, a smile finally breaking out on her face.

She took up the photograph in her hand. The trauma of the struggle with Imogen wouldn't be forgotten for a long time. It would join with her sorrow over Reed's death. She was accumulating some difficult memories.

The door knob moved slightly, and Caroline turned toward the sound.

"Good morning," Louise said, peeking into the room. "I was checking on you."

"How many times have you done that this morning?" Caroline asked. She replaced the photograph carefully on its usual spot on the table.

Louise came toward her. She had to have seen Caroline holding the picture of Reed, but she said nothing.

"I'm hungry," Caroline said. "Do you think Mattie could make me some of those pancakes which come with lots of maple syrup and butter?"

"And sausages?" Louise looked delighted to hear the request.

"Yes, Louise. Definitely sausages. And I want coffee and orange juice."

"I'm glad you haven't lost your appetite, Caroline."

"I feel as if I could eat all day."

Ben had been eager to hear the details of the death of Imogen Revel, and Hank had arrived at the police station early that morning to brief him. The sergeant had been disappointed that it was Keisha and not he who had been there at the end of the trail, and Hank didn't tell him that it was Keisha's young and athletic body which he had needed on the Cliff Walk.

Hank was tired. Sleep hadn't come easily to him. He had to do the paperwork this morning, and he forced himself to begin that tedious chore. The file with Janet Dawson's report was on his desk, along with the notes which Ben had made of his conversation with Greg Daly, the agent who had written the policy on Dockings's life. Hank read everything carefully and re-examined the documents he had found in the Waterville cottage. He fingered the packet of papers Hugh had signed so that he could put in for his retirement. The pension plan, the medical plan, and there it was, the request to continue and increase the life insurance coverage through the same carrier which offered The Camden School's group policy.

The vital clue had been in his hand that day at the cottage, and he hadn't seen its significance. All along he had been unsure of the motive for Hugh's death. Hank had considered revenge, in the person of Donald Montgomery. Hank had only thought of money as a possible motive for Imogen's death. No one had seen how there would be any profit from Dockings's death, but the money motive was a mirror's image, the truth in opposite.

Hugh had Imogen's resources, alive or dead, but she could only get his if he were dead. Which one of the ill-starred couple had first suggested the subject of their marriage? Hank had never met Hugh Dockings while he was alive, but his impression of the dead man was of someone totally concerned with his own comfort and security. The policeman rather thought it would have been Hugh who made the first move. Sailing was his passion, Claude had said, and a union with Imogen would bring the teacher retirement in the sailing town of Newport, along with a luxurious boat of his very own.

Hank still couldn't see the proud daughter of the house of Revel suggesting an alliance with the type of man he had come to see was Hugh Dockings. Hadn't Dorsey said all along that Hugh was a poor match for Imogen? She must have known it, also. Yet her plans demanded that she accept his proposal.

Now he was starting to see her plan; everything was beginning to fit in. It had been Imogen who had wanted the party to celebrate the marriage to be held on the day before the actual event. Claude had explained that because of her age his sister had wanted a quiet wedding ceremony with only the family present. At the time it had seemed a curious but understandable decision. But, knowing now that the engagement was only to make possible the purchase of the insurance, Hank was sure that Imogen had never intended to go through with the marriage. Despite the endless opportunities she would have after they were married, it was imperative that she kill Hugh Dockings before they were married. That way Imogen would remain a Revel. She would continue to use her monogrammed handkerchiefs with the large R emblazoned upon them. And she would have her million dollars.

Ben was standing in the doorway. He held a sheet of paper in his hand.

"What is it, Ben?"

"It's the property report you wanted. You know, what was in Dockings's pockets when he died."

"No keys, right?"

"No. Not even house keys."

"Well, Imogen had taken his set of school keys away from him well before the party. I'm sure of that. After Dockings had retired, he would have no need of them. He probably tossed them somewhere into the disorder of that cottage where he lived."

"She could have borrowed them from the desk in his classroom, too. The Hansen woman said he left them there."

"Imogen had all kinds of opportunity to take them. She had a key to the cottage to give me, remember? I guess we'll never know when she removed the bottle of hydrocyanic acid from the school's poison cabinet. It could have been at any time."

"I wonder how she knew to use the cyanide."

"Everyone agrees the woman had brains. I'm sure if we look in the school library at Camden or at the books in Hugh's cottage, we'll find any number of chemistry texts with the information on the lethal qualities of cyanide... everything that Dr. Peters had in his autopsy material. It works faster on an empty stomach... also quicker if alcohol is present. It was perfect for someone like Hugh Dockings. If I had the time I would satisfy my curiosity and go to Waterville to look at those books."

"Mrs. Kent will swear that she saw Imogen Revel poison the wine?"

"She saw the vial as Imogen took it from her purse. And I think she will say that Miss Revel spent a long time at the plant stand before she turned and brought the glass back to Dockings. More may come back to her memory later. Where that gold purse is now, I don't know. We'll have to search the pavilion for it, and also for the bottle that carried the hydrocyanic acid. There could be traces of the chemical in either."

"What else is there to do?"

"I've got to sit down with Claude Revel and explain everything."

"He doesn't know?"

"Louise Kent gave him some of the key information yesterday, although I wonder if he didn't suspect some of it beforehand. He was so insistent about sending his sister away, you know."

"He didn't give us any indication, if he did, Lieutenant."

"Finding the canceled check for the life insurance and talking to the agent to get the details made everything come into focus for us, Ben. That's all we needed to understand how the crime was constructed."

"Mrs. Kent must have been horrified when she realized that her daughter-in-law was in the killer's house, alone."

"Louise Kent is a strong woman. I told her everything we had while we were driving to Mon Plaisir after I spoke to you on the telephone from Kenwood. Caroline could have been killed out there on the Cliff Walk. I can't get the picture of that out of my head. She was the one who was so worried about Miss Revel. When we found Mrs. Kent she was crawling in the mud. But the look on her face wasn't one of fear." He shook his head. "She fought back. And Miss Revel was a very strong woman."

"A gym teacher, let's don't forget. She was tall and strong. She had a grip like a man's."

"I know."

"She was nuts, right?"

"I don't know if that is the clinical description, but she wasn't normal. No, she was definitely psychotic."

"Nuts then," Ben said. "A rich looney."

Hank shook his head. He didn't feel like talking about Imogen anymore. She had tried to kill Caroline, and he had fought against the image's coming into his mind all during the night. He was tired. With a nod of dismissal to Ben, he began writing his report to the chief.

Mattie had helped Louise settle Caroline into one of the ample chairs behind the balustrade on the second-floor loggia, the open-air room, which faced the water side of the U-shaped house. Caroline usually kept the door to the area locked; the loggia was too shabby for guests to use. Once there had been a huge red and white canvas awning which could be lowered from the roof's overhang against the afternoon sun. But its mechanisms had rusted, the fabric rotted, and it now lay stored in the attic.

"Are you sure you won't be too warm out here?" Louise asked, looking up as the noon sun shone high overhead. She had brought a small blanket out with her, which remained folded at Caroline's feet.

"I want to feel warm, Louise," Caroline said. She saw that even Mattie was regarding her young mistress with some concern. "I'm fine, really."

"You got so cold yesterday," Louise said, more to Mattie than to her daughter-in-law.

"I'll bring you up a pot of tea, Mrs. Caroline," Mattie said. Before Caroline could reply, the cook scurried through the door, back into the house.

"Do you want me to sit with you, Caroline?"

"No, that's all right. I really am all right. I just don't have any energy. Sitting here in the sun feels good. You do what you have to today. Isn't it a fine day to be out gardening?"

"Yes, it is. I'll go, but I'll be right outside the house. I'll come back if you want me to."

Louise left, but not before she kissed the top of Caroline's head. Caroline smiled to her mother-in-law as she gave a last look of concern back at the loggia before going inside. Caroline turned back to the view of the sky and stared at its brilliant whiteness. Below her the rugged sound of the waves pounded against the massive rocks of the Cliff Walk.

She had brought a book with her, but her eyes felt lazy in the sun, and she closed them.

When she awoke some time later she wasn't alone. Sitting next to her, in one of the shabbiest of the ancient rattan chairs, was Hank.

"How long have you been here?" She started to look at her watch and remembered she hadn't put it on her wrist. "And in that awful chair, too. It's filthy."

"A half an hour, and this chair is very comfortable, thank you."

"I want to have this porch restored, but I don't have the money."

"Well, that's important to talk about now," he said. "Have you been worrying yourself over that?"

"No. Honestly, I didn't think of it until I saw you sitting in that particular chair."

"How are you feeling?"

"Oh, O.K.."

"Ankle sore?"

"Not all that much. I don't think the sprain is serious."

He smiled but didn't answer her. She realized he was trying to keep from moving the topic of conversation to what she had experienced yesterday on the Cliff Walk.

"I expect you've had a busy morning," she said. "What time is it anyway?"

"A little after two."

"You aren't going to tell me anything about your case, are you?"

"You don't need to know any more. I put my report in this morning. You can say that this particular case is closed."

"For you perhaps," Caroline said. She was thinking now of the Revels. What would it mean to them to have the explanation of the murder come out? "Louise wouldn't let me see the newspapers, and I wasn't allowed to look at the television either."

"She's very wise, your mother-in-law."

"Do the papers know it was Imogen who committed the murder?"

"The morning papers reported that an unidentified woman was killed on the Cliff Walk yesterday, in the early hours of the evening. That's all so far. The phone's been ringing at the station all morning for confirmation of the victim's name."

"You won't give it to them?"

"We will later today. The family does have some rights to privacy, I think, until they all know what has happened."

"But then your department will name Imogen as the murderer?" She shuddered involuntarily, and Hank started out of his chair. Before she could stop him, he had unfolded the blanket and stretched it out over the trunk of her body. She watched his eyes as he moved his hands awkwardly over her. The touch of his fingers was barely perceptible as he pulled the cover onto her thighs as well.

"You should have had that on while you were sleeping," he said, resuming his seat.

"I want to talk about this, Hank." He was pretending not to understand. "If I know everything about why Imogen killed Hugh I can put this to rest." He frowned. "Have you spoken to Claude Revel? How is he? How is the family taking this?"

"I went to Mon Plaisir earlier today and spoke to Claude. He understands what happened. He accepts the truth, that it was his sister who killed her fiancé."

"I've been thinking about Claude. He was right there when it happened. Did he tell you that?"

"Caroline, I don't know why you must know this, but I see I can't stop you from wanting to. I had a very formal visit with Mr. Revel today. He was very cooperative, but he said very little in the way of facts to me. Yes, I do think he knows more about this than he has said. The possibility is very real that he saw his sister doing something to the drink. I think all along he has been suspicious about her actions. My guess is that he tried to put them out of his mind, refuse to accept that she might be culpable."

"The Revels are very proud."

"He was going to deal with it by sending her away. That seems to have been his plan. He was trying to get the family's doctor to arrange for Imogen to go to a sanitarium."

"I knew that part."

"It was when Imogen told me that she had seen Claudine at the plant stand and that she was the one who had tampered with the wine that Claude realized this thing was bigger than he could handle."

"Louise was right about Imogen all along, Hank. I still feel bad about not trusting her judgement."

"Imogen was a very manipulative person. That's clear to me now. I kept wondering why I didn't feel sorry for her, and I guess that's why. She manipulated you. In fact, she used everyone while claiming so expertly that she herself was the victim. It was all mirrors."

"Mirrors?"

"Hugh only cared for himself. We both discovered that when we went to Waterville. Dockings wasn't lovable, you said that yourself. Imogen promised him the world: the sailboat, Des Arbres. Even the honeymoon to Greece."

"We kept thinking how much Hugh was going to profit from the marriage."

"Yes, and I couldn't see, although I had the autopsy report, how the *modus operandi* fit Dockings as the victim like a glove. Only the people who knew him and his habits would use the cyanide to poison him."

"Imogen?"

"Imogen, of all people, knew he wouldn't eat anything at the party, and she knew he would drink a lot of wine. There'd be no chance of his recovering from the poisoning. He'd die almost immediately, before help could come. From the beginning, I thought the Revel women were the strong members of the family."

"But Imogen liked to say how everyone else was evil, Hank. I was remembering so much of our conversations this morning. She said Claudine was evil; her brother was evil. I suppose she thought her father was the most evil of all."

"He kept her from the money which came to mean so much to her."

"Money," Caroline said with a sigh. "She caused a death just so she could have the money."

Suddenly the reality hit her, and she felt an over whelming sadness. Her face must have reflected her anguish because Hank reached for her hands, which were resting on the blanket's soft surface. He held them tight in his own hard grasp.

"You've got to talk about what happened to you, Caroline. Not Imogen. She's beyond anyone's help now."

"I can't," Caroline said weakly.

"I want you to. Tell me all about it." He was holding her hands and squeezing his strength into them.

"When we struggled... there on the Cliff Walk... I almost felt that I could give up. Die, if she wanted me to."

"But you didn't. When I found you, you weren't afraid."

"I kept thinking... oh, you don't want to hear this." She tried to pull her hands away, but he held on to them.

"I do. Tell me what you were thinking."

"I thought about Reed and how if I were dead, I would see him again, and that would be all right." She met his eyes. "Every day I wonder when I'll stop thinking of him, Hank. When will I accept that he's gone?"

He looked as though someone had hit him. His chest bent down, and he expelled a deep breath.

"How can I keep going on like this?"

"I don't know," he said, looking up. "I think you have to keep doing what you are doing. It gets better. It must."

"I know I have to live without Reed. He's gone. He's never coming back." She heard the sound of uncertainty in her voice. She hadn't meant to sound doubtful.

"No, he's not coming back," Hank said, his voice quiet, but firm. "I'm sorry, but Reed's not coming back." She saw that Hank's face was full of sorrow for a man he never knew.

"I was the one who made him drive home that night. It was raining so hard, and he should have spent the night in Albany. Then he would never have..." She couldn't hold back her tears any longer. He grabbed her around the shoulders and hugged her as hard as he did on the day before when he had held her close to him on the Cliff Walk.

"I've seen so many accident scenes, Caroline. No one knows when one is going to happen. They're often no one's fault. No one can really prevent accidents from happening in this life."

"Louise... I feel so bad about Louise."

"Louise loves you. She doesn't blame you. I would know if she did, Caroline."

"If we'd had a child, Louise would have that. But I thought we had so much time--"

"Stop it," he said forcefully. He held her body out so that she could see his face. It was so different from Reed's, dark and rugged where Reed's had been fair and gentle.

"I'm a detective, Caroline. Louise doesn't blame you for anything. I could tell if she did. Do you believe me?" She nodded her head. Her throat felt hard and she couldn't swallow. She tried to blink and her eyes were burning, and she could only put her head against his chest to hide them.

"You're so nice to me," she said.

"I want to be your friend."

"I know that." She was afraid to look at his face.

"How can I stop loving Reed?" she asked.

"You can't, Caroline. You won't. You shouldn't."

"But then how can I ever love anyone else?"

"You will. You have plenty of room in your heart, and you will find a place for someone else."

Epilogue

The July day on Narragansett Bay was humid, and the thick air under the Newport Bridge was as still as being inside a vacuum. In the cockpit of *Fancy Boy*, Hank Nightingale worked hard to trim the sails in hopes of catching some wind. His efforts were useless.

Hank paused to wipe the perspiration from his forehead. He took off his cap and pushed his wet hair back from his face.

"We're in irons," he said, the frustration strong in his voice as he looked up at the limp sails. "I hate to do it, but I'm going to have to turn the motor on to get us back to the dock."

His sole passenger smiled languidly in his direction, the dark glasses hiding her brilliant green eyes. Caroline Kent was reclining against the exterior wall of the cabin, her hands folded peacefully across her chest. The cascading rays on her head made her pale brown hair appear golden in the sun.

"Do we have to go in now? I'm enjoying this so much."

"There isn't any wind. We can't sail without wind. Let's go back. I'll buy you an early dinner."

"I'm not hungry at all. Why don't we go out to Hammersmith Farm? That's a beautiful view of the coastline."

"All right," he said. Although he wouldn't enjoy motoring along in a perfectly good sailboat, the lack of wind was against Hank's arguing. Hammersmith Farm it would be. He turned on the motor, and the strong smell of the diesel engine filled his nostrils.

"We would have to pick the calmest day of the year to take our first sailing trip together, Caroline. And the hottest."

"I think it's lovely," she said. She truly thinks it is, he thought to himself.

"Come sit next to me at the wheel," he suggested. "You can steer."

She smiled, pleased with the offer, and slid around on to the hard seat beside him.

"Do you know which way to go?" he asked. She pointed past Goat Island toward where Fort Adams lay situated on the curve of the coastline. "O.K., here you go." He moved slightly to his right so that she could put her two hands on the wheel.

Caroline turned the wheel slightly, and he braced her with his own body as she turned with the boat. "That's good," he encouraged. Caroline smiled back. She was near enough for him to catch the familiar smell of her perfume mixed in with the heat hanging in the air. He put his nose next to her ear, taking in a deep drink of her scent.

His companion was still smiling, and he put his left arm across her back and brought it to rest in the crook of her neck where he could feel the warmth of the sun on her skin.

"Yes, that's perfect," he said.

Fancy Boy was noisily cutting through the bay, past the harbor and out toward open water, and Hank Nightingale didn't care whether there was any wind or not. He had the sensation that a marvelous journey was about to begin. And, what's more, he was sure that the woman beside him knew that, too.

About the Author

Anne-Marie Sutton was born in Baltimore, Maryland, and graduated from the University of Maryland with a degree in English. Her first love was journalism. But she fulfilled a life long dream when she published her mystery novel *Murder Stalks A Mansion*, set among the fabulous mansions of Newport, Rhode Island, where she lived for several years. Now a resident of Connecticut, she continues to spend time in Newport and to write stories set there.

Gilded Death is the second book in the Newport Mystery Series and Anne-Marie is currently writing a third, *Keep My Secret*, in which an old friend of Caroline reappears unexpectedly and once again murder and mystery haunt the mansions of Newport.

CPSIA information can be obtained at www.ICGtesting.com
Printed in the USA
270317BV00001B/3/P